DARKWATER COVE

A GRIPPING SERIAL KILLER THRILLER

DAN PADAVONA

GET A FREE BOOK!

I'm a pretty nice guy once you look past the grisly images in my head. Most of all, I love connecting with awesome readers like you.

Join my VIP Reader Group and get a FREE serial killer thriller for your Kindle.

Get My Free Book

www.danpadavona.com/thriller-readers-vip-group/

1

The dark.

This is where monsters lurk.

The loss of light forever terrified Darcy Gellar. When she was a child, she begged her mother to read her one more story, and after she finished, another tale. Anything to delay the inevitable darkness that followed. No amount of checking for monsters in the closet and under the bed comforted little Darcy. After the lights went out and she was alone in the bedroom, every shadow became a clawed witch or a man with a knife.

Now the dark is an unexpected ally. It conceals Darcy even as it traps, working in her favor.

The FBI agent's hands tremble as she swings the gun across the upstairs hallway. Four open doors bleed shadows across bare hardwood. One door leads to a bathroom. Darcy sees the sink and a drawn shower curtain. The others open to bedrooms.

He is here. Hidden in the shadows and following her with his eyes.

For over a year, Darcy and her partner, Eric Hensel, followed a trail of North Carolina murders. All girls in their teens and early twenties, women with their entire lives ahead of them, butchered by a serial killer the media refer to as the Full Moon Killer. Forensic evidence at the murder scenes proved scarce, and the few hair fibers and fingerprints the crime scene investigators discovered drew blanks. The Full Moon Killer was a ghost.

Until tonight.

Darcy realizes she is a fool. No way should she be here alone. Though she competently handles a gun, she is not a marksman like her fellow agents. Nor is she a strong or skilled fighter. Her value to the Bureau is as a researcher and profiler. She's hunted killers across the country and entered their minds to predict their next moves, but never has the duty of capturing a dangerous criminal fallen on her shoulders.

She grabs the radio off her hip before a squealing floorboard silences her. Gun raised, Darcy throws herself flat against the wall. Her breaths freeze in her chest as she searches the upstairs for movement. The noise could have come from anywhere inside the old bungalow. Sounds echo through the walls and down the vacant corridors like water droplets inside a tomb.

Darcy is here to interview Janelle DeLee, a friend of Marcy Abraham, the twenty-four-year-old office temp the killer murdered last month. No reason she couldn't question DeLee alone. But when she arrived, Darcy found the front door open and a note taped to the mailbox.

I'm upstairs, come inside.

After DeLee failed to answer Darcy's calls up the stairs, a thud shook the walls, loud enough for Darcy to fear the woman had fallen and required medical assistance. She took the stairs two at a time. At the top of the staircase, the lights shut off.

A trick. The fly had crawled into the spider's web.

That's when she knew the killer was already here.

Another moaning floorboard gets her moving. Saucers for

eyes, she slides along the wall and reaches the jamb surrounding the bathroom entryway. Something grabs at her shirt. Darcy almost cries out before recognizing the light switch digging into her back. Her heart thunders with the frenzied rhythm of a rabbit caught in the wolf's gaze. On the silent count of three, she spins past the jamb and aims the weapon into the bathroom.

Clear.

Pulls the shower curtain back.

The tub is empty. A moth flutters past her face.

The bathroom door is flimsy, but the knob and lock set are new. She considers throwing the door shut, twisting the lock, and radioing for help.

Her flashlight rests on her hip. If she flicks the light on, she'll draw the madman to her location. Instead, she edges into the hallway and walks toward the first bedroom.

The darkness sharpens her senses, attunes her to the creaks and groans of the old house. The scent of wood polish is thick, and she smells the flowery soaps and perfumes behind her on the bathroom counter.

Scratch.

The tree branch scraping the house makes her jump. Outside the window at the end of the hall, the bough extends clawed branches and dances when the wind blows.

Still blinded by the pitch-black, Darcy reaches her hand out and touches the bedroom door. A little nudge will swing it all the way open, but this is foolhardy. Better to slip into the room without alerting the killer.

But the spare bedroom is empty. Just a made bed and a wooden dresser set against the far wall.

"Darccccy." The whisper drifts down the hallway. "Come out and play."

Darcy throws herself inside the bedroom and waits. It's difficult to hear over the pounding pulse in her ears. She crosses the room and slinks down to one knee beside the dresser. The killer's breaths rasp in the hallway as she yanks the gun back and hides in the shadows.

Footsteps approach. Emboldened, the killer no longer conceals his whereabouts. He's hunting her now.

The footsteps stop outside the bedroom door. Seconds pass.

Then the steps continue through the darkness, moving away from her now.

When she hears him descending the stairs, she rips the radio off her hip. Lowering her voice, she gives her location to the dispatcher. He can't make out her words, and she repeats herself. A moment later, he confirms her whereabouts. Help is on the way.

The door slams open and blasts against the plaster. The killer outsmarted her again.

Reaching around the dresser, she squeezes off two shots, but in the deep gloom, she can't see him.

Ears ringing from the blasts, she pulls the gun back and prays her aim was true. Darcy's hands shake until she can barely maintain her grip on the weapon. In her mind, she pictures the killer on his back, bullet wounds streaming blood onto the throw rug. Yet she never heard him fall.

Fear holds her in place amid the silence.

Minutes tick away.

Maybe he retreated into another room.

Her shivers cease, and Darcy regains control of the gun. When she tries to stand, her leg cramps from kneeling too long. Listening for the killer, she rubs the feeling back into her leg and creeps out of hiding.

The silhouette of the bed stretches before her. Almost coffin-like. An empty closet with two clothes hangers beckons as a potential hiding spot. And beside the door, a coat rack she hadn't noticed before.

But it can't be a coat rack, because the looming shadow moves.

She cries out and fires the gun. But he is too fast.

She twists her body out of the way as the knife plunges into her arm and tears flesh from shoulder to elbow. The agony paints stars across her vision.

A hand grips her neck and squeezes. Choking. Pulling her down to the floor.

Three hours ago, she'd argued with her son over concert tickets. Hunter's last words were angry and hurtful after she told him he wasn't old enough to go with his friends. His door slammed. He locked her out of his life and tossed away the key.

Darcy won't die with Hunter hating her, nor will she force her teenage son and eleven-year-old daughter to bury their mother. They already lost their father and know too well of life's cruelty. She can't fail them.

Survival instinct takes over as the corner of the dresser clips her spine. She kicks out, fighting a monster she can't see. The force drives the wind from his lungs. He totters back a step and comes at her again. But she's ready this time.

The wicked blade slices at her belly as she pulls the trigger. The knife tears into her stomach. Screaming, she fires the gun again.

He pinwheels backward and collapses against the corner of the bed. The killer clutches the mattress, holding himself up, before he topples off and pulls the covers off the bed and over his body.

The pain catches up to her. She grasps at the bubbling wound and slumps against the wall, desperate to halt the pumping lifeblood. The ceiling, the walls, the crypt-like bedroom darken as the gun tumbles from her hand and cracks against the floor. She finds herself on her back, no memory of how she got there. Eyelids droop shut and blink open. Labored breathing fills the room. Her own or the killer's?

Please don't hate me for dying, she begs her children. Mom loves you.

Sirens rip the night as her vision turns black. The dark envelopes her body and pulls her into its clutches.

2

T HREE YEARS LATER
Genoa Cove, North Carolina

ARMS SNAKE around Darcy's throat and cut off her oxygen.

"Fight him."

She twists her hips and rolls, but her captor holds her firm. The man's breath is hot on her neck, the veins standing out on his arms as he pulls her chin back. The instructor, Bronson Severson, yells advice she can't discern over the shouting spectators.

During sparring sessions choke holds are illegal. Why the instructor allows the holds this time Darcy doesn't know, but if she doesn't make a move soon, she'll lose consciousness.

She feels her muscles weaken as the man strains to control her. Scrambling to slip her hands free, she drives her palm against his forearm. The momentary break of his grip is all she needs. Darcy twists and drives the point of her elbow toward his temple, pulling back at the last second so she doesn't injure him.

"Stop."

At the instructor's command, Darcy rolls out of the man's arms and jumps to her feet. Her opponent, a thirty-something policeman with a shaved head and a black beard, shakes the cobwebs out of his head. He blinks at Darcy, knowing she could have knocked him cold if she struck him flush. Darcy offers her hand, but the cop pushes himself up and stands against the wall, catching his breath.

Six women ranging in age from young housewife to golden years circle the mat. Bronson, an ex-cop with the Charlotte Police Department, jots a note on his clipboard. He has a neck like a linebacker's, his skin tanned and weathered from life beside the ocean. His chin is strong, arms chiseled from years of weight training. The fifty-five-year-old doesn't look a day over forty.

"I trust everyone observed Ms. Gellar's technique for breaking the grip of a stronger male."

Darcy isn't used to compliments. Usually Bronson spends half the class critiquing her mistakes. The man would have made an excellent drill sergeant.

"That's why I continuously stress that you keep your hands free when someone grabs you from behind. I don't care if you're sixteen or sixty-five. Drive the point of your elbow into an enemy's temple with speed and precision, and he'll give up his grip." His eyes sweep the class. When they come to rest upon Darcy, they narrow. "But hopefully the rest of you won't make the critical mistake of rolling into a choke hold in the first place. That's an amateur move, one that will get you killed in a life or death struggle."

Ah, that's more like it.

She collects her backpack and slides on her socks and sneakers as the other women file past. Using a hair tie, she works her long, dark locks into a ponytail, identical to how her daughter, Jennifer, wears her hair.

"Thanks for agreeing to be a punching bag, Julian," Bronson says, slapping the officer on the shoulder. "Tell the boys down at the office I said hi."

Julian gives Bronson a sidelong glance Darcy doesn't understand. She didn't mean to embarrass Julian, and Bronson's good-natured jabs make it worse. All she wanted to do was escape the choke hold. As the police officer changes out of his training shirt and stuffs it into his gym bag, she considers apologizing. Too late. The officer throws the bag over his shoulder and shoves the double doors open.

Darcy follows Julian outside when Bronson stops her.

"That was a dumb move, leaning back into his chest like that. You practically invited him to choke you out."

"I panicked."

"Obviously."

"Since when is a rear naked choke legal during sparring sessions?"

"It isn't."

Darcy switches the backpack to her other shoulder.

"Yet you allowed it today," she says, darting her eyes to the ring finger on his left hand.

There's no band there, but he keeps rubbing the finger as though searching for a missing item. He's recently divorced, she thinks. Three years removed from her profiler position, and she still assesses everyone she meets based on their mannerisms. There's no turning it off.

"You handled it, so no harm, no foul. I would have stepped in if you were in danger. Trust me?" He grins, and she nods. "You're showing improvement. Keep coming to class, clean up the mistakes, and soon you'll be teaching beside me."

"I doubt that," Darcy says, smiling. "But thank you."

"It makes me think you've had similar training in the past."

He raises an eyebrow, but she doesn't take the bait. Seems she isn't the only profiler in the room. Better he knows her as a single mother new to Genoa Cove and not the FBI agent who accepted an early retirement after a serial killer came within inches of murdering her. It's difficult enough to stay below the media's radar and keep reporters from hounding her children. But anyone with a search engine can find out all they wish to know about Darcy Gellar's past.

She says goodbye and exits the dojo before Bronson can probe further. In the parking lot, she unlocks her Prius when her phone rings. It's Hunter. This can't be good. Her son only calls when something bad happens.

"Hunter?"

"Can you come get me?"

His voice is shaky as though he's gotten into an altercation or just finished crying.

"Sure, but I thought Michael was driving you home today."

Michael, who lives two blocks from their house, plays on the football team with Hunter and brings him home after practice.

"Just come, all right?"

"What did you do?"

Hunter ends the call, and she regrets her accusatory tone. It's difficult to maintain neutrality. They've only lived in Genoa Cove for three months, and during the first weeks at his new school, Hunter has been in the principal's office twice, and last week a pair of teachers pulled Hunter away before he fought another boy.

Despite her best intentions, she's failed her children. She knows this. Between the therapy sessions and the anti-anxiety medications, she's been a hollow reflection of herself since the stabbing. What good is a guardian who is afraid of the dark? Now Jennifer is a freshman, and Hunter, whose previous school in Virginia held him back, is twenty months from graduation. Time moves without her. She's losing her kids.

Darcy kicks the accelerator, and the Prius lurches forward as she turns off the coast road onto the highway. It takes ten minutes to reach Genoa Cove High School, the gray brick building planted on a hill overlooking the village. The marching band practices on the lower field, and she hears the horn section blare as she coasts through the parking lot, searching for Hunter.

Members of the football team congregate outside the side exit, boys sitting on helmets, others shoving each other and laughing while a hip-hop song thumps from car speakers. A few of the players stop what they're doing and stare as Darcy drives past. Hunter isn't with them.

She spots her son in the parking lot beside a boy she doesn't recognize. Hunter's hair is dry, a sign he didn't shower. Did he even practice with the team? His heavy metal t-shirt depicts a demon-like creature breathing fire upon a city. The unknown boy beside Hunter wears dreadlocks, his face punctured by multiple piercings, a chain drooping off his belt loop. Hunter spots Darcy and bumps fists with the unknown boy. The kid vanishes into a Ford Fusion with tinted windows as Hunter drags his feet to the Prius. The door opens, and Darcy hears the words *pussy* and *scumbag* shouted in their direction. One of the football players, a barrel-chested boy with red hair, raises a middle finger. He doesn't care that Darcy sees.

Hunter tosses his bag in the backseat and slouches down without a word. She stares incredulously at him.

"What the hell was that about?"

He shrugs.

"They're dicks, okay? Let's drop it."

"Look at me, Hunter."

When he huffs and pops his earbuds in, she taps his

shoulder and fixes him with a glare that promises consequences
if he doesn't comply. He pulls the earbuds out as she stops the
car inside the loading zone along the curb. Two teenage girls in
short-shorts mingle on the sidewalk. Hunter turns his head
away from them.

"Come on, Mom. Drive."

"Not until you tell me what's going on."

Hunter sighs. His hands won't sit still, tugging at the tears in
his black jeans. That's another thing. Everything he wears is
black. His shirt, jeans, sneakers. Even his hair, dark to begin
with, is dyed to a midnight pitch.

"Why weren't you with your teammates?"

"Because Coach kicked me off the team, okay? Happy now?"

While the news doesn't surprise Darcy, it still feels like a kick
to the stomach. Hunter is good at football, and being part of the
team chipped away at the walls he'd fortified after leaving
Virginia. Hunter blamed her for the move, and rightfully so.
Tearing Hunter away from his friends before junior year forced
him to start over. New beginnings were scary during high
school. Kids labeled you as an outsider.

"No, I'm not happy. Why did the coach kick you off the team?
Did you get into a fight with one of those boys?"

"Thanks for going there. Because of course, I'd start a fight.
That's all I do, right?"

"I never said that."

"It's what you were thinking."

Darcy bites the inside of her cheek.

"Then why?"

He shakes his head. Accepting Hunter isn't ready to talk
about it, she yanks the car off the curb and drives down the hill.

"It's that stupid team rule. We're supposed to wear a shirt
and tie. I'm not dressing like a freaking geek every day until
November."

Darcy wants to tell him he looks good dressed up, but that's poison to Hunter. She might as well invoke grandma-mode and pinch his cheeks, tell him what a handsome boy he is. In her mind, the conversation isn't finished. He's being unreasonable.

"Didn't Coach Parker move you up to second string wide receiver?"

"I guess," he says, continuing to pick at his jeans.

"Then he must think you're good, Hunter. If he didn't, he'd sit you on the end of the bench and ignore you. Talk to him. I'm sure he'll let you back on the team if you're sincere."

Hunter doesn't answer. The earbuds pop back in, and she hears guitars squeal and cymbals clash. If the heavy metal sounds this loud to her, what must it be doing to his ears?

They descend the ridge. To the east, early autumn sunlight sparkles across the Atlantic as waves pound the beach. A scattering of sailboats are on the water, but only a few people dot the sand despite the beautiful weather. Blue and green waters converge with white breakers, and for the first time a hint of a grin forms on Hunter's face. Living by the ocean has its benefits.

The waves perish where the land juts out and forms a cove. Two rocky cliffs loom over the cove and block the westering sun, turning the water an oily black. She understands why the locals refer to Genoa Cove as Darkwater Cove. The water is murky under full sun and a bottomless pit at midnight.

Leaving Virginia after twenty years hadn't been easy, but there were too many skeletons lurking in those closets. Thirteen years ago, six months after entering the Bureau as a Behavioral Analyst, she lost her husband, Tyler, to an aneurysm. Hunter had been four, Jennifer only one, so she understood why Tyler's death affected Hunter more. Jennifer had been too young to carry memories of her father, whereas Hunter recalled picnics in the park and Tyler pushing him on the swing set behind their first apartment. After Jennifer was born they bought their first home, a tiny ranch in middle class suburbia, seven miles from Quantico. A year later, Tyler died on the way home from the grocery store. He was working late all week, and Darcy asked him to grab bread and eggs for breakfast on the way home. According to the doctor, Tyler died before the car crunched against the telephone pole.

For several years Darcy sensed Tyler's ghost around every corner. She entered rooms and expected to find him there, feet up on the sofa, the Redskins game on. She'd needed a change of scenery then, a new start, but she stayed, stasis being one of the universe's most powerful forces. After the stabbing and retirement, life in Virginia lent nothing but bad memories.

She sneaks a glance at Hunter. His chin rests on his elbow, face against the window. When the car shimmies over a grooved road, his cheeks jiggle. Darcy wishes he could be four again. That was when she began to lose him, she realizes. Subtle changes at first—loss of appetite, disobedience. As the years passed, he frequently spent nights at friends' houses. His grades dropped during sixth grade and cratered when he reached high school.

Taking the first turn down Main Street, she passes a gazebo set on a grassy island separating oncoming traffic. At the center of the village, a red brick road carries traffic through the commerce district. Genoa Cove is rich with old money, and this is apparent in the upscale clothing and jewelry stores. Every summer, tourism fills the coffers and boosts the village's economy, but there's enough money from the year-round residents to support Genoa Cove through a slow year. Even the local banks are powerful enough to stave off their national competitors.

She pulls into a parking spot in front of Antonia's Pizza and stops the engine. Hunter cuts the music and looks at her cockeyed.

"What are we doing here?"

"Making the most of my cheat meal," she says, climbing out of the car. Though Darcy watches her calories and bikes, she grants herself a fun meal every week. Doing so kills the cravings and gives her a reward to look forward to. She breathes deeply through her nose. "Smell that? That's heaven wrapped in dough."

This elicits a smile from Hunter. Her analogies truly suck. He tries to hide the grin by pulling his hood up, but she notices.

The waitress seats them in a booth and takes their order after a short wait. Darcy scans the faces and doesn't recognize anyone. Though she feels at home in Genoa Cove, destined to live here, she's a stranger.

The room is wider than it is long with booths along the wall and tables in the center. Stacks of empty pizza boxes sit on the end of the counter where a man and woman order two slices to go. Scents of dough, cheese, and marinara sauce rumble her stomach. She hasn't eaten since lunch, and self-defense class left her famished. A jukebox in the corner plays a song from The Chainsmokers. Darcy's head bobs along to the beat as Hunter rolls his eyes.

"You don't like your mom keeping up with new music?"

For a moment she's certain he'll slip his earbuds in, but he doesn't. Instead, he shakes his head and runs his eyes across the room. His gaze stops near the jukebox, and he lowers his eyes and places his hand over his face. Not quick enough. The pretty girl in the jean miniskirt recognized him and is coming over with her friend.

"Hey, Hunter."

"Hey."

Hunter looks like he wants to crawl under the seat. The girl is copper-skinned, dark hair teased into a bun atop her head. She leans her arms on the table with a grin that is at-once shy and mischievous. The epitome of youthful beauty, she's the type of girl who turns heads at the bat of an eyelash. Her blonde friend, heavyset and dressed in sweatpants and a Mickey Mouse t-shirt, shifts around on her feet like a child who needs to go to the bathroom.

"You must be Hunter's mom."

Darcy reaches across the table and shakes the girl's hand as her mortified son squeezes into the corner.

"Yes, I'm Darcy Gellar."

"Bethany Torres."

"So you go to high school with Hunter?"

"Eleventh grade. I sit next to this guy in Economics."

Bethany gives Hunter a playful punch on the shoulder. The boy's face takes on a strawberry coloration.

Darcy is content to sit back and let Bethany lead the conversation. The girl bubbles over with personality, yet she's genuine, not putting on a show. Everything about the girl feels natural to Darcy, from the laughter and unreserved smile to the lack of makeup. There's something between Hunter and Bethany, though Darcy doubts they are a couple. The banter is pure courtship. Remembering when she met Tyler at college twists her heart into knots, and she needs to look away until the painful memory recedes.

The small-talk concludes when Bethany's friend checks the time on her phone, a cue for Bethany to wrap it up.

"Okay, so I'll see you on the field tomorrow, yeah?"

Hunter locks eyes with Darcy, then buries his face in the menu.

"Sure thing. I'll see you there."

After the girls leave, Darcy bites her fist to keep from laughing. If she's ever seen Hunter this flummoxed, she can't recall.

"I like her a lot."

"Don't say anything, Mom."

"Come on. She's cute, and she sure seems to like you."

He grabs a bottle of red pepper and rolls it nervously between his hands.

"We're just friends."

"So, Bethany said she'd see you on the field tomorrow. How are you going to pull that off if you're unwilling to talk to Coach Parker?"

"I'll think of something."

"Is she a cheerleader?"

"Last I checked," he says. Darcy leans her head back and laughs. "What's so funny?"

"The king of death metal has a crush on a cheerleader."

"I don't."

"Uh-huh."

The waitress slides the pies in front of them. Hunter's pizza is pepperoni and extra cheese. Darcy's is a thin crust marinara with basil and a balsamic drizzle. Neither will finish an entire pie, but Jennifer will appreciate the leftovers.

"I'll make a deal with you," Darcy says between bites. She bats her hand in front of her lips to cool the fire burning the roof of her mouth. "Tomorrow I'll stop by school and talk to Coach Parker. I need to speak with guidance and get Jennifer switched into a different math class anyhow."

"I don't know if that's such a great idea."

"Give me a chance. If he's a jerk, I'll let you retire from football sans press conference."

Hunter smirks and dabs his crust in a cup of extra sauce.

"Okay, so what's the deal?"

"I'll tell Coach Parker what a great but misunderstood kid you are and get you back on the field, and you invite Bethany over for dinner next week."

"Mom—"

"This isn't a debate. Parents have the final say."

Darcy finishes the slice and wipes her hands on a napkin.

"Fine."

She reaches out, and Hunter hands her the red pepper. As she sprinkles heat across the next slice, she continues.

"And I'll speak to the coach about what those boys called you."

Hunter shakes his head and sips his Pepsi.

"Let it go. It's not worth it, and it'll only make things worse."

He's right. Darcy hasn't forgotten schoolyard rules. A bully never forgets a snitch.

Any goodwill she's gained vanishes on the ride home. Hunter escapes inside his music again, and he's out the door the second Darcy pulls into the driveway.

"Don't forget your books."

She sighs, knowing he can't hear her over the grinding guitars. She grabs his bag and lugs it with hers to the front door. At least he remembered the pizza.

Beige and silver with cardinal shutters, the ranch-style house sits two blocks from the beach. The previous owners were desperate to sell after Hurricane Florence damaged the roof and flooded the kitchen. Darcy grabbed the ranch at half of its market value and hired the neighborhood handyman to re-shingle the roof. The man also added a small deck off the back door, and it's there she likes to sit with a glass of wine while the final hour of sun turns the cove golden.

Jennifer bounces past with the phone glued to her ear as Darcy drags the bags into the foyer. If Hunter is the perpetual dark cloud which promises flooding rains, Jennifer is a tornado that strikes out of a clear blue sky. With her dark, wavy hair yanked back in a ponytail, Jennifer is the spitting image of Darcy at fourteen. Although Darcy doubts there was ever a time she could pull off jean shorts cut in a Daisy Duke-style.

"Why do you even bother to wear pants?" Darcy asks, dropping her keys on the kitchen counter. Jennifer shoots her a withering glare and ends the phone call. "No, seriously. If you're going to show that much, ditch the shorts and save me a night's worth of laundry."

"Stop," Jennifer says, dragging the word out as though someone is twisting her arm. Just as quickly Jennifer sets the phone on the counter and smiles, hands on hips, feet drawn together and back erect, a pose Darcy recognizes from her daughter's routine with the junior varsity cheerleaders. "Guess who that was on the phone?"

"Based on your outfit, I'll say the decency police. Who do I send the bail money to?"

"Can't you be serious for a second?" The yellow tank sags off Jennifer's shoulder. "That was Kaitlyn. She throws the most epic parties, and she's having another next Friday night. She's got a band and a deejay. Everyone's invited."

Darcy's heart skips. She's used to sleepovers and birthday parties organized by parents. Logically she realizes teenage parties are an inevitability, but Darcy hasn't met Kaitlyn or her parents.

"And by everyone you mean kids your age."

"Not necessarily," Jennifer says with a wink. "Kaitlyn's brother goes to community college, and sometimes he's there with his friends." Darcy raises an eyebrow, and Kaitlyn waves her hands in placation. "No, it's not creepy or anything. They have their own girlfriends. Ew, Mom."

"Will there be drinking?"

"No way."

Yeah, right.

"I'll need to speak with Kaitlyn's parents before I consider this. So you're telling me the college boys aren't there to buy you beer. They're just hanging out to talk about the cool stuff they learned at school."

"Obviously I shouldn't have mentioned it."

"It's a good thing you did."

"This is ridiculous. You let Hunter go to concerts."

"Leave me out of it," Hunter says, grabbing an apple as he cuts through the kitchen toward the den. No doubt to blow three hours playing *Call of Duty* on Xbox.

"Your brother is seventeen," Darcy says, watching Hunter disappear around the corner.

"Like that will make a difference when I turn seventeen. You only trust him more because he's a boy."

Despite Jennifer's perk, she can snap and turn nasty without warning. Darcy takes a breath.

"I didn't want to tell you this, but another girl got raped last week."

"That was in Smith Town, not Genoa Cove."

"Smith Town is only ten miles away."

"It's a dirt hole."

"When did you become an elitist?"

"We'll be totally safe at Kaitlyn's."

Darcy raises her hand to cut Jennifer off.

"No, you're going to listen. The latest rape happened after a party like the one Kaitlyn is holding. One girl walked home alone, a bad idea at night. Even when two girls walk together, a pair of males can overwhelm them. When I was with the FBI—"

"Mom, stop. You're so over-dramatizing everything. Everyone knows about the rapes in Smith Town. But nothing like that happens in Genoa Cove."

"Rape happens everywhere, Jennifer. It's not a socioeconomic problem."

"Mom, it sucks. I get it. What happened to that girl was terrible, but my friends and I are careful. There will be like fifty people at the party."

Fifty people. That doesn't comfort Darcy.

"The police never caught the rapist. He wore a mask so she couldn't see his face. The girl was only sixteen."

"Yeah, yeah. She was sixteen, and I'm fourteen, so lock me inside the house for the next four years to keep me safe. Or better yet, put me in a convent."

"Don't raise your voice, Jennifer. It's perfectly reasonable for me to check with Kaitlyn's parents and see the lay of the land before I decide."

"It's perfectly reasonable for you to be a bitch whenever I want something that's important to me. Why do you fuck my life up every time I'm happy?"

The words stun and sting. Darcy's fingers twitch as she remembers her mother slapping her across her face for cursing during an argument. She still feels the slap, red and burning. No, she isn't her mother and won't strike Jennifer, even if her daughter deserves punishment.

"You don't talk to me like that," Darcy says through gritted teeth. "Go to your room."

But Jennifer is already down the hall, stomping hard enough to jiggle the glassware. The bedroom door slams.

What the hell just happened?

Darcy sniffles and drops onto a chair at the kitchen table, running her hand through her hair as she remembers the fight with her late-mother. Was she this nasty as a teenager? Hormones at that age mess with a girl's mind, leave her edgy with a twisted belief the world is out to make her miserable. No doubt Darcy was a handful. Yet she doesn't recognize Jennifer's vicious streak as one of her own. Times like these make her wonder if Tyler's death affects Jennifer as much as it does Hunter. At least he has memories. She has nothing, just an empty hole and stories of who her father was.

Between Jennifer's blow up and Darcy's worries about Hunter and the football team, she loses track of time. Darkness creeps over the window. Hadn't it been sunny a moment ago? She checks the clock. After sundown.

At the kitchen window, she sweeps the curtains shut and hurries down the hall to the bedroom. The anxiety isn't as bad as it was a year ago when she couldn't step outside at dark without a heavy dose of medication, and the pills turned her into an empty husk. One pill became two, then three, and forced the kids to fend for themselves while Mom slumbered on the couch like a strung-out addict. It kills Darcy that her kids saw her like that. They haven't forgotten and never will.

Sliding a chair in front of her laptop, she scrolls through her bookmarks and locates the link she seeks. It's a website which allows the public to search the prison system by inmate ID or a criminal's name. She chooses New York from a menu and types Michael Rivers' ID. After three years of searches, she can type the number blindfolded.

He must be incarcerated. If the state released the Full Moon Killer, or he escaped, the news would dominate the headlines.

But she needs to know.

Only one girl escaped the serial killer: Amy Yang, a fifteen-year-old high school student who broke free of Rivers' grasp during a failed abduction behind a closed Starbucks. A resourceful girl, she ran into traffic and flagged down the first vehicle willing to stop. The killer had been new to the game then and hadn't honed his technique. Amy was lucky.

After the murderer's capture, Darcy and Amy stayed in contact for over a year, battling their demons and leaning on each other for support. The weekly phone conversations ended abruptly. Though Darcy wondered about Amy, she didn't pursue the girl, figuring Amy needed to put the horror behind her. If only Darcy could do the same.

She clicks send, and the browser churns through the data. And churns.

The search never takes this long. Something is wrong.

Darcy backs up one page and reenters the data. Studies the murderer's number until she's positive it's correct.

Enter.

Her stomach falls. In a moment, the database will return zero results, and she'll know he's free.

Finally the information loads. She slides down in her chair and releases her breath.

Michael Rivers is behind bars.

3

Hunter can't look more uncomfortable dressed up. He's buttoned the wrinkled white shirt to his neck, and a black tie flops over his belly like a dead eel. He tugs at the collar, neck red, a choked grimace contorting his face as he fights to pry his fingers under the top button.

"You have to keep it buttoned to the top," Darcy says while she turns up the hill toward Genoa Cove High School.

"I can't breathe. This shirt is so tight it's cutting off my circulation."

"The more you fight it, the worse it's going to feel. Relax. Breathe."

He punches the door. Not hard, but it's enough to make her jump.

Reflected in the mirror, Jennifer sulks in the backseat. She hasn't spoken to Darcy since the fight and won't even look at her. This morning she stomped through the kitchen while Darcy scrambled eggs on the stove. Darcy offered her breakfast, but the girl whipped open the refrigerator and snatched a yogurt off the shelf before retreating to her bedroom.

"So stupid we have to do this," says Hunter, chewing on his

thumbnail. "What's the point? How am I going to play better if I can't suck air into my lungs?"

"It's about team building," Darcy says, sweeping the hair out of her eyes. "When I played varsity field hockey, everyone had to dress up on game day. Did we like it? Not really. But when we passed one of our teammates in the hall, we kinda knew we were all in this together, and I think that made us successful. Coach Parker wants you to look the part and represent the school. Give it a chance."

Jennifer gives an exasperated sigh and jumps out of the car the second Darcy stops behind the buses.

"She'll get over it," Hunter says, dragging his bag over his shoulder.

Darcy, who'd been watching Jennifer shove through the crowd toward the main entrance, twists her head toward her son.

"I'll text you after I speak with the coach." She leans across the seat and kisses him on the cheek before he can escape. "Love you, Hunter."

He mutters the words back to her and flies out of the car as though his seat caught fire.

Merging with the crowd, he pops his earbuds in and follows Jennifer's path. Darcy waits beside the curb in case the football players harass Hunter again. A line of cars circles the lot, and the other parents will expect her to move. A tall boy with a high fade gives Hunter a cautious nod, which he returns. But a small, muscular player with spiked hair slaps his friend on the shoulder and points at Hunter. They share a laugh at her son's expense.

A horn pulls her eyes to the rear-view mirror. Behind the Prius, a businessman sitting behind the wheel of a Lambo makes an irritated gesture. Darcy gives him a wave and pulls out. She can't see Hunter or Jennifer anymore as the massing students swallow them. The sudden violent ebb-and-flow of the crowd tells her two kids are shoving each other inside the throng. Darcy cranes her head as she drives past, anxiety amping her blood pressure until she's certain Hunter isn't at the heart of the scrum.

After parking in the visitor's lot, she stops at the main office to sign in, then she's off to guidance to take care of Jennifer's class switch. The hallway floor gleams with the shine of a fresh polish, and student drawings of autumn scenes hang from the walls. As the bell rings, she wades through the sea of students toward the stairs.

The high school basement holds a gymnasium and offices for the coaches, all of whom double as teachers. The doors to the gym are closed. Inside, the gym teacher blows a whistle, and a dodge ball bangs off the door.

At the end of the hallway, Coach Parker's office appears twice the size of the others. A picture of a younger Parker surrounded by teammates and hoisting a championship trophy hangs prominently on the wall beside plaques for various coaching awards. An imposing figure, Parker's knees barely fit under his desk. He wears running shorts and a gray hooded sweatshirt. His head is shaved, and a black goatee Darcy assumes the coach dyes girds his mouth. Head buried inside a playbook, he doesn't notice her until she raps on the door.

"Help ya?"

"Are you Coach Parker?"

His eyes assess her and sneak down to her skirted legs.

"That's me. Have a seat. What can I do for you?"

"Sorry to bother you, sir. My name is Darcy Gellar." When he shows no recognition, she adds, "Hunter Gellar's mother."

Disgust crosses his face. It's quick, but she notices. Parker tosses his pencil on the desk and leans back in his chair, fingers interlocked behind his head.

"I must say I pictured you differently."

Darcy doesn't like his smile. It feels disingenuous, untrust-worthy. His gaze keeps darting to her neckline.

"How so?"

"Well, Hunter is so..."

"Dark?"

Parker snaps his fingers.

"That wasn't the word I was searching for, but it'll do." He cocks his head. "Yeah, now that I look closer I can see the resemblance. You moved to the village recently, correct?"

"From Virginia, yes." She glosses over her reasons for leaving, though Parker prods her for information. "Hunter and his sister lost their father when they were very young."

"That's a tragedy. Kids who grow up without fathers have a difficult time fitting in and often lack discipline."

If Parker intends to slight Hunter, Darcy shrugs it off.

"Hunter was four when Tyler passed. It hasn't been easy on him. He asks a lot of questions about his father—where he worked, what he was like, if he looked like Hunter when he was a teen."

Darcy's throat constricts at the memory.

"If you don't mind me asking, was your late-husband an athlete?"

"He ran track in high school. Why?"

"Fast, I bet he was. That's Hunter. Kid can't catch, but he can run like the wind."

"That's why I came to see you, Coach Parker." Darcy uncrosses her legs and leans forward. "Hunter is good at sports, especially football, though he will never admit it. He'd rather play it cool and act like he doesn't need a team."

"Your boy could turn into a fine receiver, Ms. Gellar. May I call you Darcy?"

"Sure," she says, wishing he wouldn't.

"Not quite starting material with the senior talent we have this season, but I could have seen Hunter working into that role next season. But..."

He lifts his palms and shrugs.

"He didn't wear a dress shirt and tie."

"It's required of all players. Refusal to comply results in automatic dismissal. This is a team game, not an assemblage of individuals."

"But certainly you've had exceptions over the years. For example, kids who came from less money and couldn't afford to dress up."

Parker's mouth turns up at the corners.

"Now, Darcy. A simple white button down can be had at Wal-Mart for twenty bucks. Even less if you frequent the consignment shops. And the example you gave doesn't apply in this situation. I won't pretend to know your financial situation, but Hunter clearly doesn't come from poverty. His refusal to comply with team rules is a personal choice. And a selfish one at that. You've heard the music he listens to. He's choosing individuality over the good of the team, and a team of individuals is a team of losers. Hunter let down his teammates, he let me down."

He's battling her and concocting reasons why Hunter shouldn't be on the team. Coach Parker passed judgment on the boy for his love of dark metal and can't get past his prejudice. Darcy doesn't understand Hunter's musical choices, but parents rarely do. Her own mother and father looked out the corners of their eyes when Darcy went through her Cure phase and later adopted grunge. Is today's music so different? She once attempted to listen to one of Hunter's favorite bands and gave up after thirty seconds of screeching guitars and guttural screams. Maybe she needs to listen again.

"Surely you believe in second chances."

"I do, but with Hunter it's a waste of time. I've seen the nose piercing, the sick t-shirts he wears. He's doing it for shock value. See what I'm getting at? That's not something I want representing this program. We've won two state championships in the last fifteen years, and the community takes pride in the team's accomplishments."

"What if I told you he is already complying?"

Parker snickers.

"Hunter Gellar? Dressed up? I'd tell you to prove it."

"I drove him to school myself."

"This I must see." The coach sits forward and clasps his hands on his desk. "You seem like a good mother, Darcy, and though I prefer my players come to me when they have a problem, I appreciate your candor regarding Hunter's father. I'll call my captains and ensure Hunter dressed appropriately today. If everything checks out, I'll allow him to practice."

"Thank you, Coach Parker. He won't let you down."

Parker presses the palms of his hands on his desk and stands up from his chair.

"This is Hunter's second chance. Understand there won't be a third."

Darcy stops for bagels on the way home and picks up a decaf. By the time she pulls into the driveway she regrets the beverage choice. A poor night's sleep catches up to her, and her legs feel like gelatin as she slogs inside the ranch. The air conditioning hits her with winter's breath. Someone turned the temperature too low. She adjusts it back to seventy, then she tosses her bag on the floor and lies on the couch, using her toes to pry each heel off. Propping her feet on the armrest, she drags a pillow under her head and closes her eyes.

Did she do the right thing by sticking up for Hunter? Darcy doesn't want to be one of those parents who fights her kids' battles.

A lawn mower rumbles down the block. Somewhere a dog

barks. Sunlight at the window paints the backs of her eyelids pink as the rays touch her face, melting the chill away. She trusts Hunter will return to the team, especially now that he has Bethany to impress.

Then there's Jennifer. When Jennifer gets home, Darcy will sit her down and set ground rules. Darcy is overprotective of her daughter and understands it is inherently unfair to deny Jennifer her social life. The girl has done a remarkable job making friends during the few months they've lived here. But Darcy won't allow the outbursts or the vulgar insults. Respect is a two-way street.

Sleep quietly pulls her under. It comes one breath at a time, and then she's afloat on an ocean of memories and fears which pull her into a nightmare.

In her dream, the lights flick off. She's alone in the dark. Pitch-black around every corner.

A terrible scent reaches her nose. The smell of burned flesh.

A woman splays in the corner. Blood gushes from the stab wounds on her chest and neck. A familiar symbol marks her neck—a smiley face burned into her skin by a branding iron. The FBI will find the symbol on each of the Full Moon Killer's victims.

Darcy recognizes the woman: Kelly Anne Collings, the serial killer's first casualty. Darcy and her partner had observed the body inside the Charlotte morgue, the formaldehyde smell a rancid candy that made her ill.

Why is Collings inside her home?

The ranch is silent until footsteps creep down the hall. She'd known he was inside the house before he approached. Michael Rivers.

The scrape of a knife blade against plaster comes closer. Darcy hurries through the shadows to the front door.

Jammed.

In the strange way of dreams, when she wheels around, he is already upon her.

Before she can cry out for help, the knife plunges toward her chest.

Darcy awakens screaming. The pillow lies on the floor. She's teetering on the edge of the cushions, a hair's width from falling off the couch. Pulling herself up, she rushes to the window.

Just a dream. She thought she'd left the nightmares in Virginia, but they've trailed her to the North Carolina coast and won't stay quiet.

The hot sun pulsing through the window cleanses her and washes the horror away. For several minutes she stands in the light until her limbs stop trembling and she gains control over her breathing.

Though she checked Rivers' status last night, she races to the bedroom and throws the curtains open. At the computer, she verifies the Full Moon Killer is locked away and serving a life sentence. She has contacts at the Behavioral Analysis Unit. People who will tell her about an impending release from prison. She swipes through her contacts and finds the numbers. Sitting beside the window, she taps her nail on the screen, debating.

No, she made a fool of herself last year when she called. Her former coworkers must think she's gone off the deep end.

She checks the clock. Three hours until school lets out. Add another three hours for football and cheerleader practice, and Darcy has enough time to fortify the house from intruders before she cooks dinner.

She grabs her phone and makes the call she's been putting off for three months. The woman at the security firm takes Darcy's information and schedules an appointment for a state-of-the-art home security system installation.

Twenty minutes later, she stands at the Home Depot

customer service desk. Their team will deliver and install a gas-powered generator next week.

She tells herself the generator will prove useful when the next hurricane spins up the Atlantic seaboard. And it will serve a purpose in the event of a storm. But the generator is a virtual guarantee she'll never again be stuck in the dark because of a power outage.

When the front door bangs open at six o'clock, the turkey and stuffing is finishing up in the oven, filling the ranch with the mouth-watering scents of Thanksgiving in October. Darcy sprawls on her back beside the sliding glass door, a screwdriver clenched between her teeth as she works the security bar into place. Most people don't realize the locks on patio doors are futile. A burglar with a little know-how can rattle the locking mechanism until it disengages. She twists the last screw into place and locks the bar with a satisfied nod.

Two phony alarm system signs adorn the front yard bushes. She won't need them after the installers activate her system and plant the legitimate signs.

Hunter wears a confused look. Jennifer's grin shows her pearly whites as she tosses her homework on the table.

"I can't figure out if this is Fort Knox or if I walked onto the set of an HGTV show," Jennifer says, giving her brother a high-five over the lame joke.

This is classic Jennifer. She'll hate Darcy with every ounce of her body and suddenly forget the gripe as if no disagreement occurred. It won't save the girl from a grounding, but Darcy is happy the Jekyll and Hyde routine has temporarily settled on the former.

"What are you doing, anyway?"

"This is a locking bar," Darcy tells her as she slides the mechanism open and shut. "Makes it harder for someone to break in."

"Like those signs are going to fool anyone. Wouldn't it be easier to buy a dog?"

"Take your books off the table and put them in your room," Darcy says, climbing to her feet on achy knees. Her jaw tightens, a message to Jennifer that all isn't forgiven. "Dinner is ready."

Head lowered, Jennifer retreats to her room. Darcy shifts her attention to Hunter, the boy slouched in his usual chair closest to the deck. The folded dress shirt and pants stick out of his bag. After practice he'd donned shorts and a black t-shirt with another metal band she'd never heard of on the front. His hair glistens from showering.

"Now then, how was practice?"

"Okay, I guess."

"Coach Parker have anything to say?"

"Why would he?"

"I don't know. He's the head coach, isn't he?"

"We work with the coach who handles receivers and the offensive coordinator."

"I trust there weren't any issues with your teammates."

Hunter blows air through his lips.

"Can we eat? I'm starving."

"Set the table," she says, worrying over Hunter's evasiveness. Twice she's witnessed his teammates bullying him. Is she overreacting to a couple bad eggs? Maybe she needs to back off and give Hunter space.

The tallest member of the family, Hunter doesn't require a chair to reach the top shelf dinner plates in the cupboard. As he walks three plates back to the table, Darcy opens the oven and lifts the turkey with a pair of potholders. She sets the turkey on an oval serving dish with handles on the ends and carries it to the table. On his way to the kitchen for utensils, Hunter dodges her. While Darcy places the stuffing beside the turkey, she eyes the fading orange light at the window, weary of the shorter days as Halloween approaches.

Jennifer returns wearing gray, baggy sweatpants and a half-shirt. Darcy can't fault her daughter for wanting to be comfortable, but this is her third change of clothes today, if Darcy counts the black sweatpants and t-shirt Jennifer wore at breakfast.

"After dinner, you're doing the laundry," Darcy says between bites, pointing her fork at Jennifer.

"Why me?"

"You make the most laundry, so you get to do the honors. Besides, you don't question me when I assign chores."

"Owned," Hunter grins as he sets his hand on Jennifer's shoulder and gives it a playful shake.

"And you're in charge of folding tonight," Darcy says, narrowing her eyes at Hunter.

The chore score even, the kids stop razzing one another and focus on their plates. The turkey melts in Darcy's mouth, the stuffing seasoned with just the right amount of salt and pepper. Though Darcy appreciates conversation during dinner, the only time of day she sees the kids, the lack of small talk tells her the food must be good. She hadn't expected the meal to come out so well, distracted as she was by the new locking mechanism for the deck door.

After eating, Darcy washes the dishes. Jennifer dries, and Hunter puts them away. The kids head to their rooms, but Darcy stops Jennifer.

"Have a seat," Darcy says, motioning toward the table.

Jennifer scowls but doesn't protest. Hunter shoots her a sympathetic look from the hallway before he leaves. Darcy loves that her kids stick up for each other when the pressure is on.

Jennifer sits with one leg crossed over the other, her eyes glued to the table top. She bites her lower lip and fiddles with the salt shaker.

Darcy feels as if she looks into a mirror. It's not so much the physical resemblance but the mannerisms, the way her daughter fidgets when she knows she's done something wrong, the downward tilt of her head as she braces for punishment.

"You hurt my feelings, you know?"

"I'm sorry."

The apology isn't out of her mouth before Jennifer starts crying. And it isn't a sob, but a waterfall of emotion that leaves the girl hitching and hiccuping as she buries her face in a napkin. Darcy reaches for a Kleenex and gently takes the napkin from Jennifer's hand, trading her the tissue.

"I don't know what's happening to me," Jennifer says, wrestling with every syllable. She blows her nose and stuffs the tissue into her pocket. Darcy hands her the box. "Sometimes it doesn't even seem like it's me saying things. It just comes out. I know it's wrong, and I don't want to hurt people, but I can't stop."

"Shh." Darcy strokes the hair off her daughter's eye. "You're fourteen. There are enough hormones jolting through your body to light a city block. Every girl goes through this. I did. So did Grandma."

Though Darcy's mother never admitted as much. She was forever above teen angst and immaturity.

"It doesn't make sense. This never happens when I'm with my friends. Just with you and teachers."

Darcy cringes. If Jennifer erupts on one of her teachers, the school will punish her, perhaps suspend Jennifer.

"You have problems with authority, no different from Hunter, except he expresses it in different ways. But Jennifer, you can't go around thinking the world is against you. That sort of hate eats at you until you're hollow and alone. I'm not out to get you, and neither are your teachers. I love you and Hunter more than words can express." Darcy takes a breath while she composes her thoughts. "About these parties. Understand that part of being a parent is saying no when I don't think you're ready." Jennifer slumps her shoulders and tosses another tissue into the trash. "But I never said you couldn't go to Kaitlyn's party, only that I want to speak with her parents first."

Jennifer lifts her head, face brimming with sudden hope.

"I swear to God I'll be careful and won't drink, and if things get weird, I promise I'll call and you can come get me."

"Slow down. I didn't say yes...yet."

"Okay."

Jennifer remains reserved, but she sees the light at the end of the tunnel and desires to rush forth.

"Now let's talk about your grounding."

Jennifer clicks her tongue on the roof of her mouth.

"You're actually grounding me?"

"Don't start again."

"Sorry."

"Every day after school through next week, you're to come straight home after cheer practice."

Jennifer folds her arms and glares at the table again.

"No hanging out afterward, no stopping at friends' houses. Straight home, dinner, and homework."

"There's a dance this Friday after the game."

"Tough."

"I can't even watch Hunter play?"

"Of course, you can watch your brother's game. But you're sitting with me, not your friends unless they want to join us."

"Awkward."

"That's the deal, and I'm not negotiating. Stick to the straight and narrow and I'll consider letting you go to Kaitlyn's party."

Jennifer sighs through pouting lips.

"Okay."

"Now give your Mom a hug. She's had a long day."

Jennifer leans over and hugs Darcy. They hold each other for a long time, the girl sobbing every few seconds. For the first time in forever, Darcy feels connected with her daughter. Caressing Jennifer's back, she wishes she could freeze time and stay here forever.

Then both kids lock themselves in their rooms, presumably doing homework. Probably on their phones, Darcy thinks.

Night presses against the windowpane. Darcy draws the curtain and assesses the ranch's safety. Even with the new lock, the glass door itself is vulnerable, easy for an intruder to smash through, though he'd make a helluva racket doing so.

Or not. The ranch sits on the western edge of the neighborhood loop, the house next door vacant. Would anybody hear the glass break?

Darcy can't shake the growing dread that something is wrong. Sitting beside her computer, she eyes the closet and chews her nail. A cardboard box rests on the top shelf, the sweatshirt thrown over the lid doing little to conceal the box's existence. Pulling a step stool beneath the shelf, she climbs up and hauls the container down. After setting the box on the bed, she listens at the door. It's quiet inside the kids' rooms.

She edges the door shut. Sitting on the edge of the bed, Darcy reaches inside the box and removes a manila folder containing the notes and pictures from the Michael Rivers case. She shouldn't have copied the files before leaving the Bureau, but she considers the folder's contents as protection, ammunition should the Full Moon Killer come after her again. Know your enemy.

Though she's reviewed the pictures since the investigation's nascent days, the brutality takes her breath away. The depths of the stab wounds indicate strength and frenzied rage. A twisted smiley face brands each girl's neck. Though the tag is the Full

Moon Killer's calling card, Darcy believes the symbol exists to taunt the police and FBI. The brainstorming session she'd used to construct the original profile is stuffed behind the case notes. Reading the page causes her skin to prickle with goosebumps. It's the most accurate profile of her FBI career.

White male, thirty-five to forty-five, six feet or taller and muscular. Organized—think Ted Bundy or Dennis Rader. First signs of violence displayed during childhood. Egocentric and without remorse. Lives alone in an isolated location, probably in a rural location with plenty of land. Works a solitary job, possibly a contractor.

Though Rivers had a substantial bank account thanks to inheritance money, he lived in an old, weather-beaten farmhouse. Per the profile, the serial murderer was an electric contractor and utilized his van to transport abducted women back to his house.

Studying the printed map, Darcy examines the circle drawn in red marker, indicating a 150-mile radius stretching from North Carolina down to Myrtle Beach and Murrells Inlet. Darcy was certain the killer lived inside the radius, and this also proved to be true.

Yet she cannot understand how a man becomes a mass murderer. Victims of childhood abuse struggle with demons, but the vast majority lead normal, productive lives. A small percentage become violent offenders. What sets Rivers apart is his seemingly normal childhood. No abuse, no trauma.

She continues thumbing through the notes when her phone rings. The unexpected shrill causes her to spill the gory pictures across the floor, and she gathers them up before one of her kids walks in and sees the horror splayed across the carpet.

Darcy doesn't recognize the number and considers letting the call go to voice-mail. On the fifth ring, she answers.

The woman on the phone is too distraught to speak clearly, but between the sobs, Darcy identifies the voice.

Amy Yang.

It's been a few years since Darcy last spoke to the girl. She must be nineteen by now. Darcy tries to picture the girl four years older and fails. Time moves at blinding speeds.

"It's all right, Amy. I'm right here. Slow down and tell me what's wrong."

Several seconds pass before the girl composes herself. Darcy sits on the carpet with her back against the bed and her knees drawn to her chest, the phone locked between her shoulder and ear as she returns the case folder to the box.

"Nobody believes me, and I don't know who to turn to."

"Did someone try to hurt you, Amy?"

"Yes."

"Who?"

"It was him. The Full Moon Killer."

4

Amy Yang wears polka-dot pajama bottoms and a heavy sweatshirt when Darcy arrives on her doorstep. An odd twist of fate has brought them together again. Taking a break from college, Amy works for an advertising firm in coastal North Carolina and rents this two-bedroom house in Smith Town.

They hug inside the foyer as Amy's eyes dart over Darcy's shoulder.

The young girl locks the door and throws the bolt. Inside, the house looks barely lived in. The foyer leads into the living room where a brown leather couch torn by cat's claws holds court in the center. It's the only piece of furniture in the room, and it probably came with the house. There's no TV, but this isn't unusual. Many of the younger generation find entertainment in mobile devices and don't have a need for a legacy item like a television. Darcy takes in the remainder of the downstairs. The adjoining dining room is empty except for a glass cabinet in the corner. There are no glasses or dishes inside. No table, no chairs. Across from the dining room, the kitchen is tiny but functional. The linoleum floor is old and curling up at the edges, and rust stains mar a white electric stove. No table in the kitchen either. Does Amy eat her meals leaning over the sink?

Amy escaped Michael Rivers, but she's a victim like the others. An intelligent girl, Amy seemed destined for a full scholarship at a private college. The brush with death altered the arc of her life, and now she works a dead-end job when she should be taking notes inside a lecture hall.

Despite the mild October morning, the girl draws a blanket around her arms and collapses on the couch, the space between the cushions almost swallowing Amy's tiny frame. Her legs bounce as she sits, and her gaze keeps traveling to the curtained picture frame window.

Darcy pulls an ottoman in front of the girl and sits on the edge. She places a hand over Amy's.

"Start from the beginning. Don't leave anything out."

Amy nods once. Her lower lip trembles, and she can't stop glancing at the door and windows, the house's most vulnerable entry points. Darcy recognizes the paranoia. She's lived with it since the stabbing.

Amy feels certain someone has followed her for two weeks. Temptation coaxes Darcy to remove a pen and notepad from her pocket and conduct a full interview. Old habits die hard.

"Where did you first notice the man?"

"At the movie theater last Monday. They have two-dollar matinee specials at noon, and I had the day off from work. Halfway through the movie, I got the feeling someone was watching me. I turned and saw him in the back row. I didn't think much of it at the time. Probably just a typical creep, nothing to worry myself over. Then afterward, I stopped at the cafe, and he was standing in the bushes across the street and staring at me."

The second meeting could have been coincidental—Smith

Town's population is half of Genoa Cove's—but Darcy knows better than to doubt a stalking victim.

"Did you get a good look at his face?"

Amy shakes her head.

"It was too dark in the theater, and he stayed in the shadows outside the cafe."

"Was that the last time?"

"No. Two nights ago, I toured the lighthouse with a girl from work. Every time I looked out the windows, he stood beside the ocean staring at me."

"Did your friend see this man?"

"No. He vanished when I tried to point him out." The girl averts her eyes and rubs the back of her neck. "You think I'm crazy."

"Not at all. There's a chance you have a stalker. On the other hand, it might not be a big deal. Maybe it's a guy who thinks you're cute but can't work up the courage to ask you out."

Bending over with her elbows on her knees, Amy grabs her hair.

"No, it's *him*. He got out. I can't explain how. Now he wants to finish what he started four years ago."

Darcy leans forward and levels her face with Amy's. The girl reminds her of Jennifer, steadfast and convinced of the impossible. Only five years separate Amy and Darcy's daughter. Is this who Jennifer will become in the near future?

"Amy, I checked the inmate database last night and twice again this morning. Michael Rivers will never get out of prison."

"No, he's here. It has to be him."

"He's not Houdini. Whoever is following you, it can't be the Full Moon Killer."

"I know it doesn't make sense, but it couldn't be anybody else."

"What convinces you this man is Michael Rivers?"

"Come with me."

The girl's bony fingers grasp Darcy's wrist. Amy rises and leads her through the dining room and into the kitchen where a side door Darcy hadn't noticed opens to a yard of dirt and brown grass. A junk pile of old rakes, rusty car parts, and assorted trash steams in the bushes.

But it's the red spray paint on the side of the house that stops Darcy's heart.

It's an evil smiley face, the calling card of the Full Moon Killer.

5

The ride home to Genoa Cove is fraught with confusion and creeping dread. Unless Michael Rivers is a phantom who can appear at any location, a stalker is playing a nasty game with Amy. But how did he know the serial killer attempted to capture Amy Yang? The police omitted the minor's name four years ago. Nobody knows about Amy, not even the press.

Darcy stayed with the girl until she phoned the police. Amy would have to share her past with the officers, and a few loose lips would soon spread her name to the public and media.

Darcy doubted the police would take the girl seriously. What did they have to go on besides graffiti vandalism and an unrecognizable man who might or might not have followed Amy around Smith Town?

The clock reads noon when Darcy pulls into the driveway. In the kitchen, she releases the bar and slides the deck door open. Hands cupping elbows, she walks a full circle around the house, half-expecting to find the leering graffiti painted on the exterior. There's nothing. Inside, she slides the locking bar into place and opens the kids' rooms, confirming the rooms are secure.

Hunter's window is open a crack. Darcy shoves the pane down and throws the latch.

Impulse urges her back to the computer, but she recognizes her obsession ballooning toward dangerous levels. She's doing herself no favors staying locked inside the house with only her fears as company.

After mixing a quick salad, Darcy trades her sneakers for flip-flops and dons a baseball cap. The sun is warm on her face as she crosses the street. With everybody at work, the neighborhood is silent, peaceful. On the opposite side of the loop, a sand path cuts between two grassy dunes and opens to the beach. This is why she chose Genoa Cove.

Half a mile to the south, waves pound the public beach. Here at the cove, water sloshes over the sand in hushed whispers. She's surprised to see another person on the beach. It's a large man, his back to her. A planted fishing pole juts out of the wet sand, and a taut line extends into deeper waters. He leans back in a reclining beach chair and nurses a bottle of beer.

When she kicks off her flip-flops and treads through the bathwater-warm shallows, she recognizes the man's muscular frame and close-cropped hair. Bronson Severson from the dojo.

He appears to be in a state of bliss, his face turned up to the sun, eyes closed to thin slits.

"Ms. Gellar," he says without looking up. "I thought that was you."

"Mr. Severson."

"Call me Bronson. Please."

"Only if you call me Darcy." She sits in the sand with her arms wrapped around her knees. "I didn't realize you live around here."

"I don't. Actually I'm on the west side of the village. You probably saw my truck parked down the road from your house."

"You know where I live?"

He slips a bucket hat over his head and slides the rim down to his brow.

"Yes, from your sign-up form. I recognized the street when I entered your information into my database. You're in Steve and Patty Mitchell's old house."

Darcy locks her elbows and leans back on her hands, digging her toes into the sand.

"Seems you've met everyone in Genoa Cove."

Bronson shrugs.

"Small village. Live here a few decades and you'll memorize half the population's birthdays." A tug on the line grabs Bronson's attention. He calmly removes his hat and grasps the fishing rod, almost annoyed the fish interrupted his relaxation. "So it's just you and the kids, that right?"

Darcy shifts her weight. How much does this man know about her?

"My son and daughter, yes," she says, hoping he didn't learn about Tyler.

"Hunter and Jennifer." A jolt of electricity shoots through her bones upon hearing her children's names. He notices her alarm and raises a calming hand. "My nephew plays on the football team, and I guess he was at a party with Jennifer last month."

A party? Darcy's brow furrows. How many times has Jennifer sneaked out?

Bronson, in no rush to reel in the fish, nods for several seconds, considering.

"Crap, I probably sound like a creeper. Hope I didn't throw you off asking about you and your kids."

"It's okay. You were a cop."

"A nosy one apparently." He jerks the rod, and the line goes slack. "Lost another one. For the record, Genoa Cove is a safe place to raise kids, a lot safer than Smith Town. But the area has its challenges, the occasional hurricane not being the least. Don't hesitate to call if you or the kids need anything."

The tension releases from Darcy's shoulders. Bronson is a retired police officer and her instructor for self-defense class. She should be thankful he's taken an interest in a single mother and her kids. What if Darcy was in Amy's shoes, looking over her shoulder for a sick stalker who knows too much about her past? It might be helpful to have a guy like Bronson keeping an eye on them.

"There is something you could help me with."

She tells Bronson about Amy, leaving out the Michael Rivers angle. It's a matter of time before he runs an Internet search for Darcy Gellar and learns about her infamous and abbreviated FBI career, but he doesn't need to find out yet. Amy is the one who needs protection.

"The Smith Town and Genoa Cove police departments never saw eye-to-eye, but I remember a few guys over there. Let me make a call and get back to you. At the very least, it wouldn't be a bad idea to have someone drive past her residence until this stalker thing works itself out."

"That's very kind of you."

"Not at all. We're neighbors now. People in Genoa Cove look out for each other."

Bronson packs his fishing gear and groans when he stretches. He grabs his chair and stops as if he remembers something.

"Darcy, do you have an alarm system?"

"As a matter of fact, Gilmore Security will install my system tomorrow."

"Then you did well. Gilmore is the best in the region. I'll take them over those national brands any day. What about a gun?"

"A Glock-22."

He nods.

"Fine weapon."

They walk together along the path back to the neighborhood, the sand too hot for Darcy without her flip-flops. Bronson climbs into his red Dodge pickup with another invitation to phone him at the first sign of trouble. It makes her wonder if Genoa Cove has more problems than he's letting on.

Inside the ranch, Darcy rubs the chill off her arms as her body adjusts to the air conditioning. She rummages through the refrigerator for a snack and hears a thump from down the hall.

Someone is inside the house.

The kitchen window is open. She checked every window before she left the house.

An image of the serial killer's tag on the side of Amy Yang's house flashes in her mind. As she told Bronson, she locks the gun in her bedroom safe. The noise came from her daughter's room.

Jennifer's door bangs open.

Darcy throws herself against the wall as her daughter toils down the hallway, rubbing at her eyes. She's barefoot in a SpongeBob nightshirt, her hair tousled as though she'd been sleeping.

"What are you doing home? It's not two o'clock yet."

Jennifer touches her stomach.

"Sick. Jenna drove me home." Jennifer totters into the kitchen and opens the refrigerator. Scratching her head, she considers an orange and places it back in the crisper drawer. "Word of advice: never trust fish day in a school cafeteria."

"Why didn't you call? You need to tell me if you leave school."

"I called. You didn't have your phone with you."

Jennifer fills a glass of water and tilts her head at Darcy's phone on the table.

"Did you open the kitchen window?"

Jennifer holds up her forefinger as she gulps the water. After finishing, she wipes her mouth on her forearm.

"Yes."

"Jennifer, how many times do I need to tell you to keep the house secure? You were home alone."

"Seriously, Mom. It's Genoa Cove. Who's going to break in? The Kardashians?"

"It's not a joking matter, especially with a rapist in the area," Darcy says, cranking the casement window closed. "And you're letting the hot air inside."

"I'm letting the *fresh* air inside. This place smells like an old carpet and Hunter's feet. Oh, speaking of which."

Jennifer reaches for a folded sheet of paper on the table and hands it to Darcy.

"What's this?"

"You better take a look."

Darcy unfolds the paper and feels her stomach fall out from under her. It's a note written in angry reds. Vulgarities. Homophobic slurs. Threats to beat the shit out of the target. Her hands tremble as she scans the vicious note.

"Where did you get this?"

"It was stuffed into Hunter's locker this morning. Don't worry. I grabbed the note before he saw."

"Don't worry? Whoever wrote this wants to hurt Hunter. Why would somebody write this?"

Jennifer raises her hands.

"Probably because he's dating the prettiest girl in school, and dumb-ass jocks get jealous."

"He's dating Bethany?" Darcy notices Jennifer's questioning stare. "We ran into her at Antonia's yesterday. Hunter said they were friends."

"Friends. Right." Jennifer burps into her hand. "I'm gonna yak up a fish sandwich. I'll be in the bathroom if you need me."

Darcy can't understand why Jennifer is taking this lightly. The note is hateful and shocking, a decisive leap beyond bullying. This person wants to hurt her son.

Threats of physical violence are a matter for the police. Hunter will hate Darcy for calling the authorities, and perhaps the note is only bluster and empty threats, but she won't take chances with his life.

An hour later, a police cruiser pulls up in front of the house. Darcy watches through the peephole as two officers emerge from the vehicle. They stand talking across the roof of the cruiser for a moment, then they approach the door together. She recognizes the man. Oh, hell. It's Julian, the cop who volunteered to attack Darcy at self-defense class. Won't he be pleased to see the woman who embarrassed him?

A stocky female with short blonde hair accompanies Julian. The woman rings the doorbell. Darcy waits a few heartbeats before answering so they don't think she poised beside the front door, waiting for them to knock.

"Ms. Gellar?" The female officer flips open a notepad. "You called the department about a threatening letter?"

The female's name tag reads Faust.

Julian buries his head in his own notepad. When he lifts his gaze, recognition flashes in his eyes. Recognition and annoyance, Darcy thinks.

"Yes," Darcy says, standing aside. "Come in, please."

Officer Faust waits in the foyer while Darcy pads to the kitchen. Julian runs his eyes over the downstairs and focuses on the hallway, which leads to a series of closed bedroom doors. His tongue prods at the inside of his cheek, bored.

"My daughter found this note sticking out of my son's locker at school," Darcy says, handing Faust the letter.

The female officer performs a quick scan of the letter. She

hands the note to Julian, who blinks at the letter before giving it back to Darcy.

"So your daughter didn't actually see the person who placed the note," Julian says.

"No."

"Not much to go on."

"I understand, but isn't that how investigations begin?"

"There's no way to determine if your son wrote the note himself and intended to drop it in another locker."

"What? No. My son isn't violent, and I know his handwriting, anyway. This isn't his."

"Does your son have enemies?" Officer Faust asks.

"A couple boys on the football team bullied Hunter when I picked him up two days ago."

Julian itches his lip to hide his smirk, but Darcy sees. The star of the self-defense class raised a wimp. The irony must be killing him.

"Who were the boys?"

"I don't know their names," Darcy says, folding her arms. "We moved to the village three months ago and I'm still learning names."

"Where did you move from, Ms. Gellar?"

"Virginia."

"Virginia," Officer Faust repeats, jotting down Darcy's answer. "It says in my notes you're currently unemployed."

"Retired."

"You're quite young for retirement. What sort of work did you do?"

Darcy bites her tongue. They're more interested in interrogating her than taking the letter seriously.

"Law enforcement."

Officer Faust raises her eyebrows.

"Police?"

"FBI, actually."

Another scribble on the notepad.

"Why did you move to Genoa Cove, Ms. Gellar?"

"I fail to see what my previous line of work has to do with someone threatening my son."

Julian takes a step forward. Is this an aggressive move meant to intimidate? Up close, he is larger than he seemed while they fought on the mat.

"You're probably overreacting. This is typical teen stuff, boys getting under each other's skin. No violence occurred."

"Not yet."

"Boys like to play games with each other," Julian says. "Nothing ever comes of notes like this. Clearly your son upset someone, and now the other boy is fighting back, not that threats are ever justified. It's all bluster. Give it time and this will blow over."

"It sounds to me like you're blaming the victim."

"Not at all. If you'll allow me to take the note, I'll follow up with the school and see if we can get to the bottom of who wrote it. Problem is there's no signature. Unless a witness comes forward, there's no way to prove who wrote the letter. It becomes a *he said, she said* situation."

After the officers leave, Darcy leans her back against the door and closes her eyes. She hadn't expected much to come of the letter, but she'd hoped the officers would take the threat seriously.

Hunter arrives at four. An engine guns as Darcy peeks through the window. She recognizes the tinted windows before tires squeal and the Ford Fusion jets down the road.

"No practice today?" Darcy asks, arranging a stack of mail on the table.

"Nah. Coach says we need a day to heal up before the game."

"Who dropped you off?"

"Oh, nobody. That's just Squiggs."

"Squiggs have a real name, or is he a Scooby Doo character?"

"Sweet," Hunter says crunching on an apple. He pokes through the refrigerator. "Any cold cuts left?"

"Your sister found a letter in your locker."

He freezes. So Hunter knew about the note. He shrugs, brushing it off as no big deal.

"Hunter, do you want to talk about it?"

"Talk about what? It's only a letter. Not like anything is going to happen."

She tries again, but Hunter won't budge. He skips out of the kitchen with a peanut butter and jelly sandwich. After his door closes, she considers calling around to verify Coach Parker canceled practice. She doesn't. Darcy trusts Hunter, though her son is hiding something.

The revolving doors routine continues as Darcy boils a pot of water on the stove. Jennifer shuffles into the kitchen with a bit more color on her cheeks.

"What's for dinner?" she asks.

Darcy knows her daughter well enough to spot disinterest. She couldn't care less about dinner and has something on her mind.

"Pasta."

"Better not be with a cream sauce. My stomach can't handle anything super heavy."

"Tomato sauce."

"Good."

Jennifer slides onto a chair and taps her phone on the table.

"What's on your mind?"

She pauses, biting her nail as the water percolates.

"Kaitlyn knows who wrote the letter."

Darcy sets the wooden spoon down and sits across from her.

"Oh? How did she find out?"

"Kaitlyn overheard a couple guys bragging about it outside the weight room after school. For what it's worth, I think the letter was only to scare Hunter."

"Why would anyone want to scare him?"

"Because he's new."

"You're new."

"Yeah, but he isn't fitting in."

Darcy parts the curtains, a compulsion she's followed with increased frequency since she saw the smiley face on Amy's house.

"Because he dresses different and likes loud music? That's ludicrous."

"It's more than that. The company he keeps...they aren't good kids."

"Who is this Squiggs character?"

Jennifer's eyebrows shoot up.

"You know him?"

"He dropped Hunter off a few minutes ago."

"I shouldn't say anything because I don't have proof. But most of us are pretty sure Squiggs is supplying most of the drugs in school."

The air rushes out of Darcy's chest. Losing her son to drugs is her greatest fear. Because a part of her believes it could happen. Isolated, introverted, and balancing on the edge of depression, Hunter is a prime candidate for addiction. And he learned from watching his mother.

"But Hunter doesn't do drugs," Jennifer quickly adds. "He'd tell me, I think."

Darcy makes a mental note to look into Hunter's new friend.

"What's this kid's real name?" Darcy asks, lowering her voice so Hunter can't eavesdrop.

"Benny Chilton. He's a senior."

"Chilton."

"Mom, the water is boiling over."

The hiss of water splashing onto flame brings Darcy's head around.

"Oh, shit."

She lowers the heat and stirs, calming the roiling water. Satisfied, she dumps the pasta into the pot.

"So who wrote the letter, Jennifer?"

Jennifer pinches the bridge of her nose.

"Aaron Torres. He's on the team with Hunter."

"Torres. Where have I heard that name?"

Jennifer swipes through her phone and sets it on the table as though afraid her social contacts can hear.

"As in Bethany Torres."

The pretty girl she met at Antonia's.

"Her brother, I take it."

"Her older brother, yeah. He's looking out for Bethany and thinks Hunter is bad news."

"Pot calling the kettle black, in my opinion."

"Don't call the police back, okay? Let me talk to Aaron first."

"I don't want you talking to this Aaron Torres. And how did you know about the police?"

"I saw them through the window, duh. That wasn't a good look, Mom. If the cops show up at school and start asking members of the football team questions, it could get a lot worse for Hunter."

Sweat dripping off her brow, Darcy kneels in front of Jennifer.

"What do you mean it could get worse?"

"Just let me talk to Aaron. Don't make this harder than it already is."

6

Hunter lingers in the kitchen after washing the plates, then he leans against the hallway wall, checking his messages. Jennifer locks herself in her room, hopefully not informing half the world about the letter before Darcy decides the best way to proceed.

Inside her bedroom, Darcy sips from a cup of calming tea as the clock ticks past sunset. From her nightstand, she grabs the anti-anxiety pills and rolls the bottle in her hand. Just one to take the edge off, and then none for the rest of the week. She glances at the window. The reflected face belongs to a liar.

A voice in her head urges her to check on Amy and wonders if Bronson followed through on his promise to call his friends at the Smith Town Police Department.

Hunter looks up when Darcy opens her door.

"Benny seems like a nice boy."

Hunter halts in place.

"Why do you say that?"

"Well, he's been driving you home, right?"

"Just a few times."

"How did you meet?"

Hunter crosses his arms.

"Why the interrogation? We went to a concert together last month, that's all. He's a good guy."

"Don't get excited, Hunter. I'm just asking how you came to be friends. Maybe you'd like to invite him to dinner some night."

He snickers.

"I doubt he'd be into that scene. Especially if everyone is judging him."

"It might be nice."

"Stop watching everything I do. I'm not one of your criminals."

Hunter cracks open a Coke and stalks into his room. Darcy braces for the door to slam, but it drifts shut. Still, she hears the lock twist.

That went well.

Darcy sips her tea and pulls back when the heat singes her lips. In the kitchen, night pours against the casement window. She checks the locks and peeks outside, but it's impossible to see with the lights on.

At that moment, it occurs to Darcy someone could be staring at her from the yard. The grinning face of a lunatic pressed close to the glass.

She clicks the light off and exhales. The yard is empty, tall grass waving with the night breeze outside the vacant home bordering the ranch. The moon is full, its face screaming over the cove and tinting everything it touches in a deathly silver.

Amy.

Grabbing her phone, she dials the girl's number. The phone doesn't ring. She tries again and gets the same result.

Damn phone. It's three years old and failing fast.

A moment later she's at Hunter's door. She knocks softly and receives no reply.

"Hey, Hunter, can I borrow your phone for a second?"

It takes several seconds before she hears the springs squeak as he climbs off his bed. The knob twists and the locking mechanism pops open. He leans in the doorway, his face suspicious.

"What's wrong with yours?"

"It works when it feels like it, and I guess it decided not to tonight. I want to check on a friend who's having trouble with a guy. It won't be a second."

"Yeah, that's fine. But the battery is toast. Either plug it in or make the call before it dies."

"Thanks."

He starts to shut the door, and she blocks it with her palm.

"Come on, Hunter. I didn't mean to pry. I meant what I said about inviting your friends to dinner some night. It won't be creepy. I'll be on my best behavior."

This elicits a small grin, a victory in Darcy's eyes. She waits until she's inside the kitchen before calling, not wanting her children to hear the Full Moon Killer's name. Though the call goes through, it rings several times and goes to voice-mail. Her anxiety rising, she dials again.

"Hello?"

"Amy, thank goodness. Is everything okay?"

"Sorry, I was checking around the house. I put new locks on the windows like you suggested, and I've got a guy coming by tomorrow to paint over that damn...face. You must think I completely lost it. I didn't mean to freak you out this morning."

"You're being cautious. I'd react the same way if I was in your position. But please understand Michael Rivers can't hurt anyone, not me, not you, and he'll never get out of prison."

"Then who painted his symbol on my house?"

Darcy lifts herself up and sits on the kitchen counter, feet dangling above the floor.

"I don't wish to downplay what you're going through, but I'm starting to think someone is playing a cruel joke on you. Are you certain you haven't confided in anyone about the abduction attempt?"

"Nobody knows except the police and my parents, and I'm sure my parents wouldn't tell anybody."

"Someone talked, and the wrong person found out and is trying to frighten you."

Amy's voice trembles.

"He's doing a damn good job."

"Serial killers fascinate the public," Darcy says, picking at a nail. "To some people, it's like a movie. They're bored, and I suppose a part of them wishes their town turned into a *Friday the 13th* movie. The media won't leave me alone, and there isn't a month that goes by without someone offering me a book deal."

"So what do you think I should do?"

"Exactly what you're doing. Keep the house locked and watch your back. What did the police say?"

Amy gives a mirthless chuckle.

"Not much. To them, it's just graffiti, something they see all the time."

"And you told them about the man following you and the symbol's meaning?"

"Yes, I'm an open book now. They're probably at the station laughing about the crazy Asian girl who thinks a ghost is chasing her. Nothing they can do when I haven't seen the man's face."

Darcy hops off the counter and paces the kitchen.

"A friend of mine retired from the Genoa Cove force a few years ago. He teaches my self-defense class, which is another thing you should consider. Bronson knows Smith Town cops and promised to call them, so don't be surprised if you see a cruiser in your neighborhood checking on the house."

Amy tries to reply when Hunter's phone beeps. The battery is close to zero.

"Sorry, Amy. I called you on my son's phone, and it's out of juice. If you can't reach me on my phone, feel free to use this number."

"Thank you, Darcy."

The next morning, Darcy gets her phone repaired and swings past the cove on the coast road. The beach is empty, no Bronson today. As she pulls into the driveway, a van labeled Gilmore Security Systems in cursive lettering wheels around the corner. Just in time.

Two men and a woman wearing dark blue polos and gray pants walk through the house before beginning the installation. The leader is a middle aged man with silver hair and a fit physique. He introduces himself as Scott.

They work through lunch and finish at four, and already the tension drains from Darcy's body. Why didn't she install an alarm months ago?

"The most important thing you can do is choose a passcode that is easy to remember but nobody else can figure out," Scott says, demonstrating how to arm the alarm. "Don't share the code with anybody, and make certain your children keep it secret."

Under Scott's supervision, Darcy enters the ranch and inputs the alarm code. Nerves cause her to mess up the code on the first try, but she corrects the error.

"Now," Scott says, pointing to the alarm. "If you forget the code, don't panic. We'll receive notification at our headquarters and call your house before contacting the police, so don't worry over a squad of police cars swarming the neighborhood if you screw up. On the other hand, in the unlikely event a real break-in occurs, response will be immediate. You couldn't be more protected."

Scott gives Darcy a tour around the perimeter of the house, explaining how the system monitors breaches at the windows and doors while he points out the cameras.

Then they sit in front of her laptop. She clicks the Gilmore icon, a padlock with a lightning bolt through the center, and a series of windows load.

"You can switch between the cameras and system monitor with one mouse click," he says, demonstrating. "Provided you have Internet connectivity, you can monitor these screens from anywhere. Go on vacation, visit friends, and you can always check on the house while you're away. And it's not just about thwarting criminals. You never need to worry about a burst pipe or what a thunderstorm did to your home while you were away. Click the app and check for yourself. That's what I call peace of mind."

"And if the kids throw a party?"

"Oh, yes," Scott says, laughing. "It works for that too."

For the first hour after the team departs, Darcy can't keep herself from checking the monitor screens as if they're a cool new toy. She loads the phone application, and the camera views appear. For fun, she steps outside and waves to the camera aimed at the front door. After a short lag, she appears in the picture.

"Best thing ever," she says, forcing herself to shut down the app so she can work on dinner.

The next few days are the best she's experienced since moving in. Jennifer obeys curfew and remains in a good mood. On Friday night, Coach Parker puts Hunter into the game at the end of the third quarter, and Hunter catches a pass for a first down. After the game, Bethany rides home with the family and roasts marshmallows with Hunter in the backyard. Even the dark of night fails to rattle Darcy, who realizes she hasn't taken her anti-anxiety medicine.

Three days after the installation, a skinny man with red hair and a tiny scar over his right eye knocks on the door. Evidenced by his uniform, he's a Gilmore technician. The man ensures she's satisfied with the new system, tours the ranch and ensures the alarms and cameras work, and asks her if she has any questions. She doesn't. Darcy couldn't be more happy with the thoroughness of the Gilmore team.

Amy's stalker disappears, the smiley face painted over, and the girl agrees to join Darcy at self-defense class. Bronson calls, confirming the Smith Town PD makes twice-daily checks on Amy's house.

All good things must come to an end.

It's a gloomy Monday morning with Halloween on the wind when Darcy glances through the rain-streaked window and sees the police cruiser pull curbside.

Darcy's first reaction is something terrible has happened to Hunter or Jennifer. The doors open, and Julian climbs out of the vehicle. The man who accompanies Julian wears dark blue slacks and a gray jacket. His black tie is too long and tucked between the buttons of a bargain store dress shirt. Like a private investigator from a sixties television sitcom, the man's hair parts on the side, slicked and oily. His exhausted eyes droop, his slightly wrinkled forehead marking him as a veteran of the force. A detective.

"Ms. Gellar?" The detective's face is grim, jaw grinding from side to side.

Julian flanks the detective, one hand touching the radio, the other at his side. Close to his holster.

"Yes."

"I'm Detective Ames," the man says, holding up his badge. "And you've met Officer Haines. Is there somewhere we can talk?"

Again her chest fills with butterflies as she wonders what happened to her kids. Did Aaron Torres hurt Hunter?

"Would you like to come in?"

Darcy stands aside and motions them into the foyer. They

follow her to the kitchen and take seats around the table. Julian studies the room, looking over the stack of mail between them. Darcy pulls the envelopes aside and sets them on the counter.

"Were you at home last night?"

Thank goodness nothing happened to the kids at school.

"Sure, I was in all night."

"A jogger found a woman's body beside the cove at dawn," Detective Ames says, leaning forward with his hands clasped on his lap. "Did you see or hear anything unusual last night, particularly between the hours of midnight and two?"

Darcy's heart hammers. She's letting her imagination run wild. It's a drowning incident, nothing more.

"I was asleep by eleven," Darcy says, stammering. "What happened?"

"Think very hard. Did a noise awaken you in the night?"

"Nothing. I got up to use the bathroom once, but that was after three."

"I see you have two teenage children—Hunter and Jennifer. Are they home today?"

"Well, no. They're in school and won't be home until after football and cheer practice."

"I see." Detective Ames removes his glasses and wipes them on his tie. "Would it be all right if I spoke with them?"

"Yes, but as I said they won't be home until later. You're welcome to come back."

"Not necessary, Ms. Gellar. I may swing past the school and speak with them sooner." Why would the detective need to talk to her kids about a woman who drowned two blocks from their house in the middle of the night? "How about strangers or unfamiliar vehicles parked in your neighborhood last evening? Anyone you didn't recognize?"

"No. People who want to use the beach tend to park further down the block near the cove."

"Of course. It's a shorter walk. Notice anyone at the cove the last few days who isn't from your neighborhood?"

She thinks of Bronson, but she's not about to bring the ex-cop into this.

"No, it's been quiet this week."

Ames gives an unconvinced grunt. His phone buzzes. The detective glances at it and slips the phone into his jacket.

"I'll cut to the chase, Ms. Gellar. I'm aware of your FBI career and your relationship with Michael Rivers."

Darcy glances away and touches her stomach, the detective's words twitching the old wound.

"If by *relationship* you mean I'm the agent he stabbed, then yes."

"My apologies. Not the best choice of words. But you were the agent who shot the Full Moon Killer."

"I don't understand what my previous career has to do with your case."

And then it hits her. This wasn't a drowning.

Ames pauses, then begins to speak. Darcy's world tears in half.

—————

7

Darcy has overcome a lot during her adult life, losing Tyler, surviving the stabbing, and forever battling anxiety, addiction, and a tendency to distrust people's intentions. Yet she's raised two children on her own, and despite not being the most present mother while she fought her inner demons, Jennifer and Hunter are good kids.

What's happening can't be possible: a series of rapes in Smith Town, a man stalking Amy and painting the Full Moon Killer's signature on her house, and now a woman murdered two blocks from her front door. These occurrences are linked, but she can't think straight.

By now Ames is at the school, meeting with Jennifer and Hunter. They learned about Michael Rivers and lived their own nightmares imagining what happened to their mother, but they've maintained a safe distance from the violence. Until now. Crouching beside the front door, she holds the phone on her lap and scrolls through her contacts until she locates Eric Hensel. She pictures her former partner—blonde hair trimmed short, trim for his late-forties, designer suit and shoes, round bifocals which he often wears on top of his head.

The call goes through after a short pause. Hensel answers as though he'd been expecting her.

"I was about to call you," Hensel says, short of breath as if he just ran inside.

"How can this happen again, Eric?"

"Slow down. Are you and the kids safe?"

"We're fine, but Amy Yang..."

"I know. For your information, Genoa Cove PD called an hour ago asking about you. A detective named Ames."

"I just met him."

"Yeah, he seems like a barrel of laughs. He asked a lot of questions about you and what your involvement was in the Rivers case, though I'm certain he knows exactly who you are. He also asked why you left the FBI and what you're doing in his village. I blew him off regarding your retirement. Not his business, and I hardly think it's relevant to his case. Just a second, Darcy." Eric presses the phone against his body and talks to someone. "Sorry about that. I'm training one of the new recruits. Give me a second to get to a quiet location."

Darcy hears Hensel walking, then a door closes. He's gone where others can't overhear his conversation, and this worries her. He shouldn't have anything to hide.

"Okay," he says. "Now I can speak."

"I don't understand why Ames thinks I know something. This can't have anything to do with the Rivers case. The bastard is in jail."

A pause.

"Ames didn't tell you."

"Tell me what?"

"The woman they found last night was twenty-two."

"Teens and early twenties, that's the age group Rivers targeted. But that's hardly unique to serial killers."

"Darcy, someone stabbed the woman repeatedly and burned a face into her neck."

The news rocks Darcy on her heels. It's a long time before she can stand without her legs buckling.

"You think Rivers is working with somebody on the outside?"

"The thought occurred to me. I'll make a few calls, check if anyone took an unhealthy interest in the Full Moon Killer in the last year. In the interim, stay calm, but watch your back, Darcy."

When she arrives at the cove, the police have cleared the crime scene and departed. Their footprints are everywhere, spreading across the sand as if a small army converged on the cove. Somewhere within the chaos, the killer left his footprints.

The former investigator inside Darcy awakens from dormancy. She walks the shoreline, picturing the cove in the moonlight—silver and blue, the dunes casting humpbacked shadows toward the water. The Full Moon Killer killed his victims and left his disgusting tag burned on their flesh before dumping their bodies elsewhere. This killer must have done the same, and that would be obvious to the ME and crime scene technicians.

He couldn't have murdered the woman this close to the neighborhood. Two houses sit on the other side of the dunes. Someone would have heard the girl scream.

The ocean sloshes against the shore, the sky gunmetal gray and threatening more rain. She turns from the sea and looks back toward the dunes. This is the only path to the cove unless one arrives by boat. The killer visited her neighborhood.

He located Amy, and now he's found Darcy.

A moment after Darcy punches the alarm code onto the keypad at the house, her phone rings. It's an unrecognized number, the area code the same as hers. She considers the call for a moment. It might be the police checking on her. Except it isn't.

The woman with the disingenuous, flowery voice identifies herself as Gail Shipley, lead reporter with the *Genoa Standard*.

"Ms. Gellar, or is it Agent Gellar?"

"How did you get this number?"

"What are your thoughts on the murder, Agent Gellar?"

"I don't know any details about the murder. Maybe you should contact Detective Ames at the Genoa Cove Police Department. He's handling the case."

"The markings on her neck are identical to the branding Michael Rivers put on his victims. Agent Gellar, is the Full Moon Killer back?"

The question dangles in the air unanswered.

"However you got this information, a phone call will confirm Michael Rivers remains locked in a cell outside Buffalo. If you print otherwise, you'll start a panic."

"When you came on board for the Rivers case, how long did it take before you caught him?"

Darcy pulls the iced tea pitcher from the refrigerator and slams the door.

"Why ask? It sounds like you learned plenty about me already."

"It was a year, correct?" Shipley frames the question as if it took a decade to find Michael Rivers. "Why was he so difficult to find?"

Darcy draws in a labored breath, fighting the urge to scream into the phone.

"Ask me another irrelevant question and I'm hanging up."

"It's not irrelevant. You tracked him down, so the Genoa Cove Police Department should consider your input invaluable."

"I don't work for the FBI anymore, Mrs. Shipley, and Michael

Rivers is only a threat to his fellow prisoners," Darcy says with cool detachment. Inside, she wants to explode. "Like I said, direct your questions about the investigation to Detective—"

"Given the similarities between the Full Moon Killer murders and the latest killing, do you think it's more likely we have a copycat on our hands, or do you believe Michael Rivers had an apprentice you never caught?"

"I'm not in a position to answer that question. I'm hanging up now."

After Darcy ends the call, her left hand is curled into a white-knuckle fist, her legs tensed to the brink of cramping. She tosses the phone across the table and glares at her angry reflection. When the phone immediately rings again, she jolts and spills the iced tea. Cursing, she wipes the mess before it dribbles over the edge.

"Hello," she snaps, expecting Shipley called her back.

"Darcy?"

She wipes the sweat off her brow and sighs.

"Sorry, Bronson. I thought you were someone else."

"Are you and the kids okay? I heard what happened. Terrifying somebody died so close to the neighborhood. Have you heard anything?"

"The police stopped by."

"Wait," Bronson says, alarm and confusion in his voice. "Why did they come to your house? The cove is clear on the other side of the neighborhood."

"Could be they visited all my neighbors." Darcy doesn't think so. None of her neighbors profile serial killers who brand faces into their victims' necks. She wonders how much Bronson knows about the case. "They wanted to know if I saw any vehicles on my street that didn't belong there."

"This is insane. Who visited?"

"Detective Ames stopped by with Julian."

"Ames? Can't imagine why they'd send their lead detective door-to-door."

"He questioned Hunter and Jennifer at school. I've been trying to contact them to find out what he asked, but neither kid is answering my texts at the moment."

"He's always concocting trouble in Genoa Cove. Should have worked in one of the big cities. I figure he's been waiting for something like this to happen for the last two decades so he can justify his existence. Did he tell you any specifics about the murder?"

"Nothing."

"Good. Wouldn't figure he would. Hey, Darcy, I don't want to sound forward, but if you'd like me to come over when the kids get home, it might help them to talk to a nosy ex-cop about the murders. Let them vent a little."

"Let me talk to them first and see where their heads are at. I'll get back to you by dinner time. Is that fine?"

"I'll be here all afternoon."

"Okay, Bronson. Thanks for checking in on us."

Accepting the tea can't allay her frayed nerves, and fighting the urge to jump back on the anti-anxiety pill wagon, Darcy paws through the cabinet for something stronger and pulls down a Merlot. She pours a glass and unlocks the deck door, remembering at the last second to enter the alarm code. The sun tries to break through, but the clouds keep beating it back. She wipes water droplets off the Adirondack chair and settles down with the wine.

The backyard ends with a meadow of chickweed, clover, and dandelion. Bees dart among the wildflowers, the wind drawing long ripples through the tall grass as though something black and spindly slithers toward the house. She sips the Merlot and taps her finger on the armrest.

Is the killer the same man raping young women in Smith

Town? Serial killers often begin with rape before working up to the ultimate power over life: murder.

Her phone buzzes with a received message. Initially she ignores the intrusion, caught up in her worry. Shrugging off the paralysis, Darcy calls up the message.

No words. Just a picture of a petite young woman planting roses along the side of a house.

Darcy doesn't need to zoom in to recognize Amy and the Smith Town residence. Glancing at the unrecognized phone number, she dials Amy's phone, her pulse thrumming.

Please pick up, please pick up.

Amy finally answers.

"Where are you?"

"Darcy? I'm outside my house. Why do you ask?"

"You're planting roses."

Amy goes silent for a long second.

"How could you know that?"

"Lock the door and don't open it for anybody. I'm calling the police."

The girl's voice quavers with frightened tears.

"What's going on?"

"Just do it."

When Darcy hears Amy slam the door and throw the lock, she hangs up and dials the Smith Town Police Department. The deep-voiced officer who answers sounds gruff and impatient, but he tells Darcy he'll send a squad car to check on Amy.

She should tell Bronson too.

AFTERWORD

Darcy calls Amy back and confirms the girl locked the house.
The nineteen-year-old is crying now, voice hoarse as she wipes a
tissue across her nose. Telling Amy the truth will only terrify the
girl, but Darcy has no choice. The killer might be outside her
window. She reveals the truth.

"Did you see anyone in the neighbor's yard?"

"Nobody," Amy says, the shade crinkling as she pulls it back.
"I can't see anyone outside."

"The picture was taken from behind, but at an angle," Darcy
says, recalling a mental image of the property next door.
"There's a thicket bordering the backyard, right?"

"Yes, a stand of trees above the creek bed. But the yard is
empty."

Over Amy's phone, Darcy hears the approaching siren. That
was fast.

"I'm calling my friend, the man I told you about. Stay with
the police. I'll be over soon."

Darcy checks the time. In two hours, school lets out. Until
then, the kids are safe. She texts Jennifer and Hunter and
demands they go straight to practice after school and remain

with their friends and coaches. Hunter doesn't reply. Jennifer sends a confused message, asking for details. By now the detective finished his interviews, and the entire village knows about the murder.

Jennifer's next message tugs at Darcy's heart.

Are we in danger?

Only a precaution, Darcy types back. *Neither you nor Hunter should be alone. I'll pick you up after practice.*

Darcy phones Bronson during the drive to Smith Town and tells him about the anonymous message.

"Whatever you do, don't delete the message," he says. "Let the police check the number."

Darcy understands the evidence is crucial. During her time with the Behavior Analysis Unit, she used the latest technology to track calls and messages. She doesn't tell him this, only warms a little inside when the man promises to meet her at Amy Yang's house in twenty minutes.

Two officers patrol the backyard while another pair speak with Amy in the doorway when Darcy arrives. The girl wraps the same tattered blanket around her shoulders, making her appear waif-like, destitute. The officers eye Darcy with suspicion as she bounds out of the Prius and up the walkway.

"Ma'am, I'll need you to stay where you are," the officer, a thick-shouldered man with a mustache, says.

"It's okay," says Amy, letting the blanket fall down her shoulder. "She's my friend, the woman who called you about the picture."

The second officer is thin as a rail and has a boyish face. His skittish movements mark him as a green rookie. Neither officer takes his eyes off Darcy until Amy hugs her in the doorway.

Bronson arrives in his Dodge pickup a minute after. The rookie moves his fingers toward the gun before the older partner shouts with recognition.

"The cove run out of fish early today, old man?"

Wearing a tight-lipped smile, Bronson glances between the officer and Darcy.

"I see you're letting that hamster grow over your lip again, Pinder. Shave that thing before it scares away the women."

Amy, who'd been glancing in confusion between the two men, relaxes a little when Pinder laughs at the joke. The police seem to take the situation more seriously now that Bronson is here.

"This is Bronson, the friend I told you about," Darcy says, touching Amy's cheek. "You're safe now. Bronson is a retired Genoa Cove policeman."

"Little leagues," Pinder says with a smirk.

They convene around the kitchen table, two chairs to serve the five of them. Only Amy sits, the girl trembling as Darcy rubs the goosebumps off the girl's shoulders. Amy and Darcy repeat the events of the last hour, then Darcy hands the phone to Pinder, who orders the rookie to send a copy of the message back to the office.

"Probably using a burner," Bronson says, studying the photograph over the rookie's shoulder.

A burner is a prepaid phone with no contract minutes. If the buyer pays in cash, it's almost impossible to identify the caller.

"That would be my guess," Pinder says, itching his neck. "Good for covering your tracks."

Bronson shares an unreadable glance with Pinder, before he opens the shade and studies the backyard.

"Does it look to you like he took the photograph from the trees?"

"Given the angle, he must have. Lansdale and Gracin are checking for shoe prints. If the ground is wet, we might get lucky. We'll interview the neighbors before we leave, see if anyone saw a guy hanging around the backyards. Trouble is, this neighborhood is a drug trafficking hotbed. Vehicles that don't belong here always come and go."

Amy puts on a pot of coffee for the officers. Darcy can't stomach caffeine now, her imagination centering on a man photographing her children from a nondescript vehicle parked outside the school.

When the other two officers finish investigating the backyard, Pinder sends the rookie with them to canvas the neighborhood. Darcy suggests Amy should rest while company is here to watch the house. The girl's body slumps with exhaustion, dark circles bordering her eyes and making them appear as black holes.

After Amy departs for the bedroom, Bronson leans against the counter and pops a stick of gum into his mouth.

"It's clear the girl has a stalker," Pinder says. "First she spotted the man following her through town, then the vandalism, and now he's taking pictures of her."

"But why did he send it to you?" Bronson asks, swinging his gaze at Darcy. "And how did he get your number? It's unlisted."

Bronson's words pop Darcy's head up. How did he know her number was unlisted?

"Could be this guy broke in and got his hands on Amy's phone and accessed her contact list," Bronson continues.

Pinder chews on the theory.

"That's a lot of effort just to steal a phone number. Besides, most phones don't work until you enter a passcode."

"Maybe Amy didn't set up a passcode. Not every phone requires you do."

"We'll dust her phone for prints to make sure, but it feels like a shot in the dark."

Bronson puts his hands on his hips and furrows his brow.

"A stalker following Amy sends a photograph to Darcy the

day after someone murders a young woman a stone's throw from Darcy's neighborhood. Could it be the same man?"

"It's the same guy," Darcy says, meeting Bronson's gaze.

"How can you be certain?"

"The graffiti on Amy's house, the smiley face, is the same mark the killer branded on the dead woman's neck."

Bronson glares at her, Pinder glancing between the two and waiting for an explanation.

"How could you know this? There's nothing about that on the news, and nobody I spoke to mentioned the killer branded the victim."

Indecision swims through Darcy's head. She's run from her past, hiding her head in the sand until the monsters converged on her. She's been a fool.

"Before I came to Genoa Cove, I worked for the FBI's Behavioral Analysis Unit." As Darcy speaks, Pinder narrows his eyes and leans forward, palms on the table. "My job was to hunt serial killers."

"Jesus," Bronson mutters. His eyes light with understanding. "I knew I recognized your name. Agent Gellar. You're the woman who caught the Full Moon Killer."

The surprise in Bronson's voice doesn't register in his eyes. The silence in the tiny kitchen is explosive. Pinder's mouth hangs open for a heartbeat before he speaks.

"The branding...the graffiti on Amy's wall...was that the mark the Full Moon Killer used?"

"Yes," Darcy says in a choked whisper.

She can see Bronson watching her from the corner of her eye.

"But he's in prison. Did you catch the wrong guy?"

"No." Darcy touches her belly.

The scars slashed across her stomach are the only proof she needs that Michael Rivers was the Full Moon Killer.

8

Bronson trails Darcy back to Genoa Cove, and he follows her up the walkway as she accompanies Amy into the house. The little ranch doesn't have a guest room, but Darcy determines to make do even if she needs to give Amy her bed and sleep on an air mattress. There is safety in numbers, and Darcy won't let the girl live alone with a serial killer following her.

A dark thought crawls on spider's legs across her face. Amy is the killer's target, and Darcy invited the girl into her children's lives.

Darcy checks her phone. No news from Hunter and Jennifer. By now the kids are practicing with their teams. She fights the urge to drive up the hill and throw them both into the car. She can't protect them twenty-four hours a day, and surrounded by coaches and teammates, they're safer now than they would be at home a short walk from where the killer deposited his first victim.

Darcy enters the alarm code, aware of Bronson watching over her shoulder. His eyes sweep the downstairs and narrow on the closed bedroom doors while he scopes out the ranch, walking from room to room. Amy declines Darcy's offer to pour her a cup of calming tea. Instead, she zombie-shuffles as Darcy leads her to the bedroom. With the girl settled, Darcy softly closes the door.

Finding Bronson inside the kitchen, Darcy releases a strained breath and tosses her keys on the table.

"You should have told me," Bronson says, crossing his arms.

"It wasn't relevant before this morning."

"Dammit, I knew you weren't a typical soccer mom when you broke that choke hold. But the woman who caught Michael Rivers..."

His words trail off.

"I'd appreciate it if you didn't spread the word. I've already got a newspaper writer to deal with."

"What's his name?"

"Her name. Gail Shipley." Bronson's mouth twists. "You've met her?"

"Let's just say she made a few cops' lives difficult during my tenure. She's a bulldog. Once she latches onto a story, she won't let go. It's a little disconcerting she figured out who you are."

"It's not difficult to find a person through the Internet."

Bronson nods, pondering the situation.

"What if he didn't act alone?" Darcy asks. "Michael Rivers. Some serial killers work in teams: the Furlan brothers in Italy, Fred and Rosemary West, several others."

"You knew the killer left a mark on the woman's neck, so you must be in contact with the FBI."

"I keep in touch with my former colleagues."

"What are the chances they get involved?"

"After one murder? Unlikely unless the Genoa Cove PD requests their presence. Even with the branding, one murder isn't enough to prove a serial killer exists."

Bronson's eyes flick from the window to the deck door.

"Impressive security system. Looks like the installer did a thorough job."

"Yes."

"And you said you keep a gun in the house."

She fidgets on the chair and chews her nails.

"In a safe inside my bedroom. The kids know it's there, but I don't share the combination."

"You worked for the feds and shot a dangerous murderer, so I won't ask if you still feel comfortable firing the Glock."

"There's a gun club outside Smith Town. I shoot every few weeks, just enough to maintain skill."

"Rogers Gun Club on Walnut Road," Bronson says, itching his chin. "I stop by occasionally."

They fill the uncomfortable quiet with small talk. Bronson suggests ordering takeout, but a lead brick sleeps inside Darcy's stomach. After an hour, Bronson leaves with a promise to check on Darcy after dinner.

A hushed stillness falls over the ranch, unspoken fears whispering from hidden corners. Darcy doesn't recall when she fell asleep before she awakens on the couch to a door slamming. She pops her head up as Hunter fishes through the refrigerator for a snack.

"What time is it?" Darcy groans, rubbing her eyes.

Dusk colors the window deep magenta. Darcy bounds off the couch and double-checks if Hunter armed the alarm.

"You didn't cook dinner."

"Shit, I must have fallen asleep. Ask your sister what she wants and I'll order a pizza."

Hunter sinks his teeth into a pear and chews.

"She's not here."

Darcy pulls her phone out of her pocket. Jennifer hasn't written.

"What do you mean she's not here? Didn't cheer practice let out at five?"

Worried, she dials Jennifer's phone. It rings until the call transfers to voice-mail. Darcy fires off a text.

Where are you?

The seconds seem like hours as she waits for Jennifer to reply. When she doesn't, Darcy's head spins.

"She knew to come home after practice," Darcy tells Hunter, who sends a second text to Jennifer. "I don't understand why she won't answer her phone. Where does she like to go after practice if she doesn't come straight home?"

"Check Kaitlyn's."

"I don't have her number. Do you?"

Hunter shakes his head as he sips from a glass of water.

"I know her Instagram. You could message her."

"Could you do it, Hunter? I need to make a phone call."

Hunter sends his message while Darcy phones Bronson. Full dark seeps out of the Atlantic and spreads toward the cove. Darcy explains the situation to Bronson, who slips on a jacket and snatches his keys.

"I'm sure there's a perfectly reasonable explanation," he says. "You know how kids are."

"After the occurrences of the last twenty-four hours, the worry is justified."

"Do you have a photo of Jennifer on your phone?"

"Yes."

"Send it to me. Stay put. I'm going out to look for her."

"I should call the police."

"No. They'll just tell you to wait a few hours. Kids take off with friends without telling their parents all the time," Bronson says, stepping on the gas pedal. "Let me call. I'll make sure they take this seriously."

As Darcy hangs up the phone, Hunter throws a sweatshirt

over his head and grabs the keys.

"Where are you going?"

"Kaitlyn isn't looking at her Instagram. I'll drive through downtown, then over to Kaitlyn's."

She wants to argue with him, but she needs another set of eyes looking for Jennifer. The door shuts, and footsteps approach from the hallway. Darcy almost forgot Amy, who'd slept even longer than Darcy. An oversized sweatshirt falls over the girl's shorts.

"What's all the excitement about?"

Darcy fills Amy in.

"I should have brought my car over," Amy says, wringing her hands. "You could use another vehicle now."

"God, what if the same guy who came after you targeted my daughter?"

Darcy and Amy are inextricably tied to Michael Rivers, and the profiler inside Darcy knows her daughter is a logical target. She sends another text to Jennifer, and this message drops into the bottomless pit that swallowed the others.

"She's close to my age, yes?" Amy asks.

"Fourteen."

Fear flashes in the girl's eyes. Michael Rivers attacked Amy when she was fifteen.

"Jennifer's phone might be dead. That would explain why she hasn't answered."

"But where is she? She's impulsive and makes crazy decisions, but she wouldn't take off without telling anybody when a killer is loose."

An hour passes. They're seated at the kitchen table now, Darcy unraveling fiber by fiber. She glares at the clock. By now, the post-dinner cleanup should be finished with Hunter and Jennifer locked in their rooms, finishing homework. How could things go wrong so quickly?

Then another half-hour. An overwhelming sense of dread deepens. Hunter checks with several of Jennifer's friends, and none have seen her tonight. And then Hunter isn't answering texts, either.

Didn't Bronson call the police? A second call will light a fire under the GCPD. Darcy phones the station as the siren calls of the anti-anxiety pills tempt her.

Officer Faust, the female officer who accompanied Julian to the house after the threats against Hunter, knocks at eight o'clock. The officer's presence makes Darcy worry the worst has happened, that the police found Jennifer's body dumped in a dark alleyway. But Faust is here to ask if Darcy has heard from her daughter since she went missing. Over Darcy's shoulder, Faust eyes the young girl huddled on the couch.

"Don't worry, Ms. Gellar. Jennifer is probably with a friend, and you'll hear from her soon. We have every cruiser in the village looking for her."

"I don't understand why it took you so long. If it were your kid, you'd want the police searching immediately."

Faust gives her a confused look and is about to ask Darcy something when her radio crackles with a message from head-quarters.

Faust's presence does little to calm Darcy. The police have bigger problems with a murderer loose.

Dammit. She never should have let Hunter take the car.

Faust asks all the typical questions: who are Jennifer's friends and has she ever disappeared like this before? The circle leads nowhere, and eventually Faust finishes her interview and departs to search for Jennifer.

The door closes. Then the cruiser's motor guns and fades into the night. Sickness, terror, and helplessness gather around the solitude.

Too much to handle. The bottle on the nightstand warns

Darcy to only take one pill every twenty-four hours. When she wills her hands to stop shaking, she pops two in her mouth and swallows. The effect hits her quick. The medication goes beyond dulling her senses and slurring her speech. It hollows her out and turns her numb.

It comes as a shock when the front door bangs open and Jennifer stomps inside.

Darcy yelps. Words cannot express the relief and confusion she feels as Jennifer rips her jacket off and slams it over a coat hanger.

"Where the hell have you been?"

Jennifer spins around. Anger twists her face. She swings the closet shut with a bang.

"Where have *you* been? I waited at the fucking field for over an hour for you to pick me up. Can you guess how stupid I felt standing there in the dark? Oh, and you owe me fifteen bucks for the Uber."

"Then you misunderstood. I clearly stated you needed to tell me if you didn't have a ride, and I'd get you."

Jennifer squints.

"You're taking the pills again."

"I'm not crazy, Jennifer. I never told you I'd come get you."

"You're losing it, Mother." Jennifer darts across the room and holds her phone in front of Darcy's face. "Explain this message."

Darcy swipes the phone from Jennifer's hand and fixes her with a glare that would melt most teenagers, but her daughter is not an ordinary teenager tonight. Red-faced, Jennifer is the tremor before the ground opens.

Wait at the practice field. I'll pick you up as soon as I can get there.

Darcy stares at the message as though doing so will make sense of the matter. The message appears to have come from Darcy's phone, but that's impossible.

"I never wrote this."

"Your goddamn name is on the message."

Darcy's phone rests in her back pocket. She kept the phone in her possession all day. Calling up her messages, she confirms she never sent this text.

"Number one, if you curse at me again, I'll ground you for the rest of the semester. Number two, this isn't my message. And why didn't you answer any of the texts I sent you in the last few hours?"

Jennifer swings her gaze to Amy on the couch.

"And who is that?"

"A friend. I'll explain after. What about the messages you never answered?"

Jennifer huffs and points at her battery level, a notch above zero.

"My battery died while I was waiting in the freaking dark. I had to jump the fence and plug the phone into the press box so I could order the Uber. I didn't get your messages until I was halfway home."

After Darcy sends Jennifer to her room, she sits beside Amy. The altercation with Jennifer tore a hole through the drug-induced haze, and now she sees with clarity how ugly this looks.

"Sorry you had to see that. I'm working with Jennifer, but she flies off the handle when she gets upset."

"I should leave," Amy says, standing up.

"Absolutely not. You're a guest in my house, and you're not staying alone until the police capture this guy. None of us are."

Darcy calls Hunter to deliver the news. Hunter, complaining he is hungry, wants to stop for food on the way home.

"One quick stop, and then you need to get home ASAP."

Hunter agrees.

The next call is to Bronson, who answers on the first ring. The big truck motor growls in the background.

"Jennifer made it home."

"That's a relief. I couldn't find her at the school. What on earth happened?"

Strange. Bronson drove past the field to look for Jennifer. Is her daughter lying? Maybe he passed by while she recharged her phone in the press box.

"I'll explain it all later. Listen, someone messaged Jennifer and made it look like I sent it."

"What did the message say?"

"That I'd pick her up after practice, and she was to wait at the field. I clicked on the sender and wrote down the phone number."

"Good. Read it off to me, and I'll have one of the guys at the department give it a once over. It's either a helluva joke, or—"

"Bronson, did you call the GCPD? Because when Officer Faust came here, she acted like this was news to her."

"Of course, I called. Are you questioning me?"

His words make her flinch.

"No, I'm sorry."

He waits before he responds.

"I'm the one who should be sorry. No reason for me to get upset. This is your kid. I understand how scared you must have been. Send me that number."

Darcy reads him the number after Bronson stops along the shoulder. She pictures the truck on a lonely country road, darkness rushing toward him. Damn the pills. They're playing with her mind.

"Got it. It's probably another burner number or a really dumb kid."

"I don't think a dumb kid could pull off a fake this convincing."

"True. Glad Jennifer made it home. I need to swing by my house, then I'll stop by after."

"Thank you again, Bronson."

Darcy starts a pot of coffee, anticipating a sleepless night. From the way Amy sits ramrod straight on the couch, eyes shifting every few seconds, it's clear the girl is uncomfortable and feels she has overstayed her welcome.

"We'll get through this, Amy. Here." Darcy hands her the remote. "There must be a show you like to watch. Order a movie if nothing better is on."

Amy takes the remote in one limp hand and droops against the cushions.

A laugh track follows Darcy into the kitchen. Anything is better than dead quiet while she works. She cleans a few dirty plates in the sink while she waits for the coffee. As before, she can't see into the yard with the kitchen light on, but now it's more than paranoia rippling chills down her back. A serial killer haunts the shadows of Genoa Cove, a murderer who targets women tied to Michael Rivers, and her daughter isn't taking the danger seriously.

Over the last three years, she strove to bury the profiler lurking inside her mind and put the past to rest. A mistake. To this point, she's given the police their best leads. Their only leads as far as she can tell.

Placing a dish on the drying rack, she wipes her hands on the towel and assesses the bullet points. A rapist attacked multiple young women in Smith Town, and budding serial killers often cut their teeth as rapists. All the girls, including Amy, fall into the age group Rivers targeted, as does the young woman the killer dropped on the beach.

Michael Rivers had an accomplice she'd failed to detect three years ago, or someone just found a taste for killing.

The ages of the victims tell her little. Rapists and murderers attack women outside their own age brackets. But most hunt within racial lines, which means the killer is a white male. Amy Yang is Asian, but Darcy's experiences taught her murderers see the world in black and white, no nuances or shades of gray. And Amy is a link in the chain attaching Darcy to the Full Moon Killer.

No evidence exists the killer grew up in coastal North Carolina. More likely he followed Darcy and Amy here. But the raped girls described their attacker as a white male wearing a ski mask, average size and build.

He probably followed the girls at first. The killer would want to watch them, fantasize before he acted. Did he make contact with the girls, or did he float on the periphery, a shark hunting shallow waters? Darcy places the man between the ages of twenty-five and thirty-five, old enough to have followed Michael Rivers in the news, young enough to fit in with girls in their mid-twenties or younger. Maybe he passed them in a bar or club. A fake ID will get most teenagers past the bouncer.

The text Jennifer received troubles her. It could have been a school prank, but the faked message convinced Darcy until she compared the number to her own.

She jots down another mental note. The killer possesses information technology skills.

After she pours the coffee, she rechecks the locks and alarm. Her laptop is open on the counter. Infrared cameras pick out views surrounding the ranch in sharp contrasts, the shadows exaggerated and monstrous.

"What's on tonight?" Darcy asks, sitting beside Amy. She hasn't watched television in years and keeps her cable subscription for the kids.

"I don't watch TV."

The laughs continue, but Amy never joins in, only stares trance-like at the digital pictures flashing on the screen. Darcy reaches over and mutes the volume. A stunned expression freezes Amy's face, and the girl turns her head at Darcy as though awaiting instructions.

"Amy, could you tell me why you quit school?" The girl shrugs and looks down at the hands folded in her lap. "Last we spoke, you'd won a scholarship to a private college. Am I recalling correctly?"

Amy blinks.

"How far did you get?"

"Finished my freshman year."

Darcy's approach is slow, careful. The smallest misstep will unravel the teenager.

"Sometimes we start college before we're ready. I know I did." When Amy doesn't reply, Darcy pauses and regroups. "After what happened to me three years ago, I didn't sleep for a long time. And when I did I always had—"

"Dreams."

The word hangs in the air, a black wind stirring the medication's haze.

"Yes, bad dreams." Darcy waits for a reply or reaction. When none comes she continues. "I tried to tough it out, pretended this was something I could conquer on my own. Like running to build up endurance or studying for a final exam. But I didn't have the tools to do it on my own. None of us do. I talked to someone and it helped."

"I don't want to see a psychiatrist."

"Is it the cost? I'll help you."

Sudden intensity lights Amy's eyes.

"Do you know what it's like to dream he's killing you over and over? Then you wake up, and all those girls are dead. Except I'm not. Why me? Why did God choose to save me and let the other girls die?"

Darcy leans against the backrest and closes her eyes. Survivor's guilt. Michael Rivers continues to destroy lives from a jail cell.

When Darcy blinks her eyes open, Amy falls against her

shoulder and cries. She strokes the girl's hair, kisses the top of her head as she did Jennifer when her daughter was younger. The sobs taper off a minute later, and Amy sits up.

"Sorry," Amy says, wiping her eyes with her shirtsleeve.

"There's no reason to feel guilty. Those girls wouldn't be alive today if he'd captured you, and my death wouldn't have brought back any of the victims. We're both alive because we fought back. Don't waste your second chance. Fight for the life you earned."

The teenager gives an almost imperceptible nod as she wipes her nose on a tissue. Darcy doesn't know if she's gotten through to the girl, but Amy seems more at ease in the unfamiliar surroundings.

"You want to watch more of the show?"

"I'll find something else, I think."

Darcy sips from the mug and places it on the end table. Her stomach growling, she realizes she's barely eaten in the last twenty-four hours. She pads barefoot to the kitchen and decides skipping dinner was a mistake. In the refrigerator, she grabs deli turkey, lettuce, and condiments, then slices four rolls on the cutting board.

Picking up the phone, she rings Jennifer, who sulks behind the locked door of her bedroom.

"What?"

"How about you take a deep breath and join us in the living room? I made turkey sandwiches."

"Yum."

The reply overflows with sarcasm.

"We all need to eat," Darcy says, spreading mustard on her roll. "No sense getting sick."

"Who's the girl?"

"Someone I told you about after I left the FBI. Come out. I'll introduce you."

"So awkward."

"Jennifer."

"Okay, okay."

"Have you heard from your brother? He should have come home by now."

Jennifer pauses to check her messages.

"Nada."

Darcy wraps Hunter's sandwich and slides it into the refrigerator. Calling his phone, she gets his voice-mail and leaves a message.

"You've been out long enough, Hunter. Searching for my children is starting to wear on me tonight."

Jennifer's door opens as Darcy carries the sandwiches into the living room.

"You never let us eat on the couch," Jennifer says, leaning against the entryway.

"Have a seat and feed your face. Lose another pound, and your skeleton ass will scare everyone away at Kaitlyn's party."

Jennifer's face brightens. Darcy knows her daughter deserves punishment for her latest outburst, but she also appreciates the stress they're under, Amy included. Darcy's inner psychologist acknowledges Jennifer needs something to look forward to, an escape from the constant danger.

Despite Darcy's concerns over how Jennifer will react, her daughter eases Amy into a conversation, and soon the girls are talking about music and apps and next year's festival lineup between sandwich bites. It's the only time Darcy has seen Amy smile, and she wishes she could wrap both girls in her arms and hug them close. Should her daughter reign in the explosions, she will be a leader, a teacher, an organizer. Darcy's heart warms with love and pride.

Giggles echo down the hallway while Jennifer shows Amy around the house. When they return, they decide Amy will sleep in Jennifer's room. The queen-size mattress is large enough, and Jennifer claims Amy won't get a wink of sleep in her mother's room with Darcy's snores crumbling the walls.

It's strange to see the girls hit it off, regardless of the five-year age difference, until Darcy considers the abduction attempt on Amy Yang. Amy stopped growing at fifteen and found a safe place in her mind to hibernate. In reality, Amy is a fifteen-year-old girl living on her own. The state sees her as an adult, but Darcy knows the truth.

When the talk shifts to cute boys, Darcy takes the cue to leave the girls alone and retreats to her bedroom. Locking the door, she closes her eyes and breathes, a trick to clear her mind. Theories about the killer still run through her head. If she worked as a federal agent, she'd call the prison and check the logs for Michael Rivers' frequent visitors. Eric Hensel could find out.

But Darcy doesn't need Hensel to conduct her own research. She opens two search windows on her laptop. Into one she types Michael Rivers, the other the Full Moon Killer. She cross-references both with Boolean searches for fans and message boards. The windows fill with hyperlinks. Darcy clicks on a promising link, a message board devoted to famous serial killers.

Here is the ugly underbelly of the world wide web. While most of the posters and admins discuss various serial killers with twisted fascination and academic curiosity, others tread beyond normal interest. These are the people who cheer the Manson family murders and speak of names like Speck, Bundy, and Dahmer with reverence. Darcy makes a note of these posters. They hide behind user names, but a few divulge locations. None are from North Carolina or New York.

One poster stands out. *FM-Kill-Her*. Darcy clicks on his avatar, a bloody blade against a full moon. The profile displays the poster's recent messages and most active forum topics. A red dot beside the avatar tells her the administrators suspended the poster, and a quick scan through his recent comments uncovers the disturbing post which caused his suspension.

Darcy covers her mouth. It's a short story, a disgusting piece of fan fiction written from the Full Moon Killer's point of view as he brutally murders teenage girls at a slumber party. The poster included photographs or some form of artwork, but the admins removed the pictures and locked the thread. She wonders why they didn't delete the topic, but the 10,000 views, huge numbers for a niche website, draw eyes and sell advertising.

Steeling her stomach, she forces herself to read on. If *FM-Kill-Her* left a trail of breadcrumbs, she'll follow them to the psycho's true identity. Her heart lurches. He named one of the victims *Amy*. Her murder is excruciating and brutal, the killer chopping Amy into bits as a torrent of blood splashes the walls. Nausea gurgling in her throat, Darcy searches the text for her own name. And finds it. The final victim.

She calls Hensel. The agent sounds relieved to hear from her. Though the FBI isn't involved, Hensel must be following the case.

"I've got someone you should look into," she says, saving an image of the screen in case the site removes the post.

"Shoot."

She reads him the name and web address.

"Chances are it's some lunatic who lives with his parents," Hensel says, clicking through the pages. "The odds on this being the Darkwater Cove killer are slim."

"Any way to track his real name?"

"If the FBI was involved, I'd pressure the site owner to turn over domain addresses. But we're not involved, so…"

"It's a serial killer, Eric. It's only one body, but the murder and branding are homages to Michael Rivers. This is either a crazed fan, or Rivers has someone killing for him."

"A partner."

"That's what I'm afraid of."

Hensel pauses for a beat. He's a good agent, the best investigator she partnered with. She hears him processing the evidence, and memories of working together drift back to Darcy like a favorite song from her youth.

"I'll call the lead detective on the case," Hensel says. "Maybe I can make him see what he's up against. That might be enough to push FBI involvement up the chain of command."

Finally.

"It wouldn't hurt to check with the prison and see who visited Michael Rivers over the last three years."

"Did you boss me around this much when we were partners?" Hensel chuckles. "Not to worry, Darcy. I had the same idea."

Darcy breathes easier knowing her old friend has an eye on the Genoa Cove murder. Inside the closet, she enters the safe code and opens the door. Removing the Glock, the same gun she used as a federal agent, she lets the weight of the weapon settle on her palm. Like an old friend.

She spins and aims the gun at the window, imagining the killer trying to break in. She scrutinizes the weapon and reminds herself to clean it soon. Then she places it in the safe and locks the door.

Headlights sweep across the window when she returns to the living room. Hunter? No, the lights are too high for the Prius. The thump of a truck door closing announces Bronson, and she opens the door before he knocks.

"I got us snacks," he says, raising a bag of donuts and pastries. "Sorry. It's a cliche, but the old cop in me can't pass up a late night special."

"I could go for comfort food."

His eyes search the living room. Muttered laughter comes from Jennifer's bedroom.

"Where did everybody disappear to?"

"Jennifer and Amy apparently became best friends," Darcy says, tilting her head toward the bedroom. "And I don't know where the hell Hunter is."

"Should I go out looking again?"

"You've done enough. Sit and eat. I'll put the ballgame on."

Bronson plops his heavy frame on the couch and opens the bag. Darcy returns with paper towels and hands him one. She doesn't know where to sit. Beside him, or in the recliner? She splits the difference and curls up on the opposite end of the couch. The confectionery delights taste wonderful, but she can't relax. Hunter is prone to leave the house and wander, but he should know better than to do so on this of all nights. The game ends, and Bronson checks his watch.

"It's okay," Darcy says. "No sense in both of us staying awake."

"You sure you don't want me to look for him?"

"He has the car, he's not stuck in the middle of nowhere. He does this sometimes."

Bronson studies her.

"If you're certain. Tell me when he shows up."

"I will."

He jiggles the keys in his hands. Then he's gone, and Darcy pours another cup of coffee as her phone sits in silence.

It's midnight when Hunter opens the door. He's quiet, but every nerve in Darcy's body stands at attention. His footsteps roust her from dozing. She flicks off the television.

"Why, Hunter?"

"I was just out driving and thinking."

"In my car and using the gas I pay for."

Hunter slips his hand into his pocket and removes his wallet. Darcy notices a cut on his forefinger.

"Here," he says, handing her a ten-dollar bill.

"It's not about the money. Keep it. What happened to your hand?"

He glances down at his finger and shrugs.

"Cut it somehow. I don't remember."

"Hunter, I wish you'd talk to me. Half the time you're never here, and I can't tell what's going on inside that head of yours. If something is bothering you..."

"Nothing is bothering me."

A lie. The way he averts his eyes and protectively folds his arms betrays him.

"But if something was bothering you, you'd talk to me. Right?"

"Sure, Mom."

Darcy grabs her ponytail and tugs.

"Okay. No using the car for the next week."

She braces herself for a Jennifer-like explosion, but he only nods and hands her the keys. This frightens her more than an argument. He's hollow inside and pushes everyone away, and she's losing her ability to reach him.

In bed, Darcy stares at the ceiling. The tree outside her window draws shadows across the walls as soft murmurs from her daughter's room slip through the plaster.

As sleep pulls her under, another worry tugs at Darcy. Something Detective Ames asked her.

Had she noticed any strangers or unknown vehicles parked in her neighborhood before the murder?

Yes. Just one person.

Bronson.

9

The light through the window blinds Darcy when two hands shake her awake. She jolts and sits up, gaze swiveling between Amy, Jennifer, and the clock. Nine o'clock. She overslept.

Jennifer wears a sweatshirt off the shoulder and a pair of running shorts two sizes too small for her frame. Amy dons conservative items from Jennifer's wardrobe—Adidas sweatpants and an Atlanta Braves t-shirt. It's the concerned twist to Amy's mouth that gets Darcy's attention.

Darcy sits up and pulls a pillow between her back and the headboard.

"Is something wrong?"

"There was another rape in Smith Town last night," Amy says as Jennifer hands Darcy her iPad.

The lead story on the *Genoa Standard's* website details the rape of an unnamed teenage girl in Smith Town. Darcy cringes at the byline—Gail Shipley wrote the article—and scans the text. The rape occurred between ten and eleven o'clock last night, and the only description the Smith Town Police Department has to go on is the attacker was a young, white male of indeterminate age wearing a ski mask, medium build, height around six feet. The police urge women to walk in pairs and keep to well-lit areas after dark.

"Good thing you left that hellhole," Jennifer tells Amy as Darcy hands the tablet back to her. "None of my friends go anywhere near Smith Town."

"All of my stuff is there," Amy says, biting her lip. "I don't want to go back."

"We'll go together," Darcy says, "and when we make the trip, we'll have Bronson wait outside. How many months do you have left on your rental contract?"

"Nine months. What am I going to do?"

"We'll talk to the landlord and explain that a man is stalking you. He doesn't need to know the details. If he's a good man, he'll see you as a hardship case and let you out of the contract. If not, you can look into a sublease."

A door opens. Hunter totters past, brushing the hair out of his eyes on his way to the bathroom.

"Did you hear the news?"

Darcy wishes Jennifer wouldn't show so much excitement over the Smith Town attack with Amy in the room. Hunter stops and leans his arm on the jamb.

"What news?"

"Someone attacked another girl in Smith Town."

Hunter yawns and departs without comment.

While the girls make breakfast, Darcy edges the door shut and pulls her laptop into bed with her. Exiting out of her email, she types *Bronson Severson and Genoa Cove* into the search bar. Several pages of results accumulate, the first page filled with links to Bronson's self-defense course and announcements of his retirement.

On the second page she finds a story from three years ago. Officer Bronson Severson responded to a dispute between two young males outside Katherine's Grill on Main Street in Genoa Cove. The argument turned physical, and Bronson broke one of the assailant's arms while wrestling him to the ground.

The comments section below the article turn ugly, and some posts are as recent as a week ago. The story remains a hot button topic for Genoa Cove residents. The predictable argument ensues between police supporters who believe the accused are always guilty, and those who see police brutality everywhere. As Darcy scrolls deeper into the debate, it becomes clear the vast majority of residents believe Bronson used excessive force. One poster refers to Bronson as a powder keg, an out-of-control thug with a history of brutality. Another claims his wife divorced him after he struck her during an argument.

Darcy closes the laptop. What sort of man did she invite into her home?

The shower water is cold, and Darcy remembers there's an extra body in the house. Either she needs a new water heater, or she'll have to schedule her showers at a different time of day. She wraps a towel around her body and pads from the bathroom into the bedroom. The sound of a motor brings her to the window as a black sedan moves slowly down the street as though searching for an address. Sunlight glares against the windshield and makes it difficult to see, but as the car passes, she spots Aaron Torres in the driver seat. The car stops in front of their house and idles. Music thumps behind closed windows, four boys cocking their heads for a good look at her house.

Throwing on her clothes, Darcy runs for the front door. As she hits the walkway, the sedan speeds around the corner, tires squealing and tracing long black claws across the macadam.

"Mom?"

Darcy spins around in the entryway and finds Jennifer watching from the kitchen.

"Stay inside, Jennifer."

"Who was that?"

"Do as I say. And I want to know if your brother leaves the house."

"If you say so."

Darcy still has the letter. She pulls the note out of the bookcase and taps it against her hand, considering if she should call the police. And tell them what? That a car full of teenage boys cruised past the house in broad daylight? They turned the music up on their approach. They wanted her to see.

Her phone rings as she watches the window for their return. It's Bronson.

"Hey, you never called about Hunter."

"Shit, I forgot," she says, stepping outside and closing the door. "He came home five minutes after you walked out, if you can believe it."

"Did he explain?"

"As I told you, he needs to get away sometimes. If he was drinking himself into blackouts or tagging along with the wrong crowd, I'd worry."

She remembers Squiggs, the kid she saw Hunter with in the school parking lot. Maybe she *should* worry about the crowd Hunter hangs with.

"Are you going to do anything about it?"

"About what?"

"Hunter."

"Oh. Yes, of course. I grounded him from the car, and I'll speak to him about it again later."

Darcy bites her hand. Why is she justifying methods of discipline to a man she barely knows?

"I hear birds. You must be outside."

Paranoia pulls her head around, and she searches for his pickup.

"Getting some fresh air," she says, holding back about Aaron

Torres and his friends until she speaks to Bronson and hears his side of the police brutality rumors.

"Me too. I'm finally putting in a garden."

"Good for you. Hey, I need to run to the store in the next hour. Would it be cool if I stopped by on the way home?"

"Everything all right?"

"Absolutely. I just wanted to ask you something."

He goes silent for a moment.

"That doesn't sound good."

"It's just a question," she says, staring down at an indentation in the grass bordering the walkway. A shoe print.

"Let me give you my address."

Darcy learned Bronson's address during her research, and she suspects he knows this. She plays along, reciting the address back to him when he's finished. Inside, she checks on Hunter, who is back in bed with his earbuds in. Heavy metal posters blanket the walls. Above his bed, a demon-like creature with glowing eyes slays a priest drowning in an ocean of crashing waves.

"Hunter. Hunter."

He twitches and pulls the earbuds out.

"What did I do?"

"Nothing. You plan to be around for the next two hours?"

"You grounded me from the car, so I suppose so."

"I'm running to the store and don't want the girls left alone." In truth, Darcy isn't comfortable leaving any of them alone. "Do you need anything while I'm out?"

He shakes his head and rolls over with a grunt.

Darcy has no intention of going to the store. Instead, she rolls down the window and takes the coast road, following the breakers as the sea breeze carries a salty tang into the car. It's an opportunity to organize her thoughts before she speaks to Bronson. She won't jump to conclusions, but her experience as a federal agent requires she leaves no stone unturned. She barely knows Bronson outside of the dojo, and she doesn't want a dangerous man around Jennifer and Hunter.

After driving through beach front neighborhoods for half an hour, she takes a deep breath and turns the Prius toward Bronson's house. He lives on the west side of Genoa Cove in a cookie-cutter development of two-story homes. Manicured lawns stretch in fields of green, all the houses drawn from a palette of neutral tones. A woman on a lawn tractor watches Darcy as the car coasts at a slow pace. The police department pension must be generous, Darcy thinks to herself as she takes in the upscale homes. Didn't the divorce drain his income? Bronson shouldn't be able to afford a home in this neighborhood, a thought which fills her with guilt.

The last house on the right, Bronson's house stands out from its neighbors. The red shingled roof is new, the red shutters and door contributing flashes of color to an otherwise conservative development. She parks in the driveway beside his truck and gives the door a cursory knock. When no reply comes, she rounds the house, following a stone path past an open kitchen window and a cherry wood deck off the back porch. Darcy finds him in the backyard where he's connected railroad beams to form a raised bed. His back to her, he kneels beside the garden and smooths a fresh layer of compost.

She doesn't wish to startle him, so she waits beside the deck stairs.

"Almost finished," he says.

Somehow he knew she was there.

He grabs his shovel and walks to a shed. It's too dark to see inside. When he comes back, he wipes his hands on a tattered flannel work shirt.

"And when spring arrives, I'll finally have a garden." Bronson grins, and the smile she returns feels forced and torn by doubt. "Something wrong?"

"No, no. It's been a long couple of days."

He scrutinizes her, a pair of work gloves clutched in his fist. At the dojo he wears loose fitting sweats. Until now she hasn't appreciated how muscular he is.

"Come inside with me. I'll pour you a lemonade."

The comments about police brutality echo in her mind.

"I'll stay outside. Why waste the nice day?"

Something flares in his eye. Anger?

"So we'll sit out on the deck. Give me ten minutes to clean up. I'll bring it out to you."

"You don't have to bring me a drink."

She senses his glare as he opens the door. It clicks shut, and she releases a held breath. The temptation is strong to flee while he's busy inside. Just climb into her car and drive home. What is she doing with a man who beat his wife and sent a man to the hospital?

The backyard holds a stand of apple and peach trees. All are picked clean, the leaves turning yellow and brown as if they sense winter building to the north. She flinches when the screen door bangs open, a sound like a snare drum.

Bronson wears a red Hawaiian shirt and Bermuda shorts. He grips two glasses. Ice clinks against the glass when he sets them down on the patio table.

"Wait," he says, sighing. "You didn't want a lemonade."

"It's fine."

"Drink up." He locks his fingers behind his head and balances an ankle on his knee. "So, what did you want to talk about?"

In the car, the conversation seemed so easy. She'd planned how to approach the rumors and considered responses should he react strongly. Now her hands can't sit still. Ice water trickles through her legs.

"Darcy, what's bothering you?"

"You've been a great help the last week with all that's happened." She curses her shaking voice. "And it meant a lot that you searched for Jennifer."

Though you drove past her at the school and left her alone in the dark.

"But?"

Darcy lifts her eyes and finds him staring. His hands curl and uncurl at his sides.

"I'm a mother first, and my only priority is the safety of my children."

"And you're worried about the stranger you brought into your home." She opens her mouth to reply, and he waves her off. "I'd wonder about your parenting skills if you didn't. If you need me to back off, it's fine. You're not going to hurt my feelings. I simply felt after what happened at the cove and with someone following Amy, you might want an extra set of eyes on your back."

"It's not that I...that we don't welcome the help."

"Then what is it?"

She wants to ask him how often he visits the cove, and where he'd been the night the killer dumped the woman on the beach. Darcy bites her lip and looks into the yard. Back to where shadows bleed out of the tool shed. A good place to store a body.

"I read a story on the Internet."

Bronson glares at Darcy, body tense. As if he might leap at her.

"You checked up on me."

"Yes."

He leans forward with his forearms on his knees. Close enough to smell his aftershave.

"And what did you find?"

"Understand I'm not passing judgment."

"Aren't you?" There's something dangerous scuttling around inside him. "You think I wanted to hurt that man, that I got my jollies breaking his arm? You don't know how loud that was in my ears. Like a gun went off. I'd say you've been there, but you worked behind the scenes with the FBI. You weren't a field grunt like the rest of us."

Except the night Michael Rivers tried to kill me, she whispers to herself.

Bronson sits back and closes his eyes.

"I never wanted to hurt him. I suppose the article didn't mention he had a knife." He nods when she glances at him. "Yep. Tried to wrestle it away from him, and all the time I'm holding him down, the bastard is trying to slash the other guy. I put his arm behind his back, the one with the knife, and cuffed his wrist. But he kept fighting, trying to twist his body over and turn the knife on me. His own torque snapped his arm. All I did was keep him from hurting anyone else. Of course, his lawyer didn't see things that way, and pretty soon every arrest I'd made over two decades went under the microscope. Soon people were coming forth left and right claiming I cuffed them too hard and permanently damaged their wrists, that the drug dealer I tackled in the park couldn't walk without pain. At that point, it wasn't worth defending myself, so I collected my pension and rode off into the sunset."

Darcy sips her drink. Bronson strikes her as sincere.

"There are a lot of rumors on the *Genoa Standard* forum."

"Oh, I'm aware. Like the one where I supposedly beat my wife. You saw that one, I suppose. All bullshit. She left me for the same cliched reason a lot of spouses leave cops. It's the job. The long hours, the overtime, missed birthdays and holidays. And the constant worry that an arrest might go bad, and then the cop never comes home again. I couldn't blame her, though if she'd held out another few years, I'd be around all day and she'd probably be sick of me. Thing is, we still get along well. She found another guy and has a cottage off the beach. Living the good life."

"You never had kids."

"Again, the job was always in the way."

"Do you ever regret it?" Darcy asks. "Not having kids, I mean."

"The decision was mutual. What's done is done."

"I'm sorry I pried."

"Why would I expect less from an investigator? I'm surprised you didn't run a background check the minute you stepped into my class."

"Maybe I did," she says, grinning.

"I figured. Where do we go from here?"

Darcy sets her glass down and wipes the condensation on her shirt. While she remains cautious, Bronson's story rings true, more so than Internet forum rumors and opinions.

"Let's take this one day at a time. You're welcome at the house, and to be honest, we feel safer with a retired policeman on our side."

"Even one with a history of excessive force?

"I'll look the other way this time."

The lightened mood doesn't last long.

"Did Michael Rivers only kill when the moon was full?"

She steeples her fingers and thinks back to the nightmarish year Michael Rivers butchered young girls and evaded capture.

"No. Roughly one month separates each full moon, but there's a ten-night stretch where the moon is nearly full."

"Sure."

"Rivers struck during that window. Why the lunar phase is important is a matter of conjecture, as he refused to allow law enforcement to interview him after his capture. Why do you ask?"

"The cove murder occurred two days after the full moon. If this killer is following the same pattern, his window of opportunity will close by the end of the week. Then what?"

Darcy leans back in her chair.

"If he's like Rivers, he'll vanish until the next full moon approaches. A little less than three weeks. The murders at the end of the cycle were always the most vicious. As if he wanted to ensure we would remember him."

"It's like he's a werewolf."

Bronson bares his teeth and gnarls his hands like claws. It's meant to make Darcy laugh, but it's disturbing.

Three more days, Darcy thinks. If she can keep Amy and her family safe until then...

Except she can't depend on this new killer repeating Rivers' pattern.

Inside the car, Darcy calls up the security app and checks the cameras. The pictures take a long time to view, her signal weak among the trees and buildings predominant over eastern sections of the village. She impatiently taps her fingers on the steering wheel until the data loads.

All views show an empty yard. Yet shadows in the grass catch her attention toward the rear of the ranch near Hunter's window. Footprints? She zooms in for a closer look, but the resolution is insufficient on her phone. Closing down the app, she throws the car into gear and hurries across the village.

Nobody answers when she opens the front door and calls out. After searching the house, she finds Jennifer and Amy on the deck.

"Where's your brother?"

"Sleeping."

Darcy checks the time. It's noon.

While the girls watch, she rounds the house and stops outside Hunter's window. If there were tracks in the grass, she doesn't see them now. Brushing it off as digital artifacts due to a poor connection, Darcy shakes her head and returns to the house. Her phone rings as she slides the deck door shut. Eric Hensel.

"What have you got, Eric?" Darcy asks, slipping inside her bedroom.

"Nothing good. I got the Chief of Police on the horn this morning. They're not buying the serial killer angle."

"You're kidding. The stabbing didn't convince them?"

"Apparently the girl they found, Krista Townsend, ran drugs out of Smith Town. The police haven't ruled out any possibilities, but right now they're leaning toward a drug deal gone bad."

"Nobody deals drugs at the cove. It's a private beach."

"But the killer dumped the body there. No telling where the supposed drug deal took place."

Darcy edges her door shut so Hunter doesn't hear.

"That's insane. The branding on her neck should be all the proof they need."

"It's hard to scream serial killer after one murder, especially in a place like Genoa Cove. Until they ask for our help, my hands are tied. But..."

"Yes?"

"There's nothing stopping us from checking up on our old friend in New York."

"Wait," she says, shifting the phone to her other ear. "You're interviewing Rivers?"

"Tomorrow. I'm taking Dagliesh with me."

"Do you think Rivers will talk?"

"Unlikely. But it's a chance to meet with the warden and talk to the guards. If Rivers has a regular visitor, they'll give us the lowdown."

10

The FBI's trip to New York is a failure. Michael Rivers hasn't spoken a word since his capture, and video footage shows him shuffling through the yard in a zombie state. He barely eats but somehow maintains his strong physique. The warden believes the killer's mind has shut down, and the staff psychologist agrees.

The log shows no visitors besides the tabloid media intent on interviewing the legendary murderer. It seems the nation has forgotten the terror the madman brought to Virginia and North Carolina three years ago.

The killer's favored moon phase passes, and Halloween arrives without another murder. It is easy to let their guards down, but the quiet doesn't fool Darcy. It only ratchets up her suspicion that something terrible is about to happen.

Bronson, who spends increasing time at the house, provides Jennifer's escort to Kaitlyn's party. Reading a magazine in the truck, he waits outside and ensures she doesn't leave without him knowing. Afterward he drives her home.

Amy's shell cracks and reveals hints of the outgoing, vibrant girl she was before she encountered the Full Moon Killer. No longer regressing, she seems to mature before Darcy's eyes and spends more time working around the house and less with Jennifer. On a clear, windless afternoon, she helps Darcy reposition one of the cameras to capture a wider swath along the side of the house.

Even Hunter seems to brighten. He confides with Darcy he wants to write and is looking at colleges. He turns eighteen at the end of October, and though he refuses a party, Bethany brings him an ice cream cake and a stack of DVDs. Jennifer and Amy each take a slice. Hunter and Bethany consume the rest, and Darcy leaves the living room to the two of them, where they watch movies until two in the morning. She hasn't watched Hunter laugh that hard or look so happy since he was in grade school.

A week into November, Bronson joins Darcy on the deck on a crisp autumn day. Amy is inside, browsing nearby universities on an iPad.

Remnants of a dying hurricane spin off the coast, and the black clouds in the distance draw a sharp contrast with the endless blue overhead. The cyclone is a long way off but serves as a reminder of the fury storms unleash on the coast.

"What time should I get the kids?" Bronson asks, huddled in a hooded sweatshirt. Between the two of them, they've driven Hunter and Jennifer home each day. Neither teen worries about serial killers anymore or senses the black clouds on the horizon.

Darcy checks the time—four o'clock.

"Six, if you don't mind. But I can get them if you have other things to do."

"Sit tight. I'll get them."

Teeth chattering, she rubs her legs together as the wind whips around the house and arrows toward the cove. He folds his arms and surveys the cameras, one of which focuses on the deck.

"I've been meaning to ask you something," he says, cupping his hands and blowing into them. "If it's too personal, say the word."

"Okay."

"Do you ever wish you'd stayed with the FBI?"

Darcy flicks at a fly.

"I miss the work, but I doubt they would let me near the field after the stabbing. I love participating in the kids' lives, but sometimes it gets lonely while they're at school and practice. And I worry I wasted my education."

"You could go back. Maybe consult."

"Can't go back. That door closed at least a year ago. Besides, they gave me a generous severance after the attack, and though I don't talk about it much, Tyler had a large life insurance policy. The kids are set for college, and that's the only financial concern I have."

"Well," he says, lifting a beer to toast. "Here's to a lifetime of sunny days and no bosses barking down our necks."

She closes her eyes and leans her head back. The sun fights a losing battle to burn through the cold as thunder rumbles over the sea.

Later, darkness creeps across the neighborhood, oozing between the trees and houses as Darcy sits alone in the kitchen. Bronson will bring the kids home soon, then she'll be able to relax. The moon will grow into a waxing gibbous in three days, nearly full, and the terrible waiting game will begin anew.

Her phone rings. It's an area code she doesn't recognize. Anticipating a telemarketer, she presses *ignore* and opens her laptop. The phone rings again. Same number.

"Hello?"

Quiet. Static follows like faraway lightning on an AM radio.

"Is anyone there?"

"I'm going to gut you, Darcy."

She fumbles the phone and swings her head around. Night presses against the window. It wants to come inside.

"Who is this?"

"You know who I am."

It can't be, yet it is. She recognizes the voice of Michael Rivers.

"How did you—"

"We have unfinished business, the two of us. You took away my life, and now I'm going to take everything that matters to you. How about I start with little Jennifer?"

"I can't imagine how you managed to make a phone call from prison, but I'll make sure it never happens again."

"Will you now? You're not FBI anymore, Darcy. Just another suburban pig mother lined up for slaughter. How thoughtful of you to bring Amy into your home. It will make it easier for me."

Darcy races to Jennifer's bedroom and throws the door open. Startled, Amy jumps up from her chair. She mouths, "What's going on?" The girl's eyes are white saucers.

Darcy shakes her head and eases the door shut, but as she backs away, Amy follows her into the living room. It's too late to conceal the caller. Amy reads Darcy's terror and catches herself on the couch before she crumples.

"I'm tracing the call, Rivers."

"No, you aren't. You don't have the means, nor does the retired oaf you bring into your house. Do you think he can protect you, Darcy?"

She throws open the door and steps into the yard without considering how exposed she is. The dark embraces her with cold, clammy fingers. Caresses her neck and whispers horrors into her ear. Rivers couldn't have escaped. She would know by now. So who gave the maniac a phone?

"You're making a big mistake. The FBI will talk to the

warden, and he'll find out how you called me. Why make a life sentence more difficult?"

"What makes you think I'm behind bars, Darcy? Did you ever worry you caught the wrong man?"

A shadow moves behind the vacant house and vanishes. Darcy steps inside and locks the door.

"I'm calling the police."

"Go ahead. They've had four years to catch me."

The call dies. Amy's mouth works silently as she rises off the couch.

"It's okay, Amy. Someone gave him a phone, but he can't get to us. Never again."

"I told you he was out," Amy says, her gaze wild and unfocused. "He was the one who followed me, the one who painted his symbol on the house. And now he's here."

"No, it's impossible," says Darcy, grabbing Amy by the shoulders. "The FBI visited the prison last week."

Unless Rivers told her the truth. No, she couldn't have caught the wrong man. Amy shrugs Darcy away and runs for Jennifer's bedroom. The door slams and locks.

Taking a composing breath, Darcy knocks on the door.

"Amy, don't lock me out. We're stronger if we stick together."

Sobs come from the bedroom as Darcy's pulse thrums through her head. She unlocks the safe and removes the gun. Loads the weapon. The darkness at the window looks wrong. Bloody. Dripping.

She steps outside and puts her back against the cold wall. The chill of autumn radiates through her clothes and makes it difficult to stand still. One eye on the backyard of the vacant house, she creeps beside the ranch and aims the weapon at the darkness. A branch snaps. Somewhere. In her backyard, she thinks.

Darcy searches the yard and finds no sign of an intruder, but the hairs on the back of her neck stand on end. Someone is out there. Watching.

She starts to turn and can't move her legs. They're rigid. Concrete and ice on a January night. Panic flashes through Darcy. Her fear of the dark hasn't been this debilitating since the Rivers attack. The potential that she might be trapped out here with the killer worsens the anxiety, head dizzy as her heart races out of a control.

With her free hand, she dials Eric Hensel.

"Rivers just called me," she says as her eyes penetrate the gloom.

"Impossible. How can you be certain it was him?"

"Trust me. I would never forget that voice. It wasn't a copycat, and it wasn't a prank. Michael Rivers called my phone ten minutes ago."

Hensel fumbles for a pen and a sheet of paper.

"Read me the number." She does. "And you said he called ten minutes ago?"

"Eric, somebody's in my yard."

He goes quiet for a moment.

"I'm calling 9-1-1. Keep your ass inside and don't answer the door for anyone until the police arrive."

Another sound comes from the dark. Someone stepping on dead leaves. She swings the gun toward the noise, head dizzy, arm struggling to keep the weapon still.

"Dammit, Darcy. Do as I say. The police will be there soon. I'm coming tomorrow morning."

"I can't move."

"What do you mean you can't..." He stops, realizing she's having an attack. "Hold on. This will pass."

"These attacks shouldn't be happening anymore. What if they never stop?"

"Darcy, this isn't your fault. You went through a traumatic event, and the cove murder triggered the anxiety."

She touches her wrist. Her pulse pounds at a dangerous speed.

"Listen to my voice, Darcy. I'm there with you. You're not alone. All you have to do is call your kids, and they'll help you inside."

"I can't let them see me like this."

"Shh. We'll get through this together."

The dark thickens. It crawls down her throat and constricts her breathing. Footsteps move through the yard. Toward her.

"There's somebody here, Eric. I hear them."

"Are you armed?"

"Yes."

"Then you can hold him off until the police arrive," Hensel says.

"I can't move my legs."

"You're breathing too fast. I hear you through the phone."

As her eyes interrogate the night, Hensel continues talks in soothing tones until Darcy's legs obey her. Her thigh cramps at the first step, but she's moving. Thank God, she's moving.

"You don't need to come to Genoa Cove," she says, shooting a glance over her shoulder.

"I have vacation time to spend. Darcy, I don't hear you going inside."

"Bronson is coming. I'll call you back, Eric."

She ends the call and limps along the house, gun trained on the dark.

Light sweeps across her face at the entryway. Shielding her face, Darcy hides the gun as Bronson kills the engine. Red imprints from the headlights blind her while they approach. Jennifer and Hunter push past her, Jennifer with a sarcastic giggle.

"What's the deal with Mom?"

Hunter doesn't answer Jennifer, only throws a confused glance over his shoulder at Darcy on his way to the kitchen. They didn't see the gun.

But Bronson did. He grips her by the shoulders and closes the door.

"You want to tell me why you're running around in the dark with a Glock-22?"

Darcy tells Bronson about the phone call and her conversation with Eric Hensel. The police siren screams from several blocks away.

"Stay inside with the kids," he says. "I'll check out the backyard."

"You don't have a weapon on you."

"Don't need one."

"Yes, you do. Take mine."

He stares at the gun. After long consideration, he opens his hand.

The leg cramp subsiding, Darcy finds Amy in the living room with Jennifer and Hunter. Tears streak Amy's face. The kids know about the phone call, and as the sirens grow loud, Jennifer runs to the window and parts the curtains.

Bronson returns. He opens the door as two cruisers pull curbside. Meeting Darcy's eyes, he shakes his head.

"There's nobody out there."

"But I heard someone."

"Then he's long gone. Listen, somebody at the prison dropped the ball and let that maniac near a phone."

"How did he get my number?"

Bronson itches his head and looks down at his shoes.

"The same way that reporter tracked you down. The same way every Tom, Dick, and Harry I arrested found my home address or called me in the middle of the night to tell me what an asshole I am and how he'd destroy my life for ruining his. Everything is on the Internet. Worse comes to worst, you change your phone number. Don't let it get to you."

Easy for him to say. Footsteps shuffle up the walkway. Darcy opens the door. Detective Ames arrives with Julian while two uniformed officers stand watch from the road.

"Ms. Gellar," Ames says as he peeks over her shoulder. "You received a threatening phone call and saw someone outside the house?"

Darcy gives Ames the details on the call and hands him her phone, which displays Rivers' number and the time and length of the call.

"Someone came through the yard. I went out looking, but didn't find anyone."

Ames whistles to the two officers beside the cruiser and motions them around back.

"How can you be certain it was Michael Rivers? He's in prison. Someone could have impersonated Rivers."

"I know his voice, Detective."

Ames rubs his chin and tilts his head toward the security camera.

"You got these all around the house?"

"I do."

"Then we should catch the intruder on camera." Ames lifts his radio and speaks. "Janet, I need you to run a phone number for me."

Ames holds the phone at arm's length and squints. He reads the number to Janet, then asks Darcy to direct them to the security camera footage.

When she turns around, Julian's eyebrows shoot up at Darcy's exposed gun.

"Sorry," Darcy says, slowly removing the Glock from behind her back. "I have a permit."

"That's fine, Ms. Gellar," Ames says. "Bring me the security footage, and we'll have a look at that permit afterward."

Ames swings his eyes toward Bronson, who sits on the couch with Jennifer. The detective walks past without greeting the ex-officer. Hunter and Amy stand in the kitchen entryway and watch Ames and Julian with caution.

"You see anything in the backyard, Greenbladt?" Ames says into his radio.

"There's nobody out here, Detective."

Ames sighs and puts the radio back on his hip. Darcy sets the laptop on the kitchen table. As she steps through the footage, Ames and Julian look over her shoulder. At one point, Ames bends down, hands on his knees, for a closer look. But the shadow is nothing but a large tree branch swaying from the wind. After several minutes, Ames leans against the counter.

"That's all the footage from this evening?"

"Everything," Darcy says. Humiliation tinges her voice.

"It could have been an animal," Julian says with a glare that makes Darcy feel she's wasted their time. "Lots of deer run through these parts this time of year."

"Somebody was in the backyard," Darcy says in a broken, child-like voice. "Maybe they knew enough to avoid the cameras."

Ames' face is unreadable. He's mulling over the situation, but Darcy can't decide if he thinks she's crying wolf or the victim of an elaborate prank.

"This must be Ms. Yang." Ames glances across the kitchen at Amy. Hunter protectively moves his arm around her, though Darcy doesn't find the detective hostile. "That's good, all of you staying together. Ms. Gellar, you have a state-of-the-art security system. You're quite safe."

Darcy finds it curious he doesn't include having an ex-cop around the house as an added safety measure. So far, Ames is exactly who Bronson claimed he was—a skittish detective who jumps to conclusions and overlooks obvious dangers.

"Regarding the man who called you," Ames says, "he almost certainly used a disposable phone. If his impression was good enough to fool an ex-FBI agent, he knows enough not to call using a traceable line."

Darcy grinds her teeth.

"An impression? You're brushing this off rather easily."

"Not at all. In fact, I'm quite concerned about this phone call. Until we find the killer, I have to act on the assumption he may have been the one who called you. Why he's pretending to be the Full Moon Killer, I can't say, but I assure you I'll do everything in my power to track his phone."

Ames and Julian depart with a promise to send a cruiser past the house overnight.

They're all staring at her. Hunter, Amy, Jennifer, even Bronson. Staring and judging, Darcy assumes.

"All of you, go to your rooms so I can speak with Bronson."

"We have a right to know if that maniac is trying to kill us," Jennifer says.

"You heard what the detective said. Michael Rivers is in jail."

"Then a copycat killer is out there. How is that better?"

"Jennifer, please."

Hunter walks the girls down the hallway. Amy appears on the verge of crumbling, and Darcy worries she'll only make Jennifer's anxiety worse. When the doors close, Bronson puts his hand on her hip and leads her to the couch.

"It wouldn't be a bad idea if I slept on the couch until this situation blows over."

"I can't let you do that. You have your own life."

"What kind of friend would I be if I left? I'd be just as useless as Ames and his idiot sidekick. Animals, he said." Bronson scoffs. "That sort of incompetence is another reason I left the force. I don't mind staying."

"Then take my bed and let me sleep on the couch."

He groans and runs his hand across his forehead.

"I'm not kicking you out of your own bed. Remember I was a beat cop. Back then, I dozed in squad cars at three in the morning and slept like a baby on a recliner. I'm fine on the couch."

Darcy looks at the entryway. The door is bolted. Every several seconds, the alarm system flashes a red light to indicate it is functioning.

"Eric Hensel is coming here."

"Hensel, the FBI agent you mentioned?"

"Yes, he was my partner the year we hunted the Full Moon Killer."

"GCPD didn't call in the FBI. Why would Hensel come?"

"The FBI isn't working the case. At least not until the GCPD requests assistance." Darcy touches his hand. "There's something you should know."

"Okay."

"I'm going to ask Hensel to fly with me to New York. I want to see Michael Rivers."

11

The slam of a neighbor's car door shocks Darcy awake. She sits up in bed before vertigo tugs her down to the pillow. How many pills did she take last night?

Squinting at the light, she reaches across the nightstand and grabs the bottle. She recalls swallowing a pill after the police left, but the bottle looks disturbingly close to empty. Touching her head, Darcy eases herself out of bed and winces when her thigh locks again. She limps to the shower and stands under the hot flow, one arm propped against the wall as the muscles unwind.

It's mid-morning when Eric Hensel strides up Darcy's walkway.

Her old partner took the red eye into Charlotte and looks as if he hasn't slept in weeks—eyes bloodshot and drooping, blonde hair hastily brushed by his hand, windbreaker rumpled and hanging like a snake shedding its skin.

"I got here as quickly as I could," Hensel says, shifting his briefcase to his left hand. He seems confused whether to shake her hand or hug his old partner. In the end, he does neither, and simply nods when Darcy invites him inside.

"It means a lot that you came. But I'd hate to think I wasted your annual leave."

He studies the inside of the house and blinks, stopping for a moment on the alarm in the doorway. Though Hensel looks exhausted, Darcy bets he noticed the cameras the second he stepped out of his rental car.

"Looks like you did well for yourself. Nice neighborhood, easy access to the cove." He swallows, realizing what he said. "Sorry. I wasn't thinking."

"Come inside, Eric. You've had a long morning."

Hensel sits at the kitchen table as she tidies up the counter. His shirt sleeves are rolled up and buttoned at the forearm. A *Semper Fi* tattoo with a bald eagle peeks out from below the sleeve, the former marine looking ten years older than when Darcy last saw him.

He blows on the coffee when she hands him the mug. He squints at the first sip and blows again.

"Too hot?"

"Just the way I like it," he says. "As long as it kicks me out of low gear."

His gaze flicks between Darcy and the window.

"Say what's on your mind, Eric."

"You need help, Darcy. Don't let these attacks take over your life like they did three years ago."

"I'm still seeing someone."

He leans forward and studies her eyes. She blinks and looks away.

"You're taking the pills again."

She stares down at her hands, her fists clenched from the struggle to rationalize her choices.

"Of course. It's a prescription."

"You know what I mean. How many? Two? Three?"

Darcy shrugs.

"Jesus. I'll give you to the end of the month. Get this under control, or I'm putting you in rehab."

"You don't have the authority. And anyway, I'm not leaving my kids."

"Were you there for Hunter and Jennifer three years ago? Don't go down that hole again, Darcy. You'll hurt them."

She looks away and chews her nail.

Recognizing she's upset, Hensel swings the conversation to the cove murder, Amy's stalker, and the phone call from Michael Rivers.

"They're all interrelated," Hensel says, examining the extra security measures Darcy installed. Her laptop is open on the counter and displaying camera views around the house. "Even the police concur the same guy is responsible, but they're playing the usual jurisdiction games and don't want us taking their case away."

"Seems like old times."

"I'd hoped we could build greater trust with local law enforcement by the time I retired, but inroads are difficult to pave. I'm curious. How did you connect with Amy Yang after all this time?"

Darcy lowers her voice and leans forward.

"She's asleep in my daughter's room. That's all she does anymore is sleep, and when she's awake the poor girl looks on the verge of a complete breakdown."

Rubbing a stain off the table with the cuff of her shirt, Darcy tells him about Amy quitting school and taking a job in Smith Town.

"Didn't take long for the stalker to appear," says Hensel.

"She reached out to me because the local police didn't take her seriously. How wealthy do you think Rivers is?"

Hensel thinks with his eyes for a moment.

"There was the inheritance money, but the court froze his account."

"Criminals have ways of hiding their money. Offshore accounts and shell companies to name two."

"But he'd need a way to move his money around. Rivers doesn't have computer access."

"He's not supposed to have phone access either, but that hasn't stopped him."

"You think he's paying off someone at the prison?"

"And financing our killer, yes."

"I'll see what I can dig up. So, what nuggets of wisdom did Detective Ames impart last night?"

Darcy chuckles mirthlessly.

"He's convinced the caller impersonated Rivers. But there's one way to find out."

Hensel sets his elbows on the table.

"I know what you're suggesting, and I'm telling you it's not worth it." Darcy hears the scream in his voice as he scrambles for a way to dissuade her. "Rivers isn't talking. He didn't reply to any of my questions."

"He'll talk to me."

"What makes you so sure?"

Darcy finishes her coffee and sets the mug down.

"Because I'm the one who took him down."

An army of gray, swollen clouds bank overhead as Darcy stands in the driveway, arms folded as she thwarts a wind that wants to rip the heat from her body. It's a difficult decision asking Bronson to watch the house. She's known him for less than three months, and though her kids get along with him, it feels like a risk.

As Bronson parks the pickup and climbs out of the cab, Darcy realizes she hasn't been away from Hunter and Jennifer during the last three years.

"I'm asking too much," she says, bouncing on her toes to stay warm.

Bronson yells over the wind.

"Nonsense. I planned to stay the night, so there's no problem sticking around until you return."

Lifting his gaze toward the agent in the doorway, Bronson's body stiffens. After a pause, he strides forward and offers his hand.

"You must be Agent Hensel. I'm Bronson Severson, a friend of Darcy's.".

"I'm sure she appreciates you watching the house. We won't be long, and I promise to have her back by tomorrow."

"Where are you flying out of?"

"Rocky Mount. It's the only ticket I could grab on short notice. They'll get us to DC, then we'll take another flight to Buffalo." Hensel looks over his shoulder at Darcy. "I tried to talk her out of it."

"I'm learning you can't change her mind once she sets it."

"Try partnering with her."

They grab their bags inside and escape the cold. It rarely snows this close to the coast, but Darcy expects flurries by the time they load Hensel's rental. Bronson patiently stands by while Darcy explains how to set and disarm the alarm. She's leaving the laptop so he can monitor the cameras. Her phone app will keep her connected, provided she has service where they're going.

The ride to the airport takes ninety minutes. A cold rain pours from the swollen clouds. Darcy shields her face from the spray as they run from the parking lot to the terminal.

During the flight, turbulence rocks the plane and sets her stomach on edge. When the puddle-jumper plane sets down in DC, her face is pallid, arms tingling with pins and needles.

Hensel follows her onto the moving walkway and stands aside for the rushing commuters late for their connections.

"Sure you want to go through with this?"

"I can't look myself in the mirror knowing I couldn't face him. He's behind the Genoa Cove murder."

"Sounds like you're leaning toward the apprentice theory, that he didn't act alone."

"Or he's influencing a copycat. Rivers has phone access despite what the warden told you. Let's find out who he's talking to."

Sunset hides behind a thick blanket of clouds as usable light vanishes at a distressing rate outside Buffalo. Darkness sets in when they approach the prison, a brown brick monstrosity ringed by a chain-link fence with barbed wire loops bordering the top. Darcy worries about another attack, but Hensel, reading the anxious look on her face, hooks her elbow with his and hurries her to the gate.

After security clears them, the doors open like the maw of a faceless beast, and they step into a heavily secured entryway. Hensel flashes his badge and introduces Darcy as Dr. Gellar. The heavyset guard glances at her before waving them through.

"Remember," Hensel says, leaning close so the escorting guards can't eavesdrop. "The warden is under the impression this little trip is a followup. He's asking a lot of questions about whether this is an official visit. So far I've danced around the issue, but he'll know something is up if we don't get in and out quick. All right, Dr. Gellar?"

"Absolutely, Special Agent Hensel."

Standing a head taller than Hensel, Warden Ellsworth awaits them at the end of a locked corridor. He's bald and wrinkled, black eyes set back in his head and rimmed by an expensive pair of bifocals. He regards Darcy with curiosity before turning his attention to Hensel.

"Welcome back, Agent Hensel. I trust your trip was agreeable."

"Very much so, Warden Ellsworth."

"It's unusual for law enforcement to return so soon after an interview. I would have expected a memo from your supervisor."

"Events in North Carolina force us to act quickly, Warden. Local law enforcement believes a serial killer is active near the coast."

"I'm unsure what that has to do with our prisoner, but I assure you Mr. Rivers, if he truly called Dr. Gellar, did so without my consent. I'll get to the bottom of the matter."

"There is reason to believe Rivers knew the killer," Hensel says, whispering up at Ellsworth. "As someone of your position can appreciate, we need to guard this information closely. If the media learns a murderer is in league with the Full Moon Killer, we'll have a full blown panic on our hands."

Shrewd move, Darcy thinks. Make Ellsworth feel like he's part of the inner circle and stroke his ego.

"Well, that is quite troubling, and you can be certain I'll keep the information to myself. But if you'd like one of my guards to... influence Mr. Rivers to talk to you—"

"I don't think that will be necessary, but I'll keep the offer in mind."

"Please do, Agent. No doubt you wish to complete the interview and be on your way, so I won't waste your time. But I warn you. Mr. Rivers hasn't spoken a word since his incarceration. I fear you've come a long way for nothing."

"Let's hope for all our sakes Mr. Rivers speaks to us. Is he in the interview room?"

"The guards will bring him in when you're seated and ready to begin." Ellsworth glances at his watch. "The time grows late, Agent. I wish you Godspeed."

Gray, peeling paint chafes in the interview room. A wooden

table sits in the center, the top marred by decades of scratches and scribbles. Four chairs circle the table, the designated prisoner's chair wobbling on a warped leg.

Darcy sets her hands in her lap and clasps them together. It's the only way to keep them from shaking. She recalls prison interviews during her brief FBI tenure, none conducted with a subject this dangerous. And she hasn't been in the same room with Rivers since he jammed a knife into her stomach.

A harsh buzz twists Darcy's head around. Two guards lead Michael Rivers into the room, the prisoner's ankles and wrists bound by chains. Rivers cut his hair short after the FBI captured him three years ago, but now it hangs over his eyes and down to his shoulders in greasy clumps. Shuffling into the room, Rivers grins at Hensel. It isn't until the guards sit him down that he notices Darcy beside the agent. His face freezes in an unreadable mask. Then a grin stretches to each ear. A grin that displays too many teeth.

It's quiet after the guards close the door and stand in the hallway. Darcy can't see them but knows they wait at the ready.

"Hello again, Michael," Hensel says, opening his briefcase. He removes a pen and notepad and sets his phone to record the conversation.

Rivers doesn't acknowledge Hensel. He hasn't taken his eyes off Darcy.

"I think you recognize my partner. It's been three years, yes?"

Again Rivers ignores Hensel. He perches on the edge of his chair as though he might launch across the table and sink his teeth into Darcy's neck.

Hensel sighs and taps a finger on the table.

"The warden knows you called my partner. That was a mistake. He's unhappy you subverted his command and wants to know who gave you the phone. Will you tell me, Michael? Give me a name, and I'll tell Warden Ellsworth you cooperated."

No response. His bloodthirsty, piercing eyes are the only evidence Rivers isn't comatose. His body sways, the motion hypnotic.

"Let's discuss the Genoa Cove murder and the man stalking Amy Yang." Rivers' eyes flash over to Hensel. "You remember Amy, I see. Those were the early days of the Full Moon Killer before you perfected your craft. I'll bet it bothers the hell out of you she got away. In fact, I bet you see her in your sleep and want a second chance. Trouble is, Michael, you'll never get out of here. Which is why you're working with someone on the outside. Who's trying to kill Amy Yang?"

Rivers licks his lips and runs his eyes over Darcy.

"Have it your way," Hensel says, drumming his fingers. "The warden wants to make your life difficult. You understand this, yes? I'm the only thing standing between you and a very traumatic life behind bars. So either you talk or—"

"You remember me, Michael," Darcy says, fighting to keep her voice steady. "If it wasn't for me, you'd still be free. You must hate seeing me alive, holding the power in the room while you're chained like an animal."

Chains rattle as the serial killer leans forward. He studies Darcy.

Hensel catches her eye. A warning. Only a few feet separate her from the wrath of the Full Moon Killer. Though he's chained, Darcy doesn't doubt Rivers could tear her to pieces if he got his hands on her. This is dangerous territory. She walks among tigers now.

"What must you feel knowing another man impersonates you? He copies your methodology like a plagiarist, a cheap hack." She prods Rivers for a reaction. If her words affect him, he hides it well. "He's killing by the moon phase. I always wanted to ask you, Michael. Did you widen the number of days around the full moon because you required extra time, or because you were too simple to comprehend the lunar calendar?"

He's closer to her now. She never saw him move, but his chest brushes the table. She's within the madman's reach.

"Your lack of an answer speaks volumes. I wonder, is this new killer a fan who read about you and worked up the courage to make contact, or do you have an apprentice, someone we never captured?" The grin spreads wider on Rivers' face. His chest heaves in silent laughter. "No matter. He brands the girls as you did. Soon he'll be the murderer everybody remembers. They'll forget you, Michael. They'll forget the Full Moon Killer."

Rivers thrusts forward and drives the edge of the table into Darcy's ribs. The door swings open, both guards rushing in with clubs in hand.

"It's okay," Hensel says, motioning them back. The first guard, a mountainous black man with flecks of gray in his hair, gives Hensel a doubtful look. "Michael means us no harm, do you Michael?"

The two guards back out of the room without pulling their gaze from the serial killer. Spittle drips off Rivers' lips. Blood tinges his incisors. Razor-edged like a shark's.

"You're even a bigger fool than I thought," Rivers says, throwing a glance toward Hensel to gauge his reaction. "I know what makes you tick, and I know what you're afraid of."

Darcy fights herself from leaning backward. He's almost face to face with her now.

"Whose face do you see when you sleep at night? Whose footsteps do you hear every time the house creaks? The nightmares will never end, and that fat pig cop you bed with won't protect you."

Hensel protests, but Darcy grabs his hand.

"You're not safe in your own home. Think a security system can stop me? These walls can't hold me forever, Darcy. When I get out of here, the first thing I'll do is chase down every last friend and family member you have and bleed them like stuck pigs. You'll be long dead by then, little girl, and I'll piss on your grave."

He's breathing heavy, face red and dripping with sweat.

"Are you through?" she asks, gripping the chair beneath the table so he can't see her steady herself. Yet he knows. He's learned to read her.

"You were an expert profiler with the FBI? You didn't find me, Darcy. Remember, I found you. I could have skinned women from New England to Florida for a decade if I chose to, and you never would have caught me."

"Why share the spotlight with a partner, though? Now the world will remember two killers, not one."

Fire burns in Rivers' eyes.

"I always worked alone, Darcy. You're playing mind games, and it won't work on me."

"And yet I'm alive and free, and you're locked in chains."

"Time to open your eyes. You can't even recognize the lunatic in your own home. Don't pretend you haven't seen the signs. Where do you think Hunter goes when he's *out for a drive?* The biggest shame is I'm not there to lend him the direction he needs."

"Don't speak my son's name."

"But your daughter...she's special, Darcy. How I'll enjoy spilling her blood. Do you know how lovely blood looks on the sand?"

Darcy slaps her hands down on the table and stands, the chair flying backward.

"Come near my family, and I'll end you like I should have three years ago." Rivers leans his head back and laughs. "No more fucking around, Michael. Who's killing girls on the Carolina coast, and who gave you the phone? Tell me the truth, dammit, or so help me God, I'll make your life a living hell."

"You amuse me, Darcy. But you won't amuse me for long. You have no idea who's coming for you and what's about to happen."

Darcy hurls herself at Rivers. Hensel clutches her by the waist and yanks her back as she grabs a lock of Rivers' hair. A clump comes away in her hand. The door flies open, and this time the guards won't take no for an answer. The larger of the two men eyes Darcy with contempt and terror. She's breathless, haunted by images of her loved ones bloodied and dying before her eyes.

"Let go of me, Eric."

"Not until you calm down," Hensel says, tugging her away from the table.

"I'm under control."

Hensel releases her. The guards stand ready to intervene if she lunges at Rivers again.

"Give me a name," Darcy says, straightening her shirt. "Who's targeting my family?"

"I'm done talking to you. Rest in peace, Agent Gellar."

Before the guards yank Rivers out of the interview room, Hensel motions the lead guard aside and whispers something in his ear. The guard gives him an irritated look, but Hensel repeats the message and elicits a nod from the man.

Rivers glances over his shoulder and smiles at Darcy as they lead him out of the room. The door closes, and Hensel rounds on her.

"What the hell was that about?"

"He threatened my family. I want him dead."

"We had him talking."

"No, Eric. He only talked to me. If I hadn't been here, he would have given you the silent treatment."

Hensel releases a heavy breath and falls back against the wall.

"We didn't get anything we can use. Either he had an accomplice when we caught him or—"

"You weren't listening, Eric. Rivers told us everything we need to know. That part about always working alone. His ego is too large to allow someone to share his glory. Which means the current killer met Rivers after the incarceration."

"We checked the visitor logs. Besides the media, nobody comes here to see Rivers."

"Then someone on the inside is making sure Rivers' visitors stay off the books. Likely the same guy who got him a disposable phone." Darcy sinks to the floor and wraps her arms around her knees. "Nobody threatens my family. I want that bastard dead."

"The whole world does, but that's not the way the law works. Bribe some inmate to stick a knife in Rivers' stomach, and you'll end up behind bars too. If we want to hurt Rivers, we have to catch this new killer. He's Rivers' lifeline, his connection to the world. Rivers keeps saying he can get to you from inside the prison, but not without help."

Hensel offers Darcy a hand, and she takes it, her knees achy as she steadies herself against the wall.

"So what did you tell the guard?"

"Let's just say I promised him a little Christmas bonus this year if he forgets he saw you attack Rivers. If the psychopath claims you assaulted him, we'll have two witnesses who state otherwise. Now, keep your head down, and maybe we'll get out of here with no one asking questions."

Stepping into the crisp November air, Darcy can breathe again. Her fury is a beacon of light that cuts through the darkness.

Darcy's breaths puff tiny clouds as they wait at the security gate for the guard to release them. Then they're in the rental and driving back to the airport, the long day turning into a long night. The clouds break. Stars sparkle across the sky. Hensel runs the heat on high as the Buffalo chill pours into the car.

She calls up the security app on her phone as Hensel navigates around a slow-moving vehicle and accelerates down the interstate. Exhaustion catches up to Darcy. She'll sleep on the plane no matter the discomfort. Her eyelids flutter as Hensel switches the radio to sports talk.

Until her eyes lock on the blank screens from the security cameras. What the hell?

"Something wrong?"

Hensel's voice barely registers as she swipes through the menu and ensures she's toggled the appropriate options. She reloads, and the same blank camera views fill her screen.

"Darcy?"

"The security cameras. They're not working."

"Could be a poor connection. The airport has Wi-Fi."

"It's not that. My phone shows four bars. No, something is wrong."

She dials Bronson's phone. It rings and goes to voice-mail. Clicking out of the call, she redials. This time Bronson answers.

"Bronson, what's happening there? I'm getting blank screens on the cameras."

"Power hit, Darcy. I lost all the cameras. We're in the dark here."

A sign flies by off the shoulder. Five miles to the airport.

"Wait, we can't lose power. The generator should have kicked on."

"Well, it didn't. Are you sure the generator has enough fuel?"

"Of course. We haven't used it yet."

Quiet follows as Bronson thinks. Darcy hears Jennifer in the background. She's upset.

"I'll check the generator after I calm Jennifer down."

"No. Don't leave the house."

Hensel watches her from across the car. He mouths, "I'll call GCPD."

Darcy nods her head.

"Bronson, I'm calling Gilmore. I'll get back to you as soon as I can."

"Okay, Darcy. Don't worry, I've got this under control."

Does he? From where she sits, it sounds like the world is caving in on the cove.

Hensel swings the rental onto the airport exit as Darcy listens to the phone ring. The woman who answers huffs as though Darcy ruined her night. So much for customer service. Darcy feeds the woman the details.

"It's unusual for the cameras to stop working unless the batteries go bad, but that never happens on a new system. Are you sure the problem isn't with your phone?"

"My phone isn't the issue. The man watching my house said the power is out and the security cameras are down."

"Your monitors won't work if the power is out, ma'am."

"He's using my laptop. The battery should last three hours."

Hoping for a quick solution, the woman sighs irritatedly. Because the alarm seems to be functioning and nobody is breaking into Darcy's house, the woman arranges an order for the tech crews to check the cameras tomorrow afternoon.

"Tomorrow? I paid for twenty-four-hour monitoring."

"We *are* monitoring the house, Ms. Gellar, and the alarm is operative. Now, as there isn't a break-in and the system is running properly, is there anything more I can do for you this evening?"

"You've done so much, I'd hate to ask for anything else."

Darcy ends the call before the woman responds.

"That sounded like it went well," Hensel says as he swings into the rental return lot.

Darcy calls Bronson back, but he doesn't answer. She redials and still can't get a hold of him. Calls to the kids' phones yield no results.

A creeping terror that something is wrong follows Darcy into the airport. At the check-in counter, she juggles her bag and ID while trying to reach Bronson and the kids. She doesn't hear when the counter attendant, a frail woman with glasses and hair tied in a tight bun, tells Hensel the flight is delayed.

Hensel grabs her by the shoulders on the way to the TSA checkpoint. Two harried travelers glance in their direction as they wheel bags toward the escalators.

"You aren't helping your family by thinking the worst. The weather looked bad when we left. Maybe a storm knocked out a cell tower."

"And the power, generator, and every camera?"

He sighs.

"I called the GCPD back while you got your ticket. They sent a cruiser to the house. If there was a problem, we'd have heard by now. It's been a long day, and what happened at the prison was scary. Keep it together. You'll be home soon."

But they won't be home soon. Another delay sets them back an additional hour and leaves Hensel and Darcy haggling with a gate attendant, attempting to find a connecting flight from DC to North Carolina. The best-case scenario flies them into Rocky Mount at six in the morning.

Darcy paces the terminal until the police call. The home is secure and Bronson got the power running. After she speaks to the police, her phone rings. It's Bronson.

"What happened to the power?"

"I threw the main breaker, and the lights started working again. Must have been a power surge."

"What about the cameras?"

"That's the weird part. They started working on their own before I flipped the breaker."

"I tried to call you, but I got your voice-mail. Same with the kids."

"None of us could make a phone call," he says. "Otherwise, I would have gotten a hold of you sooner to tell you what happened."

"Bronson, what's going on?"

She hears him walking to another room. A door shuts, blocking out Jennifer, who sounds like she's panicking.

"When the power went out things got crazy around here. Amy locked herself in your room and refused to come out."

Did Amy see the crime scene photos boxed inside the closet?

"Hunter found the key to the bedroom doors, except..."

"Bronson?"

"When I unlocked the door, the window was open. Amy must have panicked and run off."

"Oh, God. Do the police know?"

"Amy is an adult, and she's only been gone an hour."

"But she's not an adult," Darcy says, strolling to the window. A crew fuels a plane at their gate, but this isn't their flight. "She's a fifteen-year-old in a nineteen-year-old girl's body."

"That's not everything. Hunter went out looking for Amy. I tried to call him as soon as the phones started working again, but he's not answering."

"What are you saying? Amy and my son are both missing?"

"If he doesn't return in the next hour, I'll put Jennifer in the truck and we'll look for him together."

Rivers' words come back to her. Where does Hunter go when he leaves? She can't let Rivers into her head.

Her son isn't a killer in the making.

———

12

Three hours later, the flight to DC boards with Hunter and Amy missing. Darcy leaves messages on their phones, but she might as well be speaking in a vacuum. The male flight attendant tells Darcy to shut her phone down while they await takeoffs. She's near the front, Hensel stuck somewhere in the back of the plane with the flight filled to capacity. The man beside her is too large for his seat. Darcy leans into the aisle to buy herself breathing space. As soon as the plane lands, Darcy accesses her messages. Hunter is back home, thank goodness, but no one can locate Amy.

With a degree of guilt, Darcy sleeps through the connecting flight. Hensel shakes her awake, and her eyes open to gray daylight while the vent blows cold air on her. The plane is empty except for the flight crew. Hensel reaches into the overhead compartment and grabs Darcy's bag.

"Any word on Amy Yang?"

"Nothing."

"She's survived this long. Never discount she escaped a serial killer. Have faith. She'll show up today."

Bleary-eyed, Darcy shakes her head and follows Hensel

down the ramp. Lightning splits the eastern sky. As if the charge
tears a hole in the dark underbelly of overcast, rain pelts the car
and blurs the way forward.

"Let me drive," Darcy says, rubbing the clouded windshield
clean with her shirtsleeve. "I've slept enough."

"Nowhere to pull over. Anyhow, I caught a few hours during
the flights." A road sign flashes past. "We'll be there in twenty
minutes."

Bronson's bright red pickup is the first thing Darcy sees
when they turn the corner into her neighborhood. The truck
grounds her, makes her believe she won't topple off the spinning
world. Hensel shuts off the engine.

Wearing a nightshirt, Jennifer stands barefoot in the doorway. Circles beneath her eyes scream the girl hasn't slept.

"You have to find her," Jennifer says, throwing herself into
Darcy's arms.

Darcy drops her bag and holds her daughter and tells her it
will be okay, though recent events make her words seem empty.

"Why did she run away? She was safe here, Mom. Now she's
alone, and that man is stalking her."

"It's been twelve hours. The police know the killer targeted
Amy. They'll declare her missing and begin the search."

"We should be looking for her, not standing here waiting for
the police to do their job."

Over Jennifer's shoulder, Darcy spots Bronson in the living
room. He has his jacket on, keys jangling in his hand. He
approaches, and Darcy can't decide if she should hug Bronson.

"You made it back," Bronson says, twirling the key ring
around his finger.

Darcy sets her bag down and leans against the wall.

"Tell me Hunter hasn't pulled another vanishing act."

"Sound asleep in his room."

"Good. Are you heading somewhere?"

Bronson's eyes swerve to Hensel in the doorway.

"I'll take a drive over to Smith Town and look for Amy in case she headed back that way. Afterward, I suppose I should eat something."

"Oh, shit. I'm sorry I haven't shopped this week. I promise I'll pick up food after I shower."

"Hey, now. That's not what I meant. You're shouldering all the load you can handle. All I'm saying is I've got a refrigerator full of food and nobody's eating it. It wouldn't be a bad idea if I brought a few items over. No sense in it going to waste."

"I know what you meant. I can't think straight."

"You haven't slept. I'm amazed you still function."

After Bronson leaves, Hensel leans against the door.

"I hate to do this to you, but I'm heading back to Quantico this afternoon."

Darcy creases her brow.

"So soon? You just arrived."

"Another case popped up. Corruption this time, thankfully. I could use a break from serial killers."

"Eric, it meant a lot that you checked on my family and flew me to see Rivers."

"Not much good came of it, I'm afraid."

"After three years of having that bastard inside my head, it was therapeutic to worm into his for once."

Hensel fishes into his pocket and opens his wallet. He removes a card and scribbles a number on the back.

"This is my emergency cell. I reserve it for family, no work. If anything should come up..." He hands her the card and glances down at his shoes. "Anyhow, I'm a heel for leaving you under the circumstances. If all goes well with the case, I can be back in Genoa Cove early next week."

"You don't need to."

"Yes, I do, so don't try to convince me otherwise. In the

meantime, I'll dig into the GCPD database. Poke around a little and see if I can find a connection between local offenders and Rivers. Hey, Amy will turn up soon."

"I know."

Except she doesn't.

"Promise me you'll talk to someone. Follow your prescription."

"It's under control, Eric."

When Hensel heads back to his hotel, Darcy collapses on the couch. His presence buoyed Darcy. Now that he's gone, she unravels again.

Scott, the lead installer for Gilmore, knocks at noon and jolts Darcy out of a restless sleep. He apologizes over the cameras and gets to work, checking cables and using a meter to test signal strength. The tech specialist is a whirling dervish of activity, always running in high gear as he bounces from one corner of the house to the next.

"I can't explain it," Scott says, sliding a screwdriver into his shirt pocket. "All the signals appear strong, and I reattached the cables. I ran diagnostics on your system and determined you never lost battery power."

"What would make all the cameras go out at once?"

"That's the strange part. You might lose a camera to a faulty connection or a defect with the unit. But all of them? Not unless the battery backup died."

"It rained last night. Could a storm have knocked the cameras out?"

"No chance. As far as I can tell, the cameras never stopped working. For some reason the video signal never made it back to the main system. I have to be honest. I've installed these systems for fifteen years and never encountered an issue like this."

"Now I'm confused," Darcy says with a groan. "The same

time the cameras failed, we lost power to the house, and that shouldn't happen because I have a whole house generator."

"I can take a look if you want."

Scott follows Darcy out to the deck. The generator slumbers against the far corner of the house.

"Huh," Scott says, leaning on the deck rail. "I can see your problem from here. The cable isn't attached."

A black cable curls in the grass like a rat snake.

"It was attached yesterday."

"I'll hook it up if you want. Won't take me but a few seconds."

With no break in the line, it's clear someone unhooked the generator cable. Bronson told her last night he'd check outside. Had he examined the generator? Even in the dark, he couldn't miss something this obvious.

"I'll run back to the van and grab new cameras," Scott says, cupping his eyes from the gray light as he peers up at the camera fixed over the deck. "I don't think there's anything wrong with these units, but I'll change them out just to be sure. Should take me an hour if you don't mind me banging around out here."

The Gilmore van drives away before Hunter dodders out to the kitchen for a glass of water. His hair is a rat's nest, and he's wearing yesterday's clothes. Putting aside the dishes, Darcy tells Hunter to have a seat. He grumbles and slouches in the chair, rubbing at his head and battling a migraine.

"We need to talk, Hunter."

"What did I do this time?"

The earbuds hang around his neck. Darcy grabs his phone and pauses the music.

"You scared the hell out of me last night disappearing on Bronson, and it's not the first time. I understand you need time to yourself and what it's like to want to get away when bad shit keeps happening. But it's not safe, and you need to tell us where you are. Where did you go last night? Don't tell me you spent the entire time looking for Amy."

He shrugs and itches his neck. His shirt collar slumps down, and Darcy notices a purple bruise between the neck and shoulder. It could have happened playing football, but Darcy can't tell for certain.

"Come on, Hunter. Talk to me."

"I drove past her house in Smith Town like I said, and then I kept looping down the coast road and back to the highway, passing her house each time. After that, I cut through the village and drove down Main Street."

"And then?" He stares at his hands. "What did you do the other three hours?"

"Just...drove. And walked, I guess."

"Walked where?"

"Everywhere. Like I went past those new apartment buildings on the west side of Smith Town. I figured maybe she'd be down there."

"Hunter, that's a high crime area."

"I wasn't scared."

"I don't care if you weren't scared. It's dangerous. And why did you shut me out? You ignored my calls."

The silver window light turns his face ashen, dead.

"I had the phone off."

"Why?"

"Can't I relax for five seconds without someone always calling me? Fuck."

Darcy flinches at his raised voice.

"That was unnecessary."

"I didn't mean to swear."

"You're grounded from the car for another week. Hunter, do you want someone to talk to? There's a good doctor on the other side of the cove."

"I don't need a shrink."

"Then talk to me. Or your sister. Or—"

"Bronson?"

"Would that be a problem?"

Hunter's jaw shifts.

"It's a little weird how much time he spends here. I mean, it's not his house. It's yours, right?"

"Hunter, Bronson likes you and Jennifer. It's a good idea to have a man around the house, especially an ex-cop, keeping an eye on everyone until the police catch whoever killed that girl."

"He's not Dad."

His words make her wince.

"Is that what this is about? Hunter, nobody wants to replace your father."

She reaches over and brushes the hair off his brow. His eyes are red and infused with an injury Darcy hasn't recognized until now.

"I still think about your Dad, Hunter. I never stopped loving him or wishing he was here with us. From now on when you feel overwhelmed, please come to me. Let me help."

Hunter nods.

"I'll try to do better."

"Oh, honey, you're doing the best you can. We all are. Stop beating yourself up." Darcy sorts through a stack of mail on the table. Ironically, the first bill from Gilmore arrived. "What do you have planned today? Bethany hasn't been around much. How about you call her over?"

"I don't know. She's busy with student council meetings. If I can't take the car..."

"Not this week."

"Then I thought I'd walk down to the cove and follow the shore toward the public beaches. See if Amy came through."

Darcy peers out the window at the gray sky.

"The weatherman says no rain this afternoon, but you better take a jacket just in case."

"Sure."

Darcy hugs Hunter before he locks himself in his room. She drops the car keys in her pocket, figuring she has an hour to canvas the town before picking up groceries for dinner. She warns her daughter not to answer the door for anyone but Bronson. The only response is a sniffle.

When Darcy returns from the store with groceries, night creeps down and darkens the autumn sky.

And Hunter hasn't come home.

13

We all reach a breaking point, a point at which the slightest tug drags us from balance to insanity. Darcy is here now.

Calling Hunter's phone proves to be fruitless. It rings inside his bedroom, where she finds it under an open bag of potato chips. A shooter video game plays on the computer screen, Hunter's abandoned avatar gunned down as other players fire at each other from dilapidated buildings and bunkers. Like most teenagers, Hunter values his phone, and she can't understand why he left without it.

"Jennifer, did you hear from your brother? Jennifer?"

The floor creaks inside Jennifer's bedroom, then the door slowly opens, Jennifer still in her nightshirt and tipped against the jamb. Her face is drawn, eyes rimmed by red, hauntingly lifeless. Gloom blankets the room, shades drawn, an iPad providing the only light. I shouldn't have left her alone, Darcy thinks.

"He left two hours ago."

"Did he say where he was going?"

"Hunter never tells me anything anymore."

The door drifts shut and locks.

"Hey, Jennifer. Why don't you help me in the kitchen?"

"I don't feel good."

"I know it hurts. After dinner, we'll look for Amy. It's a small area. She couldn't have gone far."

"She's never coming back."

"Don't say that."

"You know it's true."

Darcy tests the knob and rests her head on the door. Releasing a breath, she drags herself into the kitchen and puts away the groceries. She can't bring herself to cook with Hunter missing. Again. And it's getting late.

A text arrives from Bronson. He's on his way. She tells him she's leaving to search for Hunter and to keep an eye on Jennifer.

Throwing a windbreaker over her sweatshirt, Darcy hurries past neighbors' houses toward the cove where Hunter said he was going. Lights flicker on inside homes. Mr. Gibbons, an overweight, balding man wearing glasses and a cardigan sweater, rakes leaves in front of his Cape Cod.

"Evening, Mr. Gibbons."

He stretches his back and leans the rake against an elm tree.

"Evening."

"Have you seen my son?"

"Can't say that I have. Did you check the beach?"

"Heading there now. Thank you."

Shadows pour across the narrow pathway at the end of the neighborhood. Trudging through the sand, Darcy folds her arms and hurries toward the cove. A slice of sunset clips the trees and colors the water bloody, the beach empty. A pile of driftwood collects on the south end of the cove where the ocean pushes over the sand. Footprints along the water lead from the cove toward the public beach, and when she examines the prints, she recognizes the Nike lettering imprinted on the sand. Hunter wears Nike sneakers. Another set of footprints follow the same path. Did Hunter meet someone on the beach?

The bushes rattle. Darcy spins back to the path. Too dark. Her eyes can't penetrate the shadows.

"Hello. Is anybody there?"

A gust of wind whips sand into her face. She twists around and covers her eyes until the gale passes. The water is black, depthless.

The driftwood shifts and tumbles. Darcy backs away, wishing she'd armed herself before leaving.

"Who's there? Hunter?"

Wind moans over the water, the sound of banshees.

Darkness shifts behind the pile of driftwood. Darcy turns and runs for the path, the bordering tree limbs whipping at her face and body as she veers off course. Laughter trails her. Or is it the wind?

Darcy breaks into a sprint and doesn't slow until she reaches the neighborhood. Casting nervous glances over her shoulder, she hurries up the driveway to her home. Bronson's truck sits at the end of the drive, blocking in the Prius.

She issues a silent prayer that Hunter is inside, but the knowing look Bronson shoots her from the kitchen tells Darcy her son hasn't come home.

"You need to talk to him," Bronson says. He removes a package of hamburger from the refrigerator and slaps it down on the counter.

"I already did."

"He doesn't listen. Darcy, I don't want to play parent here."

"Then don't. You don't know what he's been through."

His face twists. Just as quickly Bronson turns placid. He's good at concealing his rage.

"You're right. I shouldn't have suggested..." Before she knows what's happening, Bronson pulls her into a hug and rubs the backs of her shoulders. "I didn't mean to upset you. If you want me to leave, I will."

"No, none of us want that."

Part of her wants to pull out of his grasp because this feels wrong, but she settles against him.

"You sure? I'm getting the cold shoulder lately from Hunter and Jennifer."

"It's not about you. Between the murder and Amy missing, neither kid can process what's happening. Hell, I'm not sure I can. Deep inside, they want you around."

"I wish I could believe that."

"Give them time."

Bronson holds her at arm's length.

"How much do they know about what happened to you three years ago?"

"It's on the Internet. There wasn't a point in hiding the truth."

"But they understand Rivers is in jail and can't be responsible for what's happening in Genoa Cove."

Except Rivers is responsible. He knows Darcy's every move and who she brings into the house.

Darcy and Bronson grill hamburgers and eat in the kitchen. Jennifer won't leave her room, so Darcy fixes her a small plate and sets it on the girl's desk. When she retrieves the plate after dinner, Jennifer hasn't touched her food.

Seven o'clock comes and goes with no sign of Hunter. Then eight. But he opens the door after nine and sets his house keys on the counter as Bronson and Darcy glare at him from the kitchen.

"I checked around, but nobody saw Amy," Hunter says.

When he starts toward his bedroom, Darcy blocks him and sets her hands on her hips.

"It's too dangerous to be out after sunset. You're eighteen, but we're amending the rules as long as you live in this house."

"Why are you angry? I told you I was going for a walk. You didn't have a problem with it."

"From now on, I want you home before dark. And you better bring your phone and leave it on so I can reach you."

"It's almost winter. It'll be dark by the time we get home from school."

"Tough. Until it's safe in Genoa Cove—"

A knock on the door brings Darcy's head around. Red and blue lights sweep over the window.

As Darcy searches Bronson's face for an explanation, the bedroom door opens and Jennifer inches into the hallway. This is a horror story, and Jennifer knows how it will end.

"Go back to your room," Darcy says over her shoulder.

Ignoring her mother, Jennifer shuffles down the hallway, eyes glued to the front door.

Darcy opens the door as Detective Ames prepares to knock again. Julian stands by his side, the intensity in his eyes making Darcy flinch.

"Detective? What's the meaning of this?"

Ames holds a folded sheet of paper with WARRANT OF ARREST written across the top in bold and black.

"Ms. Gellar, is your son here?"

"My son...Hunter?"

Hunter stumbles toward the doorway as Bronson slides behind the boy. As if to block Hunter should he try to run. Julian reaches for his handcuffs.

Her instinct to protect her son rules her actions. Darcy braces her arms against the entryway and blocks Ames' passage.

"Please, Ms. Gellar. Don't make this more difficult than it needs to be."

"This is insane. I'm not letting you inside my house."

"We have a warrant," Ames says, pointing to the paper. "I need you to stand aside."

"Not until you tell me what this is about."

"Ma'am, I won't ask you again. Stand aside."

Darcy lifts her chin, but Hunter touches her arm and slips into the doorway.

"It's okay, Mom."

"Hunter, you can't go with them."

"I'll be all right."

Julian and Ames crowd the door while the confusion distracts Darcy. Jennifer screams behind Hunter as Julian handcuffs her brother. Ames locks eyes with the boy.

"Hunter Gellar, you are under arrest for the murder of Amy Yang."

An icy chill lances into Darcy's chest. She grabs the threshold to keep from falling, and Bronson moves to support her.

"Amy's not dead! She can't be. My son isn't a killer."

But he is, Darcy hears Michael Rivers whisper from the shadows. The signs were there.

"You have the right to be silent. Anything you say can and will be used against you in a court of law. You have the right to an attorney."

"Oh, he'll have an attorney," Darcy says, throwing herself toward the two policemen as Bronson tugs her back. "Hunter, don't say anything. I'm calling a lawyer. We'll meet you at the station."

Then she watches Ames and Julian lead Hunter to the car. A pair of officers outside a second cruiser provide backup as Julian pushes Hunter's head down and forces him into the backseat.

"He's not resisting," Darcy cries. "Leave him alone!"

The door slams. Ames gives her a sympathetic glance over the cruiser before he slides behind the wheel. The two cruisers weave out of the neighborhood while Mr. Gibbons watches from his front lawn. Gibbons meets Darcy's eye and turns away, locking his door behind him.

"How could you let them arrest Hunter?" Jennifer grabs Darcy by the arms. Her nails leave sickle moon shapes below Darcy's shoulders. "You just stood there and let them take him away. Do something!"

Bronson lays a consoling hand on the girl's shoulder. She shrugs him off and falls wailing into Darcy, Jennifer's words drowned by sobs, though Darcy hears Amy's name.

She imagines Amy, the beautiful girl a daughter to Darcy, butchered on the cove, Hunter locked in a cell and charged with the murder.

"Who's the best criminal defense lawyer in Genoa Cove?" Darcy asks over Jennifer's shoulder. "Better yet, give me someone from Smith Town, someone who isn't afraid to get his hands dirty."

Bronson rubs his chin.

"Breck Appleton is good. I'll get you the number."

When Darcy, Bronson, and Jennifer arrive at the police station, a female news reporter with an audio recorder in her hand darts between the cars.

"Shit," Bronson mutters. "The Standard already heard."

Darcy recognizes Gail Shipley from her photograph on the newspaper's website. The middle-aged woman wears her blonde hair teased in a bob. Though she's a writer, her makeup job is to television standards. Her heels click against the pavement as she rushes toward them.

"When did you find out your son murdered Amy Yang?"

Bronson throws his bulk between two SUVs to block Shipley as Darcy locks elbows with her daughter and rushes into the police station. The woman's hysterical questions chase them through the entry doors.

Inside, a drunk woman curses while a small, female officer leads her down a hallway adjacent to the front desk. A buzzer sounds, and the door at the end of the hallway unlocks and opens. The male officer manning the desk looks like he chose the wrong career after high school and spent the last twenty years regretting it. His shirt wrinkled, face long and dragging, he grimaces at Darcy and Jennifer before he spots Bronson. His mouth hangs open for a second before he clicks a stack of papers on the desk and files them in a folder.

Another officer, a graying man with a mustache, eyes Bronson from the hallway.

"Hey, give me a second," Bronson tells Darcy.

Bronson confers with the officer while Darcy sits on an uncomfortable wooden bench with Jennifer slumped against her shoulder. Bronson leaves for fifteen minutes, and when he returns, he gestures Darcy toward the far corner of the room. Jennifer gets up, but Darcy raises a hand and tells her to stay put.

"What do they have on Hunter?"

Bronson glances around Darcy toward the officer at the front desk, who watches them from the corner of his eye.

"As long as Hunter keeps his mouth shut until the lawyer gets here, they'll let him go."

Darcy falls back against the wall and touches her forehead.

"Finally, some sanity."

"The evidence is circumstantial. None of it would hold up in court. But I should warn you, the police have damning information on Hunter."

"Such as?"

"The police found Nike shoe prints along the beach that match the pattern Hunter wears. Ames can demonstrate the size is the same, but there's no way to prove he's the only person in town who wears that style and size."

"Okay, what else?"

"The police say Hunter met Amy before she moved in with you."

Darcy hears Rivers' voice again. Hunter found Amy online and stalked her, and when terrorizing Amy didn't satisfy Hunter, he murdered her.

"No, they never met. I never took the kids to see Amy after she called."

"Not even online? A message board, perhaps."

"It's possible. How can they prove Hunter knew Amy?"

"A phone call. Ames got hold of Hunter's phone. Hunter allowed him to examine the phone, figuring he had nothing to hide. The call log shows Hunter phoned Amy at 4:05 PM on the twenty-first of October. This was prior to Amy moving in, correct?"

Darcy's mouth goes dry. What is she missing?

"Yes, but I don't see how Hunter could have known Amy. They lived in separate towns. Wait...I called Amy, not Hunter. My phone wasn't working, so Hunter gave me his to borrow."

"You'll want to tell the lawyer as soon as he arrives. Did you take your phone to a repair shop?"

"Yes. I have the receipt and work order."

"Good. But, Darcy...Are you aware of a band called Angel Devoured?"

Darcy scrunches her brow.

"Should I be?"

"Hunter is a fan. Ames talked to Coach Morgan at the high school, and Morgan says Hunter wears an Angel Devoured t-shirt, so often he needed to speak to Hunter."

"The shirt and tie fiasco. I remember. But listening to hard rock doesn't make you a violent person. They're grasping at straws."

A female officer walks past with a Styrofoam cup of coffee. Bronson waits until she moves on.

"Ames found a picture on the back of the band's last album. It appears to be the same image the Full Moon Killer uses to brand his victims. The same mark they found on Amy Yang."

Darcy turns toward the wall and cups her mouth with her hand.

"It's still not enough to pin Amy's murder on Hunter. They can't think he's worked with Rivers since the incarceration. Hunter was only fifteen."

"Your lawyer will have a field day with Ames, but the evidence might be sufficient for them to hold Hunter until morning."

"No. I won't allow them to lock Hunter in a cell all night. I want to see Ames."

"That's not a good idea. Wait until Appleton arrives."

It's too late for Bronson to change Darcy's mind. Detective Ames appears in the hallway where he confers with a police officer holding a manila folder. When Ames turns around, Darcy stands in front of him.

"I want to see my son."

"You will."

"You'd better not be interviewing Hunter without a lawyer present."

"When his attorney arrives, you'll be the first to hear."

"You're making a big mistake, Detective. You can't believe Hunter committed these crimes."

"I gather evidence, Ms. Gellar. The court will decide if Hunter is guilty." Suspicion narrows Ames' eyes when he glances at Bronson. "But you wouldn't know anything about the evidence. Right, Ms. Gellar?"

"If you hold Hunter overnight, I'll sue the village."

"Why don't you come back to my office?"

"Is that a nice way of placing me under arrest?"

"Consider it a courtesy."

Darcy looks at Bronson, who raises one shoulder as if to say, it's up to you.

"Fine, then. Let's talk."

Bronson sits with Jennifer, the teenager groggy and subdued. The glares of the other police officers are accusatory, palpably aggressive. For some insane reason, they're all convinced Hunter murdered Amy.

Ames' office is small and cluttered. A beige coat that has seen better days hangs from a rack. Two photographs on the desk lend the only splashes of color inside the gray and brown rectangle—a picture of the ocean at sunrise, and the rolling green hillocks of a golf course. Darcy notes Ames doesn't have pictures of a spouse or family, no birthday cards or children's drawings thumb-tacked to the wall.

Ames slides a stack of folders and papers aside so he can see her across his desk. He slips a pair of reading glasses on and examines a note. He scowls and tosses the note into the trash, setting the glasses on the desk.

"So, you knew the deceased well, Ms. Gellar?"

"After the abduction attempt, Amy and I kept in touch for about a year. She was in therapy. We both were."

"But you lost contact?"

"Amy stopped calling and didn't respond to my messages. We both were in dark places and trying to find our way home. In Amy's case, I think I served as a constant reminder of what happened. She needed distance."

Ames rocks back in his chair and taps a pen on the armrest.

"But that changed."

"When the stalking began, yes. She believed Michael Rivers escaped and was following her."

"At the Smith Town residence."

"That's correct."

"How close is Bronson Severson to your son?"

The line of questioning stuns her into silence.

"The kids only met Bronson a few weeks ago," says Darcy.

"But sometimes he's alone with Hunter and they talk."

"Bronson drives Hunter to school or back from football practice when he has time. I don't understand what this has to do with a murder implication."

"Does Hunter spend a lot of time in Smith Town?"

"I know where you're going with this. The two villages interconnect. It's not unusual for residents of either village to spend time in the other."

"Witnesses have seen Hunter in Smith Town."

"Walking, I'm sure. It's not a crime to clear your head."

"What does Hunter need to clear his head of, Ms. Gellar?"

"Save it for the court case. I studied the Full Moon Killer for a year before the FBI captured him. And I just visited Michael Rivers, but I gather you knew that too. Hunter is not your killer. The man you seek patterns himself after Rivers, right down to the branding. That he's targeted Amy and me suggests he's motivated by revenge."

"Because you put the Full Moon Killer away."

"And since it's personal, he must serve Rivers. He's either a crazed fan or an accomplice."

His elbows on the desk, Ames rubs his face and groans.

"This is fascinating. But it's all conjecture, not fact. At eight o'clock this evening, a boater discovered the body of Amy Yang at the cove, two blocks from your house. Shortly after, we received an anonymous call claiming Hunter argued with Amy moments before the boater found her. Now, pretend you're still an agent with the FBI. Would you pursue Hunter?"

"An anonymous caller. It could have been the killer. He seems intent on destroying my family. You believe Hunter did this, so that means my son wants to ruin me and his sister to serve Michael Rivers. That's illogical."

"You know better than me. After all, you profile serial killers. But I have a theory."

"You better have more than a theory when we go to court."

"Stay with me for a moment. Hunter's early life was traumatic after the death of his father. Then he reached his teenage years, and Michael Rivers tried to murder his mother. The case garnered worldwide attention. That's a lot for a boy to swallow."

"Don't shame me for capturing a murderer."

"I wouldn't dream of it. But your son doesn't live in a vacuum. These events traumatized him.

"It doesn't make him a killer. Your theories are half-baked and grounded in conjecture."

Ames crosses his arms.

"Hunter saw the crime scene photos in your closet."

Darcy's heart skips. She'd hidden the notes and pictures from her children, understanding the negative psychological effect they would have on Hunter and Jennifer. She was a fool not to lock them in the safe.

"He told you this? You weren't supposed to interview Hunter yet."

"Hunter is an adult. If he divulges a fact or two without his attorney present, that's his prerogative." What else did Hunter tell Ames? "Hunter studied the Full Moon Killer's methodology using your own notes, and tonight he murdered Amy Yang."

"I think we're finished here. Make sure you share this iron-clad evidence with Hunter's lawyer."

Breck Appleton hustles into the station when Darcy rejoins Bronson and Jennifer. The lawyer is younger than she expected, a fit forty-something wearing a gray pressed suit and carrying a black briefcase. His introduction is short, then he strides down the hallway and through the locked door.

"You want something to eat?" Bronson asks Darcy.

"Maybe something for Jennifer. I'm not hungry."

While Bronson runs across the street to a deli, Jennifer snoozes, her head on Darcy's lap. Darcy brushes at her daughter's hair, reminded of times she soothed her children to sleep: Jennifer dozing in her rocker, Hunter's cars and trucks jumbled beneath the coffee table. And Tyler in the recliner sipping coffee and watching the game or reading a book. Tyler. He'd know what to do now. Darcy wipes a tear off from her eye.

A woman slides onto the bench beside them. The crone stinks of cigarettes and sweat, a tattered scarf clinging to her long, frail neck. Her smile displays decayed and missing teeth as she peers down at Jennifer.

"Pretty, pretty girl."

"Thank you," Darcy says, wishing Bronson would come back from the deli. Though the woman seems harmless, Darcy frets over how Jennifer will react if she awakens and sees the thin face leering down at her.

"This is no place for a little girl. Did she get into trouble?"

"We're just waiting for someone."

"That's good, because if you get in trouble, my boy will get you."

"Excuse me?"

"My son."

The woman digs into her pocket and removes a crumbled muffin inside shrink wrap. Extending her hand, she almost shoves the muffin into Darcy's face.

"This is for the girl. She's hungry."

"I can't take your food."

Ames jogs into the waiting area and gives an exasperated sigh.

"Mom, what are you doing here?"

Detective Ames' mother? He locks eyes with Darcy for a moment, and an apology passes between them. Worse yet, his mother has pulled him out of the interrogation room with Hunter and Appleton.

"I brought you a snack," Ames' mother says, shifting her open hand toward her son. "You work all day and never eat. It'll make you sicker than this poor little girl I met."

"You shouldn't have walked here by yourself. It's not safe in the village." Interesting Ames would say the village is dangerous. With the supposed killer trapped inside the interrogation room, the community should breathe a sigh of relief. "Let Milligan drive you home."

"Not until you have something to eat. You're thin as a rail."

"Okay, Mom. But you need to leave. I'm in the middle of an important meeting."

"Always saving the world," she says, half-limping, half-shuffling to Ames. She drops the plastic wrapped food in his hand. "That's my boy."

Ames gives her a half-hearted hug and tilts his head at the officer named Milligan behind the desk. Milligan rounds the desk and takes the woman's arm before walking out of the station.

Awkward silence passes between Darcy and Ames before he spins on his heels and hurries back to the interrogation room. Jennifer stirs, lifts her head, and asks what happened. While she explains, Bronson returns with two white paper bags redolent of condiments and onion. He's brought sandwiches for the three of them.

"What was Ames' mother doing here?" Bronson hands Darcy a bag. "Changing her kid's diaper?"

"You know her?"

"I remember her. Crazy as a loon. Easy to see where her son gets it from."

Darcy coaxes Jennifer to eat while forcing herself to nibble on her own sandwich. They finish as Appleton glides down the hallway. Darcy rises.

"Their case is paper-thin," Appleton says, donning his jacket. "They'll drop the charges, they have no choice unless further evidence arises. The DA is strong-arming the police to make an arrest, and Ames knows he doesn't have enough for a conviction."

"Will they let him go tonight?"

"Technically, they can hold someone overnight without charging him. Right now Ames is being stubborn, but I think he sees this is a dead end." Appleton tugs his shirtsleeve up and reads his watch. "I need to meet with a client in Smith Town. I should be back in a couple hours."

Midnight comes and goes. Darcy's back throbs, impossible for her to get comfortable on the bench. Bronson took Jennifer home at eleven, and Darcy feels like she is behind enemy lines, the department dead set on concocting proof that Hunter is a copycat murderer.

Ames, pale and barely able to keep his eyes open, springs

Hunter at two in the morning. He warns Hunter not to leave the village.

"Are you dropping the charges?" Darcy asks, shrugging on her jacket.

"For now."

"Why are you so determined to prove Hunter did this? You're banging a square peg into a round hole."

"Good night, Ms. Gellar."

Genoa Cove is an empty shell, no sign of another vehicle as Darcy navigates through the village. The night sky consumes light and leaves a wasteland of infinite darkness. Hunter won't talk. He taps his phone on his knee, exhausted yet wide-awake. Hunter won't sleep tonight, and neither will Darcy.

At the house, Bronson snorts and sits up when the door opens. Rubbing his eyes, Bronson watches Hunter slog to his room as Darcy slides beside him on the couch.

"How did it go?"

"Well, they let him out. Ames dropped the charges, but I'm sure he's angling toward another arrest. He's like a bulldog who won't let go of a steak. Appleton thinks the DA is pulling Ames' strings."

"District Attorney Hebert is up for reelection next year. If the police don't apprehend the killer, the public will blame him."

"That doesn't justify what they did to Hunter." Darcy yawns and leans her head on a pillow. "Lord, the things Ames said. He thinks Hunter snapped or something because he found the crime scene photos from the Rivers case in my closet."

"You still have them?"

"The FBI frowns on that sort of thing."

Bronson rubs her shoulder.

"Mums the word. Is that what happens with people who become serial killers? They snap because of a traumatic event?"

"Every case is different. Rivers came from a normal

suburban family in Virginia. Two parents, a cat and a dog, no alcoholism or abuse. He started early. The neighbor caught him outside with a magnifying glass."

"Ants?"

Darcy's mouth twists as though she bit into a lemon.

"Spiders. Rivers looked for the biggest spiders he could find. He liked it when their abdomens caught fire and exploded."

"Disgusting."

"The family cat disappeared when Rivers was twelve. His mother was on to him by then and suspected he killed the cat. She gave the dog up for adoption before he could hurt it. There was a rape accusation in high school, then a second in college. Neither charge stuck. The kid was sick but smart. Maybe some people are evil."

Bronson is sound asleep and snoring on the couch when Darcy hobbles into the living room at the break of dawn. She hasn't slept. Every bone in her body aches as she squints at the light streaming through the windows. On her way to the kitchen, she senses something is wrong. And a memory surfaces. A noise she heard in the dead of night when she was half-asleep. Wrapping a blanket around her shoulders, she cracks open the door.

The car drips with red paint. Someone scrawled MURDERER across the driver side, the tires punctured and flat. Paint covers the windshield where some genius wrote DIE ASSHOLE.

She curses, stepping onto the lawn.

The vandals are long gone, not that she expected them to hang around after the sun rose. The front door squeaks, and she spins around to find Bronson watching her from the entryway.

"I guess I should have expected this," Darcy says, picking up a stone and hurling it into the trees with a frustrated grunt. "But hey, it's a gorgeous morning, and they spared your truck."

"Easy now. The damage is superficial."

"Apparently the assholes didn't realize they're on Candid Camera. Of course, the cameras probably failed as soon as the shit-show started."

But they hadn't. Darcy scans the predawn footage and stops when a car pulls to the curb. The time stamp reads 4:06 AM when four large boys wearing sweatshirts with the hoods drawn over their faces converge on the car. But the camera catches a face. Aaron Torres, Bethany's brother. This is the same crew who drove past the house.

"Not very intelligent, are they?" Bronson says, sipping on a cup of coffee. Almost appearing amused, he points at the largest boy. "That's Sam Tatum."

Darcy winces when Tatum, a lineman judging by his imposing frame, raises a boot and kicks out the taillight. That was the noise she heard. What would have happened had she responded? Would the boys have fled to their car and raced out of the neighborhood, or might something horrible have occurred? Some boys cross lines and turn violent when alcohol is involved, and their erratic stumbles tells Darcy these boys were very drunk.

"Those little pricks," Jennifer says, nudging between Darcy and Bronson. "What are we going to do for a car now?"

"Grant's Body Shop down on Schuyler will take care of the damage," Bronson says. "In the meantime, we've got my truck."

An hour passes before the police arrive, and Darcy looks ready for a war when the cruiser pulls beside the vandalized Prius. Arms folded, jaw working from side to side, Darcy watches as Julian clambers out of the vehicle. He's the last cop she wants to see.

"You called about damage to your vehicle?" Julian asks as though he doesn't notice the crushed taillight, dented body, and spray paint. "This the car?"

"Great observation. Can't put anything past the Genoa Cove PD."

"It's a simple question, Ms. Gellar. No need to get surly."

"Yeah, this is the car. It's the only vehicle in the driveway with MURDERER painted across the side."

Julian mumbles something and rounds the Prius, recording his observations as he goes.

"About what time did the vandalism occur?"

"4:06 AM. It's all on video."

"Your security cameras caught the person who did this?"

"Persons. Four boys, to be exact. Would you like the see the video, Officer Haines?"

"Hey," Bronson says, pulling Darcy aside. "Don't bring the police into this. Turn it over to your lawyer and force the parents to pay for the damage."

Darcy ignores the advice and pushes past Bronson.

Clenching his jaw, Julian follows Darcy into the kitchen while Jennifer shoots him a death stare from the couch.

"That's Aaron Torres," Darcy says, gesturing at the boy when his face turns toward the camera.

"It might be," Julian says, squinting his eyes. "The picture is awfully dark."

"You can't be serious. Well, okay. Look at his vehicle. You can read the license plate."

"Can you? Go back a few frames." Julian jots three letters on his notepad. "Do you have a better shot than that? I'm not seeing the entire plate."

"Oh, for God's sake. I'll read them to you." Darcy recites the license plate number.

Julian reaches around Darcy and clicks the zoom feature. It takes him an uncomfortably long time to compare Darcy's version with what he sees on the screen, then he pockets the notepad.

"I need a copy of the video."

"Can you take it on a thumb drive?"

"Or you can email it to me. Whatever is most convenient."

"Sure, the video will take a few minutes to download."

The bedroom door opens. Julian's eyes follow Hunter as he heads for the bathroom.

"While you work on the video, I'll write up the report so you have it for the insurance claim."

"Are you going to arrest Aaron Torres and his friends?"

"I'll take care of the situation." Down the hall, the bathroom door clicks shut. "I'd like to do a walk-through of the residence and make sure the kids didn't break inside."

Bronson blocks the hallway, arms folded.

"Not without a warrant," says Darcy.

"Ms. Gellar, I'm not out to get you."

"No, you only arrested my son on circumstantial evidence to be neighborly."

"Fine, then. Would you like me to examine the property from the outside? That would save me from filling out a second report if you discover damage after I leave."

Darcy agrees, but she keeps one eye on the monitors while Julian surveys the exterior. He spends a long time in the back-yard beside the deck. When she finishes copying the video, she walks the thumb drive out to Julian.

"No additional damage, but you'll want to examine the property yourself in case I missed anything. Oh, and your generator cable is unplugged. Better plug it in before we get another storm."

Darcy's feet go cold as Julian walks out to the cruiser. The Gilmore tech reattached the generator cable. She watched him do it.

While Bronson is outside keeping an eye on Julian, Darcy accesses the security video archives. Twenty-four hours ago, before someone murdered Amy Yang and spun Darcy's world off its axis, the video displays the cable attached to the generator. Twelve hours later, darkness turns the picture gray, yet she sees the cable intact. Now she fast-forwards to 4:06 AM when Aaron Torres and his Neanderthal crew vandalized the Prius. The cable is on the ground. Yet Torres never unhooked the generator.

Rewinding the footage at high speed, Darcy watches the pictures blur past until a shadow catches her eye after midnight. A man behind the house wearing a dark sweatshirt with the hood pulled up. He keeps his face averted from the cameras. He knows their locations. After he unhooks the generator, he steps out of view. Darcy searches for the man on the other cameras, but he's a ghost.

She was at the police station when the man came. Bronson was home with Jennifer.

Bronson tails Julian into the house. When the officer hands her the damage report, she tells Julian to watch the video. Bronson stands behind them, his face emotionless.

"So this man came to your house and unhooked the connection to your generator, but he didn't break in or cause additional damage."

"It's not the first time," Darcy says. She tells him about the power outage, the trigger that caused Amy to flee.

"No way to determine who he is from the footage, but I'd like a copy of the video all the same. And I want to sweep for prints around the generator."

After Julian leaves, Darcy stares at the screen for a long time. Is this the killer?

15

Midnight. The witching hour.

Sirens awaken Darcy and pull her out of bed and to the window. Emergency lights flare across the pane, and she thinks the police are coming to take Hunter away again. The police cruiser shoots past, followed by another. Distant sirens announce more are on the way as she slips into her clothes.

Bronson already stands at the picture window in the living room. His head turns toward her, and she rushes past.

"Wait, Darcy."

Outside, the night air thickens with humidity, warning of a storm. Branches rattle with the wind.

"They're heading to the cove," Darcy says, pulling a jacket on. "You know what that means."

Hunter and Jennifer appear in the doorway. Darcy knows Hunter has been inside all night, and she's sick with guilt for questioning his whereabouts during another murder.

Jennifer's eyes are glowing moons.

"Is it happening again?"

Before Darcy can answer, Jennifer pulls free of Hunter and slams her bedroom door.

"Stay with the kids," Darcy says to Bronson.

"Don't go down there."

"I have to know."

The moment she steps onto the driveway, it hits her. The dark suffocates and stiffens her body.

As if Darcy can outrun her anxiety, she breaks into a sprint as Bronson's shouts follow her through the neighborhood. Another cruiser blows past with a gust of wind, lights whirling with the siren off. Between the trees lining the pathway to the cove, torches dance and throw angry reds and oranges across the sand. The cruisers can't reach the cove without veering toward the public beach and driving across the shoreline. Taillights whip around the corner as the police vehicles converge on the municipal parking lot.

The sand tries to swallow her sneakers. As she staggers onto the cove, Ames whips his head around and scowls. Two officers flank Ames, though it is too dark to make out their faces. A crumpled bulk sprawls beside the water. Torso hacked, one arm hanging by a flap of skin. Gulls swoop down, and one officer shoos it away.

Darcy starts toward the victim, a young girl, and Ames raises his hand and moves to block her.

"This is a crime scene, Ms. Gellar. You need to leave."

"It's another stabbing, and there's a smiling face burned into her neck," Darcy says, trying to see around Ames.

"Go home to your family."

"Hunter was home with me all night, Detective."

"You certain of that? It looks to me like you just woke up. Now move aside, or I'll charge you with interfering with my investigation."

Flares protrude from the sand. A wind gust tears the flames

sideways and illuminates the teenager's face. Darcy has seen this girl. She's a student at the high school. Darcy passed her in the hall outside the guidance office.

"Ms. Gellar, please."

Darcy lifts her eyes to the nearly full moon, its eerie glow rimming a break in the clouds.

"He's getting more active, Detective. This guy thinks he's the Full Moon Killer, and you can expect more bodies until you catch him."

"Why would someone take up the mantle for a serial killer?"

"Why did Manson's followers murder innocents? How did Jim Jones convince his inner circle to poison 909 civilians in Jonestown? Whoever the killer is, Michael Rivers directs his actions from a jail cell in Western New York. Why aren't your officers monitoring the cove?"

Ames' face reddens as he steps toward Darcy.

"Our force is stretched to the point of breaking, especially with your kids going missing every night. How many overtime shifts can you ask these officers to take?"

"Then set up cameras. Round up volunteers. Do something besides blaming my son. He's suffered enough in his life without you destroying what's left of him."

Ames opens his mouth to reply as Darcy turns her back and struggles down the path.

"Stay out of my investigation," Ames yells over the growing wind.

A figure in the night twists Darcy's head around. A woman down the beach, watching the police from the shadows. Gail Shipley.

Darcy quickens her pace. Even if the woman spots Darcy, she can't pursue unless she backtracks through the public beach area or cuts through the crime scene. And Ames will give Shipley hell if she tries.

Darcy's house is lit like a landing strip when she arrives. Bronson's shadow passes across the living room window. During the walk home, she felt eyes on her back, a black presence watching her in the dark. Inside, she bolts the door and checks the windows in the kids' rooms.

"The vic was a teenage girl," Darcy whispers to Bronson. "I recognized her from school."

"Better not let the kids know."

"God, Bronson. Why is this happening?"

Bronson pulls her into his arms, and she goes willingly, nuzzling her cheek against his strong shoulders. His cologne is reminiscent of leather with a splash of flowers. Odd. Why is he wearing cologne in the middle of the night?

"So you saw the girl. Darcy, I'm sorry. No matter how many bodies I saw, I never got used to it. Do you want to talk about it?"

She doesn't. Something else bothers her.

"Step outside with me."

He nods. Talking on the couch, Hunter and Jennifer cast furtive glances at Darcy and Bronson.

Darcy shivers and zips her jacket as her body readjusts to the cool air. Lights from the police cruisers flicker in the distance like somber fireworks.

"What do you need to tell me?"

Darcy locks her gaze on him.

"You didn't hear the man or see him on the monitors when he detached the generator last night."

"No, Darcy. I was sound asleep. I'm sorry I can't watch the house twenty-four-seven."

"And the night the power went out. You were awake then, and somehow you missed this guy unhooking the generator, knocking out the monitors, and killing the power."

"I don't know what you expect. Are you blaming me?"

"No, but it doesn't add up. You were a cop for two decades,

and you didn't catch sabotage occurring under your nose. You didn't even hear Aaron Torres and his goon friends bashing away at my car last night."

"Did you? Why am I listening to this? I cart your brat kids around and don't say a word when they lash out. I'm not their father."

Tears blur Darcy's eyes.

"No, you're not."

"Maybe I should leave and let you cool down."

"Nobody told you to leave, and I don't need to cool down."

"Yes, you do. And when you do, you'll see I'm only trying to keep you and the kids safe." He twirls the car keys on his finger. "Listen, I'm a phone call away. But I think I'll sleep in my own bed for the rest of the night."

Her mouth hangs open while he presses the key fob. The lights flash, and then the big truck arrows into the night, the motor growling as he guns the engine.

What the hell just happened, and why did she start a fight?

A small group of neighbors convene down the road, speaking in hushed and frantic tones. Mr. Gibbons stands among them. He points at Darcy's house, and a woman puts a hand over her mouth. They believe Hunter is the killer. Between newspaper articles and police gossip, rumors spread and become truth in the court of public opinion.

Sneakers scuff against pavement. Running toward the driveway, Gail Shipley holds a recorder aloft like a holy artifact.

"How do you explain another murder occurring after the police released Hunter?"

"Stay the hell off my property, Gail."

Shipley pauses, noticing the vandalized car. Darcy cringes when the reporter photographs MURDERER in bloody lettering.

"He's branding the girls like the Full Moon Killer. Did you teach Hunter about Michael Rivers?"

Darcy slams the door in Shipley's face. She can hear the reporter barking questions outside, but the woman doesn't bang on the door.

The living room feels vacant, cavernous without Bronson. The bedroom doors stand closed. Darcy throws her jacket on a hanger and sits down at the kitchen table. She could use another pill, enough to knock her out until morning. Instead, she spins the laptop toward her and watches Gail Shipley on the monitors. Darcy allows the intrusion for now, but if the woman ventures into the backyard, she'll notify the police.

Shipley gives up after a minute and walks toward the neighbors grouping in the middle of the street. They turn to look at Shipley and bob their heads when she pulls out a pad and asks questions. Darcy can only imagine her neighbors' clickbait-worthy comments.

He was a quiet boy. You have to watch out for those types.

Did you know he listened to heavy metal bands who sing about devil worship and human sacrifices?

Why, no, I didn't. But that explains where the violence comes from.

Opening the browser, Darcy searches for Angel Devoured, the dark metal band Hunter likes. Examining images from their latest album, Darcy discovers the evil smiling face Bronson told her about. It's similar to the Full Moon Killer's tag, but there are differences. The drawing on the album appears cartoon-like in comparison, and the grin quirks higher to one side. It's not the same. Bronson is wrong, as are the police.

Darcy closes the laptop. She can't look anymore. But it's a sleepless night.

The towing company arrives for the Prius the next morning, and Darcy understands the reason for the delay. The village hates Darcy and her family and the angel of death they summoned to rain hell down on Genoa Cove. A hundred dollars per day earns her a beaten Subaru while the body shop repairs the damage. A rip-off, but she can't be without transportation.

Inside, everyone's nerves link to detonation devices. Jennifer explodes when she doesn't find oat milk in the refrigerator. Hunter is a trapped rat, clawing at the walls.

The sun shines today, heedless of last night's bloodshed. Hunter needs to leave. Walk. Exorcise his demons, or at least keep them at bay. Caving in, Darcy sends him to the store with twenty dollars for Jennifer's milk and tells him to use the rest to pick up something fun.

"Like?"

"Ice cream, frozen pizza, some disastrous comfort food," Darcy says, smiling through thin lips. "And come right home after."

She watches through the window as Hunter follows the meandering road toward the village center, thankful the neighbors aren't outside. Thirty minutes later, Detective Ames pulls into the driveway. Julian accompanies Ames, but he stays in the vehicle. Ames spends too long scrutinizing the sparkling red plastic from the busted taillight pockmarking the blacktop. Then he straightens his crumpled suit jacket, the same one he wore at the police station, and follows the walkway to her door.

"Detective," Darcy says, opening the door.

"Is Hunter at home, Ms. Gellar?"

"He's at the store. That doesn't break the rules you imposed."

Ames turns his shoulders and surveys the neighborhood. He runs a nervous hand through his hair.

"May I come inside?" Darcy pauses. "I'm not investigating."

But any damning evidence the detective discovers inside becomes fair game.

"Okay," she says after consideration. "What about your partner?"

"This won't take but a minute."

Ames wipes his shoes on the mat, though the day is dry. She offers him a chair at the kitchen table, but he prefers to stand.

"Can I offer you some coffee," she asks. "Or something to eat?"

She flinches, remembering his mother at the police station.

"No, but I want to apologize for my mother. She lives in an assisted living community up the road from the station, but she's allowed to wander."

"You don't have to explain."

"Well, the police station is no place for a woman battling Alzheimer's."

"I'm sorry."

Ames opens his mouth and stops, considering his words.

"But I'm not here about my mother. You told me something at the cove. Last night. This guy is copying the Full Moon Killer."

"That's right."

"And Michael Rivers targeted young girls."

"Teens through middle-twenties, yes."

"The girl's name is Becca Crowley, a junior at the high school and a member of the varsity cheerleaders. Hunter knew Becca."

He pauses for her reaction, but she doesn't take the bait.

"You said this wasn't an investigation. It's a small school, Detective. Hunter knows a lot of girls."

A lot of girls who fit the killer's type, Rivers whispers.

"I have eyewitness accounts of Hunter arguing with Becca Crowley two weeks ago. I find it curious, because someone saw Hunter yelling at Amy Yang moments before her death."

"Would these eyewitnesses happen to be Aaron Torres and other members of the football team?"

"Does Hunter ever become violent when he's angry?" Darcy

opens her mouth and stops. Ames is steadfast in his insistence Hunter killed Becca and Amy. "Ms. Gellar?"

Ames' stare pierces a hole through Darcy. Gone is the aw-shucks routine he used to enter her home, and now she sees the wolf beneath the sheepskin. A knock on the front door saves her. His gaze doesn't falter until the second knock, and Darcy swings her head around. Julian stands at the door and looks pointedly at Ames. The detective excuses himself and strides with a clipped, irritated gait to the door. He steps outside, and Darcy watches them talk in the driveway. Julian says something that makes Ames turn his head and stare into the window. Darcy steps into the shadows of the living room, though Ames must sense her watching.

After Julian returns to the cruiser, Ames straightens his jacket and touches his chin. When he opens the door, Darcy feels the floor drop out from under her. Something horrible happened again—she reads it in his eyes.

When he speaks, she clutches the wall to keep from falling. Hunter is in the hospital.

16

The waiting area for the emergency room is sparse of people, save for a woman in the corner watching her toddler drive a toy truck over a throw rug. Darcy sits in an uncomfortable plastic chair that is murder on her back. Jennifer sits a few chairs away, one leg crossed over the other and nervously kicking.

Detective Ames is in the lobby with an officer Darcy recognizes from the station. After the two men speak, the officer disappears down the corridor and Ames motions at Darcy.

"Besides the vandalism, what do you know about Aaron Torres?" asks Ames, the bluster gone. Contrite, he's a beaten man.

"Not much," Darcy says, shifting her stance so Jennifer can't read their lips. "Hunter dates his sister, and Aaron doesn't like it."

"How do you know?"

"Jennifer found out Aaron wrote the note."

"The one she found sticking out of Hunter's locker."

Darcy nods.

"He drove through our neighborhood and stared at the

house like he wanted us to see. He had three friends in the car with him."

"Did you recognize any of their faces?"

"No, but he also had three boys with him when they sprayed my car, so I have to believe it was the same crew." Darcy bites her lip to halt the tears. "Four on one, that's the rumor on social media. And kids are laughing about it. What kind of man are you if you need three friends to attack someone?"

Ames doesn't answer. There are no words of comfort when an act of hate sends someone's child to the hospital.

"Oh, and that claim that Hunter argued with Becca Crowley," Darcy says, rounding on the shrinking detective. "She bullied Jennifer at cheer practice, and Hunter saw and stepped in. That's what big brothers do. As for Aaron Torres, I don't care how wealthy his parents are. I want the kid arrested for what he did to Hunter. The same goes for the other three."

Darcy's hands clench into fists, nails dig through her jeans.

Ames excuses himself when the double doors push open. A dark-skinned doctor with glasses on the tip of his nose walks toward Darcy.

"Ms. Gellar?"

Jennifer crowds beside her. Darcy's heart races as the doctor glances down at the clipboard.

"Hunter is groggy but responds to questions. You'll be able to visit him soon."

"Is he going to be okay?"

"The CT scan confirmed a concussion and a brain bleed. I want to stress the bleed is slight, but a concussion is a traumatic injury to the brain. We need to take it seriously."

To Darcy, the room feels smaller, the walls closing in.

"Is the damage permanent?"

"With rest and proper treatment, most concussions clear up on their own. His reaction time and reflexes are a little slower on his left side than his right, and his balance is likely to be shaky for a few days."

"What about the bleed? Can't a brain bleed cause seizures?"

"It can, and we're monitoring the bleed. We'll keep Hunter overnight and make sure the bleed stops. If I were to guess, he'll be able to go home tomorrow afternoon."

Thirty minutes later, Darcy and Jennifer visit Hunter. He wears a hospital gown, and a tangle of colored wires like alien appendages stretch from his body to a machine. The medical staff cleaned the blood off his face, and the swelling doesn't look as bad as it had when the paramedics brought him to the hospital. But this is her son. It rips her in half to see him broken. She steels herself, recalling how bad she looked after the stabbing. She survived, and so will Hunter.

"Hey, baby."

Hunter gives a thumbs up and winces when he tries to smile. Cupping her arms, Jennifer stands beside the monitors, her jaw working back and forth as a tear tracks down her cheek.

"The doctor says you can go home tomorrow. That's good news, right? I'll stay with you tonight."

"No, don't," he says, groaning. "It might be three in the morning before they move me into another room."

She wants to ask Hunter why Aaron would do this. What would drive a boy to these extremes? She can't. Bringing up the fight will only upset Hunter, and the next several hours are critical if he is to recover without long-term effects.

"Well, I'm your mother, and I'm not going anywhere until the doctors send you home. How is your head?"

He turns his face away and settles into the pillow.

"I want my music."

"That's not a good idea with a concussion. Nothing loud for a few weeks."

"Then let me sleep."

"Okay."

Jennifer leans over the bed and kisses her brother on the cheek. Darcy does the same, holding her hair back and trying not to disrupt the confusing array of wires.

Guilt gnaws at Darcy when she leaves her son. But they're not alone. Her heart pangs when she sees Bronson in the entryway.

"Everything all right?" Bronson asks, shifting on his feet.

"Nothing is all right."

"He's a tough kid. Hunter will heal."

"Yeah, so another group of bullies can attack him outside school or on the street. I hate this village. I shouldn't have brought my kids here."

Bronson doesn't know what to do with his hands. He brings one forward as though he means to touch her arm, then he shoves them into his pockets.

"We had a misunderstanding earlier," Bronson says as Jennifer sits away from them, chewing a nail.

"I yelled at you. It was wrong to take my frustrations out on you. We...I appreciate everything you've done for us."

"Can I drive you home? It's not a good idea for you to drive when you're upset."

"No, I'm staying with Hunter. I won't sleep a wink if he's alone."

"Then let me take Jennifer back to the house. I'll hang out until you get back with Hunter."

"Are you sure? That won't be until tomorrow afternoon."

"I want to help. I owe you."

Overhearing the conversation, Jennifer rises from her chair and clutches Darcy's arm.

"Then I'm staying too," Jennifer says.

Darcy shakes her head.

"There's no reason for both of us to be here. The doctor says

Hunter will be okay. Let Bronson take you home. You can stay up late and watch a movie."

Jennifer rolls her eyes, but she follows Bronson through the automatic doors.

It's after midnight when Ames returns. Darcy isn't happy to see him, and she wishes Bronson was here to act as a buffer.

Darcy stays in the room when Ames questions Hunter. It's the first time Hunter acknowledges Aaron attacked her son. They followed him to the grocery store and jumped Hunter from behind, two of the boys holding his arms while Aaron and Sam Tatum punched and kicked him.

"This never would have happened if you and Officer Haines had taken the letter seriously," Darcy says, her eyes fixed on Ames.

He continues to interview Hunter as if she hadn't spoken.

"What precipitated the fight?"

"Don't answer that," Darcy says. "This was an attack, not a fight."

"Hunter, why did Aaron Torres attack you?"

Hunter shrugs.

"He said I'm a druggie and that I killed those girls, and he doesn't want me near his sister."

Ames thumbs to an empty page in his notebook.

"What difference does it make why Aaron did it?" Darcy asks, hanging onto the chair so she doesn't leap up and scream in the detective's face. "There's no excuse. Aaron Torres and his gang should be in jail, unless you think being different justifies classmates jumping you from behind."

"I'm not justifying the attack, Ms. Gellar."

Hearing the commotion, a male nurse hurries into the room and glances between Ames and Darcy.

"I heard shouting."

"We're about finished," Darcy says, holding the detective's stare.

"If you can't keep your voices down, I'll have to ask both of you to leave. Our patients need rest."

"You know," Darcy says, standing up to Ames. "I think it's time you left. Arrest Torres, or we have nothing else to say to you."

Ames looks from Darcy to Hunter.

"You're an adult, Hunter. Your mother can't stop you from talking to me."

"Leave," Hunter says, twisting onto his side and staring at the monitors.

Ames watches Hunter.

"You heard my son. Get the hell out."

17

No amount of fortifications keep a castle safe from breach.

Though the hospital staff locks down the corridors at night, Darcy remains on edge. Security patrols the entrances, and the staff corrals visitors into the waiting rooms. Most visitors go home, but Darcy's place is here. With Hunter. Even though she can't see her son, knowing he sleeps at the end of the corridor lends her a measure of comfort.

The clock on the wall reads midnight as she thumbs through a magazine. She's read dogeared copies of People and Time from cover to cover, and now she busies herself with Sports Illustrated. But the words have no meaning. Worry prevents her from focusing on the pages.

A woman in a flower-print dress snuggles inside her coat and sprawls on a chair, her bare legs jutting out like wooden oars. Technicians push squeaky-wheeled carts past the room every few minutes, and a heavy antiseptic smell clings to the walls and worms inside Darcy's clothes.

Darcy's head bobs when her phone rings. She fumbles the magazine and checks the caller ID. Eric Hensel.

The woman across the room stirs and mutters something in her sleep as Darcy grabs her bag and hurries from the room. When she reaches the end of the corridor, she answers.

"I just heard about Hunter," Hensel says, his voice hesitant. "I'm so sorry, Darcy. What happened?"

She tells Hensel about the attack.

"What do the doctors say?"

"No broken bones, but there's a lot of bruising. Hunter has a concussion, and the CT scan showed bleeding on his brain."

"All right, then. My nephew whacked his head on the floor playing basketball last year and lost consciousness for a minute. The doctors found a brain bleed. The hospital kept him overnight for observation, but they cleared him the next morning and sent him home."

"How long did the symptoms last?"

"As I recall he experienced headaches and light sensitivity for a month. My sister got him into a sports medicine and concussion clinic outside Richmond. I recommend you do the same. Hunter will need therapy, physical as well as psychological. Concussions are no laughing matter, but treated correctly, kids recover in a month or two."

"Thank you, Eric. I'll find a clinic as soon as we get out of here."

A doctor speaks to a nurse at the far end of the hall. They eye Darcy before continuing their rounds.

"I spoke to Ames an hour ago. After the latest murder, the GCPD is bringing the FBI into the case."

"It's about time."

"No guarantees who they'll assign, but I'm pushing the director to send me to Genoa Cove. I wish I was there to help tonight. This corruption case took longer than expected."

"Don't be sorry. Your old partner is tougher than she looks."

"This must be hell on your daughter. She's probably worried sick, and she's cooped in a hospital all night."

"No, Bronson took Jennifer back to my house. He's staying the night and keeping an eye on her."

A pause.

"You there, Eric?"

"Darcy, I don't want you to think I'm snooping around, but I looked into Bronson Severson. Did you know the GCPD forced him to retire?"

"Does this have anything to do with the police brutality accusations? I read about the fight. Two men outside a restaurant in Genoa Cove. Bronson told me the instigator resisted arrest and broke his arm trying to pull free."

Hensel makes an unconvinced groan.

"Did he lie to me?"

"Ames mentioned Bronson," Hensel says, digging out the notes he took. "He didn't like Bronson hanging around your kids."

"Ames is trying to railroad Hunter for these murders. Trust nothing he says."

"I'm keeping an open mind, but Ames says it wasn't a fight Bronson responded to. The guy's name was Vic Deneris. According to the detective, Bronson earned money on the side working as hired muscle. He was in league with another goon cop in Smith Town. Name was Pinder."

Pinder. The officer who responded to Amy Yang's call in Smith Town.

"To make a long story short," Hensel continues. "If somebody owed you money, or you wanted to leave a permanent mark on the dude bedding your wife, you called Bronson. The department tried to pin Bronson down for years, but he had a smart attorney."

"Was his name Appleton?"

"Bingo. Bronson didn't break up a scuffle. He made a premeditated attack on Deneris. The other supposed fighter was just a bystander. He tried to break it up and got pulled into the scuffle. It took two cops to pull Bronson off Deneris, and Ames claims Bronson broke the guy's arm on purpose."

Darcy sits against the wall and rubs her forehead.

"Are you sure the story is accurate?"

"It's all hearsay. From what I understand, Bronson Severson wasn't the most popular guy in the department. Could be bad blood between Bronson and the cops who blew the whistle, or maybe Bronson was a bad cop and the officers knew."

The call ends, and Darcy feels short of breath. Ames' story can't be true. If it is, Jennifer is alone with a disturbed, dangerous ex-cop who worked for criminals. Darcy reviews her memory and recalls Bronson's sudden mood swings. She barely knows the man.

Returning to the waiting room, Darcy texts a message to Jennifer.

Are you still awake?

It doesn't take long for her daughter to respond.

Can't sleep. How's Hunter?

He's resting now. Doctor says he's doing better. Will do more tests in morning.

Can he come home then?

Yes. Where is Bronson?

Jennifer doesn't reply for a minute. Is she checking on him?

Sorry. Chatting with Kaitlyn. Bronson is asleep on the couch. Why?

Just wondering. He's been under a lot of stress. Try not to bother him, okay?

Why would I?

No reason. Just let him rest.

Darcy taps her thumb against the screen after Jennifer signs off. She doesn't trust her neighbors to look in on Jennifer. If it wasn't in the middle of the night, she'd suggest Jennifer spend the night at Kaitlyn's.

She puts the phone away and picks up another magazine. Then her eyes pop open, and she jolts awake, realizing she fell asleep. Light pours through the window as Darcy stretches her back and glances around the room. The woman left, but the corridor is alive and bursting with staff.

The doctor gives her good news. Another scan shows the bleed stopped. Hunter will take anti-seizure medication as a precaution, but he can go home soon. As she leaves Hunter's room, a pretty girl steps from the elevator and stops at the nurse's station.

Bethany. Aaron's sister.

This is the first Darcy has seen of Hunter's supposed girlfriend. Why hasn't she visited until now?

Darcy wipes her face clean of resentment when Bethany spins away from the station and angles toward Hunter's room. The girl pulls up when she sees Darcy between her and the door.

"Ms. Gellar, how is Hunter?"

"Better now. It was a long night."

Bethany's smooth demeanor cracks, and the tears burst forth like a dam break. It's not an act, and realizing what the girl must be going through slams Darcy back on her heels.

"I don't know why Aaron did it," Bethany says between sobs as Darcy holds her. "He said it was to protect me, like I need protection from Hunter, but I don't believe him."

"Why did your brother attack Hunter?"

Bethany shakes her head and swipes a tissue across her nose.

"There's something wrong with him. He's been so...angry. Like my parents caught him drinking with Sam over the summer and took his car away, and Aaron punched a hole in the wall. And last month, after he had a bad practice and coach told Aaron he wasn't starting the next game, Aaron came home and started screaming at Mom and Dad like it was their fault. Then he slammed the door and took off, and nobody could find him until he returned in the morning. None of us wanted to go near Aaron, because it looked like he might explode again or..."

"Go on," Darcy says, thinking Aaron's violent tendencies fit the killer's profile.

"I don't think he would harm us, but he needs help, and my parents won't accept that he's getting worse. And now he's in so much trouble. What's happening to my family?"

Over Bethany's shoulder, Darcy watches a nurse approach with a concerned expression.

Darcy mouths, "She'll be okay," and the nurse nods and returns to her station.

"Maybe now Aaron will get the help he needs," Darcy says, her arm over Bethany's shoulder as she leads her to a pair of chairs.

Bethany hitches and coughs into her hand.

"I keep picturing my brother in jail and worrying someone will hurt him."

"He's not in prison, Bethany. Hunter will be fine, and Aaron will get better with counseling."

Except Darcy knows some kids never get better. Michael Rivers didn't.

Bethany stays with Darcy until the doctor releases Hunter. Darcy gives them space while Bethany clings to Hunter, and more tears fall before she obeys her parents' edict to come home.

The ride home is funereal. Hunter turns away and rests his head against the seat, his legs drawn up and his shoulders slumped, defeated. Jennifer isn't responding to messages. Darcy repeats the mantra that her daughter is asleep, yet she remembers what Hensel told her. Who is Bronson, and is Jennifer safe with him in the house?

The music on the radio fails to calm her nerves. She silences the volume and opens the window.

"The lawyer will make sure Aaron and the other boys get the punishment they deserve."

"It doesn't matter," Hunter says, staring out the window at the shops.

"It matters. If they let Aaron get away with hurting you, he'll go after someone else."

"No, I mean it doesn't freaking matter. You never listen. It will never stop, and Bethany's parents will make her break up with me. You think they want a loser dating their daughter?"

"You're not a loser."

"To them I always will be. To Coach Morgan and everyone at school. Why did you make us move? Neither of us wanted to come here."

"Jennifer is adjusting, and if you give it time—"

"No, Mom. I won't adjust to everyone hating me because I didn't grow up in Genoa Cove and don't wear the same stupid designer clothes they buy."

He bites off a curse and slams the side of his fist against the seat back.

"You wish you were still in Virginia."

"I wish I were high, to be honest."

Darcy swings the car to the curb and glares at Hunter.

"Why did you say that?"

"Because it's true. Wouldn't you want to get high if everyone said you were a loser and wanted to beat you up?"

"That boy I saw you with at school. Squiggs."

"Stop it, Mom. He's not the school pusher. That's just

another rumor some asshole started because Squiggs is an outcast like me."

She walks on a razor's edge. Saying the wrong thing will push Hunter away, and she'll lose him again. But in his own way, he's opening up to Darcy, and she wants to grab his hand before he plunges back into the dark chasm he's so reliant on.

"When I was your age, I used to sneak behind the garage with Aunt Vivian and get high."

Hunter twists his head toward her. It's plain on his face he doesn't believe her.

"You and Aunt Vivian. Got high. Right."

"I know it's impossible for you to accept, but your mom used to be a teenager, even if that was back in the dark ages."

"Before electricity." A hint of a grin curls one side of his face.

"Prehistoric times, yes. Kids drink, and you can't go to a party without someone passing a joint around. And I'm a total hypocrite for telling you not to party like I did, but it's not worth the risk, Hunter. Especially now that you've had a traumatic brain injury."

"Concussion."

Darcy checks the mirror and pulls the car into traffic.

"A concussion *is* a traumatic brain injury. Take care of yourself, and you'll be fine in a month or two. Keep taking chances, and you risk permanent damage."

"I can't picture you and Aunt Vivian drunk and passing a joint."

"Squiggs gets you marijuana. Be honest."

Hunter puts his feet against the glove compartment and taps his fingers on his leg.

"What if he does? Think he's the only one who can get it?"

"Look at me, Hunter. Do you do anything harder? Don't lie to me, because I'll know."

"Not really."

"Not really?"

He lifts one shoulder.

"It was just one time."

Darcy long suspected Hunter experimented, but the cold reality terrifies her.

"What did you take?"

He lowers his head and mutters.

"Jesus, Hunter. Did you say Adderall?"

"It helped me, okay?"

Darcy wants to pull the car over again, but her adrenaline pushes her to drive, don't stop, keep him talking before she loses him again, no matter how horrifying a path the conversation takes them down.

"Do you realize how addicting Adderall is? Hunter, I interviewed addicts who used Adderall as a replacement for meth amphetamine."

"Don't be mad, please. I only did it because…"

"You can tell me, it's all right."

A choked sob pulls her eyes to him. She can't remember the last time he cried.

"Because I can't stop dreaming of Dad. Okay? Are you happy now?"

The wave of emotion that strikes Darcy splits her heart.

"I miss your Dad too. I miss him terribly, and I feel guilty when days pass and I haven't thought about him. But a drug won't make you better, Hunter, and it won't bring him back. If you want to remember your father and keep his memory alive, the last thing you want to do is take something that will make you forget."

"That's what you do."

The reply dies on her tongue. He's right.

Hunter watches life fly by through the window.

"Why did he have to go?"

Darcy's hands grip the steering wheel, knuckles white as she turns out of the village and onto the coast road.

"I wish I had an answer. Life is too short. Do the best you can, and hold on to the people you care about, because we can't depend on tomorrow."

He pinches the bridge of his nose and wipes his eyes with the back of his hand.

"Thank you for telling me, Hunter. Do you want to talk to someone?"

"I told you, I only did it once."

"About Dad. Do you want to talk to somebody about your father?"

Darcy expects Hunter to fire *no* back at her. When he doesn't, she glances across the car. He watches the ocean, the water a sparkling azure, sand smoothed and carved by the relentless wind, gulls cawing and swooping as an elderly man and woman walk hand-in-hand through the breakers. And it hits Darcy that he craves the happiness he's only observed to this point. After Tyler's death, Hunter built walls and kept others out. But those walls closed on him with each passing year and became a prison.

She wants him to say *yes*. Therapy pulled her out of purgatory after the stabbing, but memories drag her back. The attack will always affect her, just as Tyler's loss afflicts their family, but accepting help is the first step on the road to recovery.

From the coast road, she turns the car into suburban sprawl. The cove is visible ahead. Even under the noonday sun the cove creeps a shade darker than the adjacent ocean.

Entering their neighborhood, Darcy's blood pressure ratchets higher. This is enemy territory. To Genoa Cove, Hunter will forever be linked to the murders.

Bronson's pickup truck butts against the garage, the red coloration devilish against the ranch's neutral exterior.

"Let me go inside first," Darcy says, stuffing her hands into her sweatshirt pockets so he doesn't see them tremble.

"Why?"

"Jennifer isn't feeling well. I don't want you to get sick."

She hasn't convinced him, but Hunter slumps down on the seat and rests his head against the door while she unlocks the house.

A chill touches her in the entryway. Drapes block the light, the ranch bathed in gloom. A ticking clock keeps beat with the dark.

A shrill beep causes her to jump. She forgot to enter the alarm code. Shaking fingers press the buttons and reset the unit.

The couch is a silent shark amid the gloom. She can't see Bronson from the entryway. Stepping across the floor and into the living room, she peers over the cushion.

Careful. Quiet. The blanket lies rumpled at the foot of the sofa. But Bronson isn't here.

Edging down the hallway, she listens. The bathroom door is open, the blue tiled floor fading to shadow. An icepick hammers at her throat as she approaches Jennifer's door. Turning the knob, she finds the door unlocked. It opens on well-oiled hinges and reveals a small body curled under the covers.

Darcy skips Hunter's room and slides toward the door at the end of the hall. Her bedroom.

She presses her ear to the door and hears nothing. Twisting the handle, she opens the room to sweeping darkness. The curtains cloak the window. She'd left them parted.

A hand snatches her ankle when she steps forward. A scream poises behind her teeth when Bronson jolts up from the floor and tosses the blanket aside.

"Holy hell, you scared me," he says, his breaths coming quick.

She tugs free of his grip as he looks apologetically down at his hands.

"What are you doing in here?"

"I figured I'd wake up before you came home." He touches his watch and checks the settings. "Damn alarm didn't go off."

"I checked the living room and didn't know where you were."

"Oh...yeah." Bronson rubs the grit from his eyes. "I should have asked first, but I didn't want to bother you at the hospital. I couldn't sleep with the streetlight in my eyes. Let me grab my stuff and I'll get out of your way."

Bronson itches his neck and reaches for his pants. Darcy turns her back, but when she faces the door, she spies the cardboard box of files and photos from the Michael Rivers case on the floor.

"Did you go through my things?"

She whirls on him. He's dressed except for his socks and sneakers, which he pulls on irritatedly.

"Darcy, I only slept in your room to get away from the lights. Why would I go through your belongings?"

She points at the box, the top askew. Through the crack, Darcy notices the folder of photographs is near the front, not at the back where she left it. She always stuffs the pictures behind the case files as a last ditch measure should Jennifer or Hunter peek inside.

"That box was in my closet on the top shelf."

"What box? I don't know what you're talking about?"

"My case files for the Full Moon Killer."

Bronson blinks. In the gray light seeping around the curtain, his eyes look wrong. Unhinged.

"Why would I give two fucks about your case files, Darcy? You know, I'm tired of your accusatory tone."

He climbs to his feet, and she sees how large he stands. A full head taller, arms and shoulders country-strong. His fingers curl into fists and uncurl.

"I find you sleeping in my bedroom and going through my belongings, and you're the one who's offended?"

His lips sweep back to reveal his teeth. A mad dog's leer. He's a time bomb. It takes all her will to keep from flinching.

Then the anger leaves him, and he shakes his head as though breaking free of unseen tethers.

"You're right. I should have asked you first. I meant no offense. It's clear I violated your space. But that box." He taps the box with the toe of his sneaker. "I swear I didn't put it there. Until now, I didn't even realize it was on the floor. No way would I go through your old case files. I mean, you broke a few hundred government rules by taking them. How would the FBI react if you shared them with me?"

The front door opens and clicks shut.

"Mom? You okay?"

Hunter.

Bronson's eyes snap to the hallway. Hunter's shadow moves across the floor.

"I think you should go," Darcy says, handing Bronson his knapsack. The urge is strong to rip it open and make certain he hasn't taken any of her belongings.

"Darcy, I—"

"Get out."

Bronson tosses the knapsack over one shoulder and holds her eyes before he pivots and stomps past Hunter. The front door slams, jiggling the jewelry box on her dresser.

"He didn't touch you, did he?"

Darcy's shoulders slump. She sits on the bed with her head in her hands.

"No, I just didn't want him in my room."

"What was he doing in your bedroom?"

Touching his arm, she says, "He came in here because he couldn't sleep on the couch. No harm done, but he's never coming back. Don't worry about Bronson."

The big truck motor fires up. The rumble worms through her stomach and sends a shiver down her back. Her spine relaxes when the truck fades down the road.

But that doesn't stop her heart from racing throughout the day whenever a pickup passes the house.

G lock-22. Holstered and concealed beneath her leather jacket.

Darcy isn't taking chances when she drives to Amy Yang's calling hours in Smith Town. Despite her reservations about the body shop, she retrieved her Prius earlier in the afternoon. The mechanics did an admirable job—the vehicle shows no damage, and the new windshield is pristine—but she pictures the bloody slurs scrawled across the car whenever she looks at it.

Though the police watch the cove at all hours, she can't leave Hunter and Jennifer alone, so Jennifer is spending the night with Kaitlyn, and Darcy agrees to allow Squiggs to come over. Strength in numbers, though she distrusts Hunter's friend and suspects he convinced Hunter to try Aderrall. The most difficult decision is telling her kids, especially Jennifer, they can't go see Amy. She worries what the community's reaction will be if Hunter pays respect to the girl they claim he murdered.

"Let her family say goodbye," Darcy told them while she changed into presentable clothes. "We'll visit her grave together and bring flowers. Amy liked pretty things. It would have meant a lot to her."

Darcy stands at the back of the room while a handful of coworkers and distant family pay their respects. She didn't know Amy's parents passed.

When the room clears out except for two female cousins sitting in the back row, Darcy approaches the closed casket. The emotion that pours out of her is sour and furious and shrouded by conflict. She should have kept in touch with Amy over the years.

To hell with Michael Rivers. She'll watch Rivers and the Darkwater Cove killer burn when this is over.

A tap on the shoulder spins Darcy around. She stares at an older version of Amy Yang. The resemblance is so strong she would believe the girls were twins.

"Are you Agent Gellar?"

"Yes. But it's Darcy Gellar now. I retired from the FBI."

Dressed in a black dress with matching stockings, the girl shifts her feet and wrings her hands.

"I'm Keisha, Amy's cousin on her mother's side. Amy talked about you. She said you helped her live."

"Helped her live?"

"After she tried to take her life last year, yes." Keisha's eyes widen, and she touches her mouth. "I'm sorry. I thought you knew."

"Amy tried to commit suicide?"

"Last year. After her parents died. It was a car crash in Florida. Very sad. She took pills, too many. Luckily Amy's neighbor found her and rushed her to the hospital."

Darcy swallows the growing lump in her throat.

"She never told me."

"Amy didn't smile for over a year, and then she found you. She loved your daughter."

"Jennifer."

A tear trickles from Darcy's eye.

"Yes, that was the name she gave me. I don't see her, though."

Darcy runs her eyes over the casket.

"I didn't know..."

"What to expect? I understand. Only her aunt, my mother, saw the body. There was nothing the funeral home could do." Keisha reaches into her purse. "Here. This is a picture of Amy when she was happy. Jennifer would like to keep it, yes?"

Keisha says goodbye and leaves Darcy alone with Amy's remains. The picture jiggles in her hand. She doesn't need Keisha to confirm Amy was fourteen when the picture was taken. The hopeful, inquisitive smile belongs to a girl who hasn't met Michael Rivers.

The Excellent Cafe, a green painted structure with a large picture window overlooking Hamlin Street, spills light across the sidewalk at the end of the block. Soft acoustic music mingles with street sounds when a man pushes the door open and crosses the street. She could use a coffee, and being surrounded by people in a well-lit room, four walls to keep the monsters at bay, nudges her down the sidewalk.

Looking over her shoulder at the Prius beside the parking lot fence, Darcy clicks the key fob. The gun rests on her hip, an old, reassuring friend that makes her less afraid of the night. Antonia's Pizza, the restaurant she took Hunter to before the horror began, stands one block to her right, and she can smell the dough from here. The rest of the stores are closed for the night —the independent bookstore, a dress shop called Willow, Love of Pete's gifts and cards. She passes the dark windows when she hears the pickup truck growl behind her.

She ducks into the alley. Back against the wall, she waits and breathes as the big engine grows louder. False alarm. The blue 4x4 speeds down Hamlin Street.

Darcy curses herself when someone kicks a can in the alley. The shadow slides behind the dumpster as another truck shoots down the road.

"Who's there?"

Shoes scuff the crumbling blacktop, but the man doesn't answer.

Ducking out of the alley, Darcy hurries toward the cafe. It seemed closer a moment ago, and now the building appears to drift away. Footsteps emerge from the alley, and Darcy knows someone is following her.

Before the shadowed figure rounds the corner, she darts into a storefront shaded by a black awning. Listening, she doesn't hear the man approaching as she removes the gun from her holster. Then the footsteps begin again. Closer than before. Moving uncertainly as though searching.

The car engines disappear. All Darcy hears is her heart pounding as the steps close in on the storefront.

Darcy raises the gun as the man emerges from the dark.

"Don't move."

The man gasps and raises his hands.

"Wait—don't shoot, don't shoot."

The lamplight catches his face. Darcy holsters the weapon. Her neighbor, Mr. Gibbons. Panic twists his face. One hand clutches his chest.

"Why are you following me?"

"What? No, you're mistaken. I was just coming out of the parking lot and—"

"I profiled murderers and put dozens of criminals behind bars with the FBI. Don't lie to me."

Gibbons waves his hands.

"Okay, okay. I followed you, but that's all."

Darcy narrows her eyes and takes a step forward. Gibbons edges back on his heels.

"Tell me why. Speak."

"Look, you have to believe me. It wasn't my idea. Becca Crowley's father came to my house and wanted to know where you lived. He said your son killed his daughter, like he murdered that Japanese girl who lived with you."

"Chinese, and her name is Amy Yang. She was a fighter, strong. Unlike you. My son is innocent, and the more time you waste blaming him instead of helping the police search for the real killer—"

"The police arrested your son. I saw them handcuff the boy and take him away."

"And they let him go."

"Only because you got that lawyer from Smith Town. That Appleton." Gibbons spits the name. "Assault and battery, rape, dope dealing, murder. It doesn't matter. If you have money, Appleton will keep you out of jail. Just like he did that crook you took into your bed."

Darcy bumps chests with Gibbons and backs him against the window. A mannequin wearing a bathing suit and sunglasses looks down on Gibbons from behind the glass. Anger colors his cheeks, and he flinches as though he wants to shove her back.

"Try it, Gibbons."

When he reads the animosity in her eyes, he scurries out of the storefront, arms pinwheeling.

"Move, Ms. Gellar," he says as he backs away down the sidewalk. "The entire village knows what your boy did. Don't think your neighbors won't make things right."

"Is that a threat?"

Gibbons turns and flees. He disappears into the alley before Darcy decides if she should pursue.

She falls back against the glass and bangs the back of her head against the window in frustration. Hunter is right. Darcy forced her family to move to Genoa Cove and invited hell into their lives. Bullies at school, a disturbed ex-cop living under their roof, Amy's death, and a maniac trying to kill her. Her appetite gone, Darcy pulls the keys from her pocket and runs to the funeral home's parking lot.

The faster she gets home, the sooner she can get her family away from Darkwater Cove.

19

Jennifer isn't happy when Darcy picks her up at Kaitlyn's, but the explosion doesn't occur until Darcy tells her they're moving.

"Just when I start to make friends, and now you're moving us again? You're ruining our lives."

"I'm trying to save our lives," Darcy says over her shoulder as she turns into their neighborhood.

Lights shine from her neighbors' homes, the walkways bathed by outdoor floodlights. They're afraid Hunter will murder them in their sleep tonight.

Jennifer is screaming when Darcy stops the car in the driveway. Darcy wants to wheel around and scream back at her daughter, but she bites her tongue. Hunter sits on the couch. The television is on, but he's not watching, just staring at the moving pictures, not comprehending. And he's alone.

"Hunter, where's Squiggs?"

Hunter shifts on the couch and takes his feet off the coffee table.

"He took off. Probably had better things to do then watch me pop Ibuprofen."

"Pack a bag. We're getting out of here."

Hunter twists around and glares at Darcy.

"Going where?"

Darcy releases a held breath.

"I don't know. A hotel, maybe cousin Laurie's house."

"Laurie lives in Georgia."

"Exactly. The farther away from Genoa Cove, the better."

Hunter grits his teeth when he stands, but he maintains his balance. Jennifer's arms are folded, her bag at her feet, eyes ringed in red from the latest outburst.

"What's your problem?" Hunter asks his sister.

She huffs and stomps to her bedroom.

"Nothing except for Mom destroying my life again."

Jennifer grips the doorknob, intending to slam the bedroom door with teeth-rattling force.

The lights flicker.

Darcy peers at the recessed lights as they dim and pulse. A whirring, mechanical noise comes from outside. The generator.

And another sound. Someone is in the backyard.

"Stay away from the windows," Darcy orders as she pulls the curtains shut.

Jennifer creeps into the living room, her anger forgotten. Genuine terror masks the girl's face. She moves beside Hunter, who protectively puts an arm around her shoulder.

Pulling his sister with him, Hunter follows Darcy to the kitchen.

"Mom, is someone outside?"

"I'm checking the cameras."

But when she calls the security cameras up on the laptop, a series of blank windows fill the screen. Unwilling to accept the system failed again, she clicks the mouse and jams her finger down on the escape key. Nothing. She's blind to the night.

"Call 9-1-1," Jennifer says, her face buried against Hunter's chest.

Darcy's jacket lifts when she reaches for her phone, revealing the holstered Glock-22. Both kids take a step backward as she removes the weapon and makes a beeline for the deck door. She clicks the backyard floodlight on, and for a moment, she swears a shadow darts off the corner of the house.

Straining to see into the dark, she dials the police. A squad car is on the way. Her next call is to Gilmore Security Systems. The same woman who treated her rudely last time takes her information. Since Darcy has already called the police, there's nothing more the woman can do, but she promises their technology specialists will be in touch first thing in the morning. A lot of good that will do Darcy. She plans to be in Georgia before sunrise.

The first siren begins seconds later. Another echoes the call from the opposite end of the village.

"Into the hallway," Darcy says.

Neither Hunter nor Jennifer protest. Both are too scared to question Darcy. This is the safest area in the house, Darcy thinks. No windows, no entry points or lines of sight from the yard. She'll defend her family until the police arrive. The wait isn't long.

Julian is the first on scene as Darcy watches through the peephole. Officer Faust accompanies Julian again, and both keep their hands near their weapons as they approach the door. The second cruiser containing Detective Ames and another officer pulls in front of the curb. Ames takes charge and directs Julian and Faust to search the property.

When Darcy opens the door, Ames surveys the house over her shoulder as though he expects someone besides her children. His gaze halts on Hunter, then swings into the living room and kitchen.

"Everybody okay, Ms. Gellar?"

"For now." The dark silhouettes of her neighbors line the street, curious and watching. If the police weren't here, Darcy doesn't trust how she'd react to their accusatory stares. "Would you like to come inside, Detective?"

He scowls at her sarcasm and follows her into the living room where she recounts the power dimming and generator turning on.

"But you didn't see or hear anyone outside?"

She swallows a nasty retort.

"I saw something...a shadow, I think."

Ames breathes irritatingly through his nose.

"Were you home all evening, Ms. Gellar?"

"No. I was in Smith Town for Amy Yang's calling hours."

"But your children were alone in the house."

The cock to Ames' eyebrow tells Darcy her motivations don't add up. Why leave her family alone with a serial killer in Genoa Cove?

"My daughter visited another girl's house, and Hunter wasn't alone. His friend stayed with him."

Ames scribbles the information and glances at Hunter.

"Does your friend have a name?"

Hunter meets Darcy's eyes, and Darcy nods for him to continue.

"Benny Chilton, Squiggs," Hunter says, rubbing the back of his neck.

"Chilton was here."

The name rolls off Ames' tongue with distaste. Darcy wonders how many times Chilton's name comes up during drug investigations at Genoa Cove High School.

"Yes, sir."

Ames exhales and jots Chilton's name on the pad when the

door opens. It's Officer Faust with Julian standing behind her in the entryway.

"Detective, you better look at this."

Ames opens his mouth and stops. Faust's body is rigid, her face pale.

"Excuse me for a moment," Ames says, following the officers through the doorway.

Darcy hurries to catch up, earning her an angry glare from the detective.

"Stay inside, Ms. Gellar."

"This is our house. Whatever happened, I want to know about it."

Security lights flare the backyard like a noonday sun as Faust's flashlight dances over the exterior. Ames rounds the house and studies the wall. As he reaches for his radio, Darcy pushes past him.

The Full Moon Killer's sinister grin drips in red paint on the side of the house.

20

The overnight bag packed and waiting inside the bedroom door, Darcy rubs her eyes and watches the CSI team through the window. Sun brushes the trees in hostile oranges and reds, the long night over. Pulled back to her FBI days, Darcy observes as they dust for prints and investigate the yard, one of them bending low and placing an item in a plastic evidence bag.

They won't find anything. The killer is a ghost, a shape-shifter.

As the CSI crew packs their belongings, Detective Ames reappears with a fresh cup of Dunkin in his hands. Of the three officers who responded last night, only Julian remains.

Darcy steps back from the window before Ames notices her, but it's too late. He nods and raises a second cup, offering it to her. She shakes her head and twirls around when the floor squeaks. It's Hunter.

"You packed?" she asks.

He yawns and tilts his head at the gym bag beside the front door.

"We're coming back for the rest of our stuff, right?"

"When it's safe."

"When will it ever be safe, Mom?"

He rustles the mop of hair atop his head and returns to his room. Visible through the open bedroom door, Jennifer curls asleep on her bed. Arm and leg twitches indicate her dreams aren't peaceful.

Vehicle doors close and an engine rumbles. Watching through the window, Darcy waits until the CSI van pulls out of the driveway. Julian sits in the cruiser. When Ames walks up the driveway toward the door, Darcy opens the closet and stuffs Hunter's bag inside. She waits three full breaths after he knocks.

"We finished up. I have to be honest, I doubt the crime techs found anything we can use."

"I'm not surprised," Darcy said, poking her head through the open door so he doesn't think she's inviting him inside.

"Look, I can't rule out anything. The killer could have painted that face, or it might have been kids screwing with you."

"You think kids figured out how to disable the security cameras?"

He glances down at his shoes and rubs his shoulder.

"Not likely. I take it your system is up and running again?"

"Just like magic, isn't it? The police arrive, and the security cameras suddenly work."

"It only takes a signal jamming device and a little know-how to disable your cameras. Many of the new systems use proprietary frequencies so they aren't easy to jam, but criminals always find a way."

As if the detective's theory summons them, the Gilmore Security Systems technology team arrives, parking their van behind Ames' cruiser. Julian watches them through the mirror as they pile out of the van with their testing equipment.

"And Ms. Gellar," Ames says, moving aside for the workers. "Remember what I said about not leaving Genoa Cove."

How did he know she planned to flee? Darcy and Hunter waited until the police went outside before packing.

Marylin, the young, blonde girl leading the team, is apologetic, and her willingness to help diffuses Darcy. As her crew members drag a ladder across the lawn, Marylin promises Darcy she'll give Scott a full report of their findings.

But as Darcy expected, the Gilmore crew finds nothing wrong with the cameras or the alarm system. An hour later, they finish packing the van while Marylin stands with Darcy in the driveway.

"The police suggested somebody used a signal jamming device to disrupt the cameras," Darcy says. "Does that sound right to you?"

"We use our own frequency settings at Gilmore, so while it's possible, it's unlikely someone figured it out."

"The house switched over to generator power right before we lost the cameras."

"That wouldn't affect the security system. Have you experienced frequent power outages?"

Darcy rubs the morning cold off her arms.

"More than I'd prefer."

"Huh. I interned with Genoa Electric before I got the Gilmore job. I'd be happy to look at the breaker."

"I'll show you where it is."

"Derrick, I'm going inside to see the breaker box. I'll be back in a second."

Derrick waves to Marylin and tosses his bag into the van.

Darcy leads Marylin to the laundry room. The breaker sits between the wall and the washing machine, and Marylin needs to squeeze through sideways. Despite the bright confines, she flips the box open and shines a flashlight over the breakers. Her brow arches.

"What is this device, Ms. Gellar?"

Darcy edges through the gap and crowds beside Marylin. A small black box is affixed to the main breaker. Every few seconds, a green light flashes. A chill rolls down Darcy's back.

"That wasn't there when we moved in. What is it?"

Marylin scratches her head and angles her face beside the black square. She reaches out and pulls her fingers back, afraid to touch the device.

"I have no...honestly, I've never seen anything like it before." Darcy gives Marylin room as the girl wiggles away from the breaker box. "You should call the police back. That looks like an explosive."

Darcy is certain it isn't a detonation device. She worked alongside bomb squads and can recognize a detonator, but she doesn't blame Marylin for panicking.

"I bet anything it sends a surge."

Marylin nods as she edges toward the hallway.

"That could disrupt your power. Like I said, Ms. Gellar, you really should call the police."

Craving answers, Darcy tells Hunter to watch the house while she drives to the station. During the ride, she kicks herself for not teaching Hunter to fire a gun. Twenty-four hours ago, she would have relied on Bronson to keep her kids safe. Never again. In the past, she didn't make grave judgment errors. She would have identified Bronson's violent tendencies from the first time she met him. Now she groped blind through the darkness, her learned skills fading. Eric Hensel and the FBI cannot arrive soon enough.

Detective Ames tells the front desk to send Darcy into his office the moment she arrives. She finds him behind the desk, eyes weary and a fresh cup of coffee in his hand.

"You haven't slept, have you, Detective?"

"There will always be time for sleep."

He sets down the coffee as she slides the blinking device in front of him. She's wearing protective gloves, not the high quality brand the FBI and crime scene investigators use, but sufficient to keep her prints off the evidence.

"What the heck is this?" He reaches into his desk and slips on his own pair of gloves, then he picks up the little box and tilts it under the light.

"I found it attached to the main breaker. If I'm not mistaken, it disrupted my power."

"For what purpose?"

"To cause confusion and make people think I'm insane, I assume."

He places the box to his ear.

"I don't think you're insane, Ms. Gellar."

"No, but you think I raised a murderer."

Darcy's skin crawls. The killer broke into her house and bypassed the security system. Ames sets the box aside and picks up his phone. A moment later, a thin man wearing a CSI windbreaker retrieves the unknown item.

"You have a cousin in Georgia. Laurie?"

Darcy's back stiffens.

"How did you know that?"

The detective steeples his fingers and rests his elbows on the desk.

"I put myself in your shoes. Where would I go if my kid got into trouble and my family was in danger?"

"We *are* in danger, Detective."

"Which is why I'm asking you not to run. Leave Genoa Cove, and I can't protect you."

"You're doing a helluva job protecting us now. The killer painted his signature on my house, our friend is dead because the police targeted the wrong suspect, and my son spent a night in the hospital with a brain bleed and a concussion. And now my neighbors are harassing us. What are you doing to keep my family safe?"

Ames squints at Darcy.

"Who is harassing you?"

Darcy recounts Gibbons following her through Smith Town.

"He made it clear Genoa Cove residents wouldn't let Hunter get away with murder. They've convicted him without a trial. Who knows how far they will go?"

"I'll talk to Gibbons." Noting the incredulous expression on her face, Ames raises his hands. "You worked for the FBI and understand I have no grounds to arrest Gibbons. But having the police show up on your doorstep adjusts your attitude. In the future, I suggest you don't go anywhere alone."

"I promise I won't go anywhere unarmed."

He clears his throat and drums his fingers on the desk.

"Regarding what happened to Hunter..." Ames opens his desk drawer and studies a sheet of paper. "Aaron Torres is out on bail."

"You've got to be kidding. When did you release him?"

"Last evening."

"So he spent what—a few hours in jail?"

"We're monitoring Mr. Torres, but I wanted you to know."

"Aaron was out in time to vandalize our house last night."

"Unlikely he'd take that risk, considering the scrutiny he's under."

"And if I see Torres and his running mates drive past my house..."

"You're to call us immediately. But he won't get away with what he did to Hunter. He'll stand trial, and so will his friends."

Ames' assurance rings hollow, and it takes less than an hour for the harassment to begin again. Darcy turns into her driveway in time to catch Eric Hensel wrap his arms around Hunter on the front lawn. He holds Hunter from running off as Darcy screeches the tires and leaps from the car.

"Hunter? What's wrong?"

The boy's earbuds crank a speed-metal beat, his face twisted. A killer's face.

"I don't know this guy. Tell him to let go of me!"

"Easy, Hunter," Hensel says. Though the FBI agent is slight of build, his arms ripple with muscle. "Nobody's going to hurt you."

Hunter fights until Darcy grips his arms. She barely recognizes her son. Finally, the boy collapses in Hensel's grip.

"They're gonna hurt Bethany," he says, his head hanging, chin against his chest.

Darcy lifts his chin.

"Who? Who's going to hurt Bethany?"

One arm grasping Hunter, more to keep the boy from falling than holding him back, Hensel hands Hunter's phone to Darcy. The text came from an anonymous number, but Darcy is certain Aaron Torres sent the message.

If she is too stupid to stay away from you, she's next.

"I'll kill him!" Hunter screams, fury lending him the strength to fight again. It takes both Hensel and Darcy to stop the boy. "I swear to God I'll tear him apart."

"Get him inside," Darcy says, and together with Hensel, they drag Hunter to the door.

One last glance over her shoulder confirms what Darcy suspected. Gibbons is on his front lawn watching. And he's recording Hunter's outburst with his phone.

21

Darcy needs to get Hunter under control.

Ten minutes pass before Hunter's fire smolders and Darcy trusts he won't hurt Aaron Torres. Yet she reads his eyes and fears the worst is to come.

While Jennifer and Hunter whisper in the hallway, Darcy confers with Hensel in the kitchen. Hensel sees no point in tracing the message. Aaron is disturbed and violent, but he isn't stupid enough to send a threatening message with his own phone.

"I need to get back to my partner," Hensel says, pulling the car keys from his pocket. "Hunter seems okay now. Will you call me as soon as you hear anything?"

"I will. Stay in touch, Eric."

To Darcy's surprise, Julian, the last person she wants to deal with, climbs out of a vehicle in front of the house. Did Hensel or Jennifer call him? Then Darcy remembers Gibbons capturing Hunter's explosion on video. Once Julian sees the footage, he'll take Hunter away.

"We agreed not to call the police," Darcy says, swiping the curtains closed.

Jennifer looks at Darcy and lifts her shoulders while Hunter buries his face in his hands, resigned. Darcy groans as Julian walks up the driveway. Gibbons yells to the officer, but Julian waves him off and continues to the door. Dressed in blue jeans and an unbuttoned plaid shirt over a gray athletic t-shirt, Julian wears civilian clothing. The vehicle parked at the curb is a Dodge Charger, not a GCPD cruiser. Darcy yanks the door open and stares bullets into Julian.

"What?"

"I'd like to talk to you, if you'll give me the chance."

Darcy folds her arms and blocks the doorway.

"Whatever Gibbons told you, Hunter became angry because Aaron sent another harassing message, this time threatening his own sister. My son did nothing wrong."

Julian raises two placating hands.

"I'm not here about Hunter, but if Aaron Torres is bullying your son again, I'll look at the message." She braces her arms against the jamb, daring Julian to walk past. "Ms. Gellar, please. We got off on the wrong foot."

"Why should I let you inside my house? The last time I trusted an officer from your department, Detective Ames tried to pin Becca Crowley's death on my son."

"You don't have to let me inside. We can talk outside, if you prefer." When she refuses to budge, Julian looks back at Gibbons, who gives up and sulks back to his house. "I know Hunter didn't kill those girls, and Ames knows it too. Please, let me help."

Darcy chews her lip, then she waves him through the door. When Julian crosses the border into enemy territory, Jennifer turns her back on him. Hunter snatches his phone off the table and heads toward his bedroom.

"Not so fast," Darcy says, holding out her hand. Hunter mutters something under his breath and gives her the phone.

In the kitchen, Darcy slides the deck door open for Julian.

"Sit on the deck. I'm pouring myself an iced tea. I've got another glass if you're thirsty."

"No, I won't take up your time."

Darcy shuts the door after he leans back in one of the Adirondack chairs. He glances back at the house, suspecting she locked him out. Bracing herself for the encounter with Julian, Darcy craves something stronger than tea. She settles for the cold drink, to which she adds two ice cubes. On the deck, she shifts her chair away from his and maintains a cold distance.

He stares out at the yard. When his eyes run along the house, they stop on the gruesome smile leering at them on the wall.

"You mentioned something about helping us, Officer."

Julian clears his throat and itches nervously at his knees.

"Understand what I'm about to say is off the record. If our conversation goes south, and you use it against me in a court of law, I'll deny every word."

"Not exactly extending an olive branch, are you?"

He leans forward and rubs his face as though doing so will clear his head. A lawn mower buzzes down the block. The air is redolent of dead leaves, and when the wind blows, they scratch and crawl along the road.

"We were wrong to accuse Hunter."

There's a quiet confidence in his admission that forces Darcy to take notice. She sets the glass down on the arm of the chair, hard enough to make him flinch.

"Then why did you?"

"The DA is pressing the chief for an arrest. Detective Ames is a good man and a solid cop, but he's got the DA and chief screaming at him in each ear, and multiple callers claimed to see Hunter with the deceased at the time of the attack."

"Let me guess. The callers remained anonymous."

Julian's grimace is tight-lipped, pained.

"They did."

"When you responded to the letter in Hunter's locker, you blew it off as typical teen stuff. Had you taken the threat seriously, Aaron wouldn't have attacked Hunter. Now the kid is free on bail. Neither you nor Ames strike me as thorough investigators."

"You don't make apologies easy, Ms. Gellar."

"You owe my family far more than an apology."

"Yes, I do. Not that it justifies my error, but the coach and principal both backed Mr. Torres. Hunter's outbursts convinced them he is capable of hurting others, and four students came forward about his argument with Becca Crowley."

Darcy swirls the tea, her grip tightening around the glass.

"That doesn't make him a serial killer. It's pathetic how quick Genoa Cove is to implicate my son. I guess when you don't fit in or come from money, this village chews you up and spits you out."

"Here's the deal. I'm convinced Torres made the anonymous phone calls. Ames sent the recordings to a speech recognition specialist. If he matches the voice to Torres, we'll bring charges."

"Did it ever occur to you Aaron might be the killer? He fits the profile—violent outbursts, superiority complex. And he has motive. He doesn't want my son near his sister, and Hunter is a convenient fall guy to cover up Aaron's crimes."

Julian shakes his head and leans back.

"Aaron Torres deserves jail time and needs psychological evaluation, but he's not our killer."

"I saw him drive past our house, and you have video evidence of Aaron and his thugs vandalizing our car. The cove is a five-minute walk from here. He knows the area well."

"While I can't account for his whereabouts when Amy Yang was murdered, Torres has alibis for the other two killings."

Julian spots the angry reply forming on Darcy's lips and raises his hand. "The alibi didn't come from his friends. Coach Parker claims he was with Aaron on the night of the first murder, and while Coach Parker is a lot of things, he wouldn't risk lying over a matter this serious."

"And his second alibi?"

"Aaron's parents say he was home all evening working on a paper for school."

"Sounds like an open and shut case."

"More sarcasm, Ms. Gellar?" Julian's eyes drift to the grinning signature on the wall. "The killer targeted you. While Aaron Torres has a problem with your son, there's no motive for him to make it personal with you. The messages they painted on your car were meant for Hunter. You had it right from the beginning. It's a copycat killer, and he's working with Michael Rivers. Your son is innocent."

An invisible weight slides off Darcy's chest. Finally, the GCPD listens to reason.

"And Ames is on the same page?"

"He is."

"How do you plan to catch this killer?"

Julian squints his eyes and scans the tall grass swaying beyond the property line. He's thought this through.

"The killer is local to Genoa Cove. He murdered three girls, stalked Amy Yang, and sabotaged your home. He might not be from here originally, but he lives close by. The attacks are personal, and that leads me to believe he followed you from Virginia."

Darcy frowns.

"If this was my case, I'd look at new renters, someone who showed up in the last four months. I'm the only person tying him to the village. He'll leave after I'm dead."

"I agree we should focus on renters. I'll call work and have them start a search for new apartment leases."

"Not apartments. Houses. Michael Rivers preferred privacy, a quiet location he could bring his victims without attracting attention."

"Like a place in the country."

"Or on the edge of the village."

Julian pulls his phone from his pocket and dials.

"Hey, Faust. Search house leases in Genoa Cove and Smith Town...that's right...and pay close attention to renters who signed contracts during the last four months." He puts the phone to his chest and leans toward Darcy. "Males in their twenties and thirties?"

"Definitely. Look for someone with a background in technology or electricity. He knew enough to beat my security system and mess with the power supply."

"You hear that, Faust? Okay, and if nobody matches the profile, expand the radius to the entire county...right...I'll get back to you after I leave Ms. Gellar's."

Darcy studies Julian. He's working on his own time and taking a personal interest in her case. His face is boyish and kind, but she's learned not to let looks deceive her. And too many things don't add up. Julian has seemed outright hostile to her since the first day he appeared at her door. Trust must be earned.

"I don't get you, Officer."

"What is it you don't understand?"

"We've been at a crossroads since that day at the dojo. The looks you gave me each time you investigated the house...I have a hard time accepting you want to help me now."

Julian peeks over his shoulder as if he fears someone is listening. He shifts the Adirondack chair and faces Darcy.

"It had nothing to do with self-defense class. To be honest, you impressed me. But later I passed judgment on you without doing my homework. But I want you to know my issue wasn't with you."

"If you tell me your issue was with my son, that won't make me trust you."

"No, it wasn't Hunter."

Bronson. If half of what the department accused him of is true, she can understand why Julian held Darcy's character in suspicion.

"Why take part in Bronson's class if you think so little of the man?"

"His is the only women's self-defense class in the village. I did it to help all of you, not because of Bronson. Plus, I want to keep an eye on him. He may have retired from the GCPD, but the man still earns good money."

"He had ample opportunity to plant that box and disrupt my security system."

"Believe me, Bronson Severson is a person of interest in Genoa Cove."

22

Sunset is bloody and chilling, the day's warmth vanishing when the final rays dip below the land. Darcy watches through the window as darkness pools and spreads between the houses and below the trees.

The Virginia Cavaliers sweatshirt conceals the gun on her hip as she parts the curtains. No sign of Bronson or Aaron Torres, but her instinct tells her trouble waits in the dark.

"Mom?"

Jennifer peeks her head out of her bedroom. Darcy drags the curtains shut.

Jennifer sits on the end of her bed when Darcy enters the room. Even during the day her room is gloomy. With night settling over the cove, Darcy can barely discern Jennifer's dresser, where the new photo of Amy leans in a wooden frame that says *Friends Forever* across the bottom. A part of Darcy's heart breaks. Clothes litter the floor and hang off the bed. Jennifer needs to clean her room, but now is not the time to argue. Darcy recognizes depression. She's looking into a mirror and reliving the last three years of her life.

"How are you doing with all of this?" Darcy asks, brushing Jennifer's hair with her hand.

"Tell me the truth. Are we moving again? I don't want to go to Georgia."

Darcy sits beside Jennifer and pulls her daughter close.

"It's not safe here, Jennifer, and half the village wants to hang Hunter."

"But the police believe Hunter now, and you said the FBI would catch the killer."

"Agent Hensel was my partner. He's the best investigator I worked with."

Jennifer picks the lint off her sweatpants.

"Then he'll catch the guy, and when the police arrest the killer, everyone will know Hunter is innocent."

"I hope so, hon, but some people can't admit when they're wrong or change their opinion. What if somebody tries to hurt your brother because they think he got away with murder?"

"Not everyone is like Aaron Torres, Mom."

"I can name at least three boys who agree with Aaron."

"They're football assholes. If the police do their job and put Aaron back in jail, he won't be a threat anymore."

Darcy's eyes wander to the door when Hunter leaves his room. Darcy wants to tell Jennifer everything will be okay, but she knows better. Will the GCPD push the assault charges against Aaron? The police won't take Hunter's concussion as seriously as they might a broken bone or stab wound. The Torres' lawyer will ensure the assault is a misdemeanor. At most, the court will sentence Aaron to six months in county lockup. Good behavior will reduce the length of the sentence. And that's if the court doesn't believe Aaron's assertion, which his friends back up, that Hunter started the fight and Aaron defended himself.

She does her best to put Jennifer at ease but knows her

daughter can smell a lie. Darcy will have to uproot her family. Again. And Darkwater Cove will leave new nightmares imprinted on their memories. But they can't run forever.

When Darcy leaves the bedroom, Jennifer is curled under the covers with a pillow over her head. A teen movie is on the television, the light from the screen drawing long shadows that lunge off the walls.

In the living room, Darcy resumes her vigil. The Kemps walk their terrier, and a light over the garage illuminates Mr. Gibbons' driveway. Otherwise, the neighborhood is quiet. Feeling her eyelids droop, Darcy makes a pot of coffee and dials Laurie's number in Georgia.

Her cousin answers on the first ring. Darcy pictures Laurie, her blonde hair tied back in a ponytail, ripped jeans painted on. She's surprised Laurie isn't out at this hour.

"That's crazy," Laurie says, who follows the Genoa Cove news. "You know why they haven't caught the killer, right?"

"No."

"Because the FBI lost their best agent three years ago. You could come stay with me. The kids would like it down here. Lots of hiking trails and kayaking, and we've got another month of decent weather before the winter blahs set in."

"I can't picture Jennifer in a kayak. The paddles might ruin her nails. Hunter maybe."

"There's a mall sixty minutes up the road if she needs to invoke her inner shopper."

"Sounds great, but I can't take you up on it just yet. Perhaps soon."

"Is it true what the news says? The killer is copying that Michael Rivers psycho you caught?"

The motor of a big truck rumbles past the house. Darcy rushes to the window as the burning glow of taillights swing around the corner.

"You there, Darcy?"

"I'm here. Someone drove past the house."

"Getting a little paranoid, aren't we? I'm one to talk. Some creeper followed me through the park last week. I thought I ditched him, but I swear I saw the same guy outside work the next day."

Darcy paces the floor.

"Wait, did you say someone is stalking you?"

"Relax, cousin. It was probably nothing. Just some guy who wanted my number and chickened out."

"Laurie, you need to take this seriously. If a guy is stalking you, call the police."

"You worry too much. Hey, I swear I'll call the cops if I see him again. But I'm telling you, he's just a loser looking for a date."

Another vehicle turns into the neighborhood. Bass thumps from the speakers as it draws nearer.

"I gotta go, Laurie. Remember what I said. Call the police if you see him again."

Laurie says goodbye as Darcy races back to the window. The black sedan stops halfway up the street, the motor revving, headlights off.

Go away, she whispers. But the car moves closer, creeping along the rows of mailboxes. When it passes beneath a streetlight, she recognizes Aaron Torres' sedan. Shutting the curtains, she stands with her back to the wall, heart racing. In the kitchen, she watches the car exit one camera view and enter another.

Issuing a silent prayer Hunter wears his earbuds and doesn't notice the approaching vehicle, Darcy opens the sliding glass door and steps into the night. The music is louder outside. Each drum thump reverberates through her teeth and skitters down her neck.

She rounds the house, sliding along the outer wall. Dew

slicks her sneakers and chills her feet, and her breath forms condensation clouds. The black sedan is even with the house when she reaches the corner. Using the Prius as a screen, she rushes to the rear bumper, staying low.

Torres stops. He's blocking the driveway.

Darcy explodes out of her crouch and gives the boy no time to react. He looks up at her with wide eyes through the driver side window as she fixes the Glock on his forehead. Nobody rides with him. She motions with her free arm for him to lower the window.

He looks too scared to move.

She gestures with the gun, and the window lowers.

"You looking for Hunter, Aaron?"

"Put that thing away. Are you crazy, lady?"

"Crazy enough to put a bullet in your head if you hurt one of my children."

"You shouldn't make threats. My parents will sue the hell out of you."

"Why stop there? Call the police, Aaron. You're not supposed to be anywhere near our house, so they'll love to hear you blocked my driveway. And they don't have to take my word for it because you're on camera." Darcy points at the security cameras along the front of the house. "Wave and say hello."

The cameras startle the boy.

"Oh, come on, Aaron. You knew they were there. The lawyer must have told you after we caught you vandalizing my car."

"I don't give a shit about the cameras. I haven't done anything. But you're the one who'll get arrested when the police see you aiming a gun at me."

"That's a chance I'm willing to take. But you'll have to report me, Aaron. Be sure to let the police know you paid us another visit."

"Fuck off, you stupid whore."

Darcy snickers and leans against the door. When he shifts into drive, she reaches through the window and snatches him by the shirt collar. She taps the gun against the sill.

"Let me make myself clear. If I catch you near my kids or hanging around my property, I'll put an end to your sorry existence. Do we have an understanding, Aaron?"

Darcy jumps back from the car as he guns the motor. The black sedan bullets into the night, flying around corners until she doesn't hear the motor anymore.

23

Two pills. One Glock with a .40 caliber Smith & Wesson cartridge tucked under the pillow.

Darcy awakens to hazy light at the window and a bender headache that makes her question if she only took two. She wants to stay in bed, pop another anti-anxiety pill for breakfast like she did during those dark days after Michael Rivers came into her life. But staying in bed makes her a sitting duck, and medicating her fears away won't save her from the wolf at the window.

She dresses in sweatpants and a windbreaker and walks the neighborhood until she wraps her head around last night's encounter. Aware of the lunar calendar, Darcy assumes the killer must strike soon. The moon reaches waning gibbous in two nights. He's running out of time.

That the police aren't beating down her door suggests she scared Aaron Torres into silence. Thankfully, none of her neighbors are outside as she breaks into a jog.

Rousing Hunter and Jennifer out of bed proves difficult, but she ignores their protests and drags them down the highway to the river walk, a boardwalk-style shopping and restaurant area.

Hunter discovers the coin-op video game arcade, where he blasts zombies and aliens into the netherworld. Jennifer falls in love with the designer shoe outlet. Afterward, they enjoy burgers, fries, and extra-thick milkshakes on a park bench overlooking the river. It's a rarity for her children to smile and forget their real life horrors, and Darcy wishes she could bottle the moment.

When they return, Eric Hensel's rental is in the driveway. Hunter lowers his head and passes Hensel without acknowledging him. Jennifer is too busy dragging shopping bags into the house to notice.

Darcy sits with Hensel in the kitchen while the kids return to their caves. The judgment he passes is cold and unforgiving when she tells him she chased off Aaron Torres.

"You could do time for that, Darcy. You can't pull a gun on an unarmed kid and expect the judge to understand."

"Torres wanted Hunter to come outside," she says, slicing an orange and handing him half. "He would have hurt my kid if I hadn't been there to stop him."

"In your opinion. Good luck proving his intent." He tosses the peel into the garbage and wipes his hands on his pants while she rolls her eyes. "Look, I get it. We both know Torres wanted a fight. All I'm saying is you've finally earned some goodwill with the local police. Don't give them a chance to turn on you."

"This morning was the first time I've seen my kids happy in weeks. Coming home, it was like popping a balloon. I should have kept driving, Eric. Screw Ames and his edict to stay in Genoa Cove."

"That wouldn't solve anything. You think this killer won't follow you to another city? He tracked you to the Carolina coast."

Deep inside she knows Hensel is correct, but Darcy pictures the car windows down and the California sun beating through the windshield. The other side of the country or the other side of the world. A moving target is harder to kill.

"I may have underestimated Ames," he says.

Darcy looks up.

"What makes you say that?"

"He's sharper than the *just-another-career-cop-nearing-retirement* routine he sticks to. You can count him as an ally."

"You really believe that?"

Hensel rinses his hands at the sink.

"I do. We're closing in on the killer."

"Any suspects?"

"A few."

"But you're not sharing."

"Not until I'm sure you won't try to take him down by yourself," he says, winking. He glances at his watch. "Which reminds me, I need to get back to the station. You haven't heard anything from Bronson Severson, I hope."

"Nothing."

"Good. Let's keep it that way." Hensel dries his hands and pockets his wallet. "You're still the best profiler I ever worked with. You should be the one giving briefings to the locals."

A memory surfaces like a lost wedding ring in a shallow pond, and Darcy recalls the many profiles she gave to police and sheriff departments during the hunt for the Full Moon Killer.

"Let me see the suspect list, and I'll be happy to help."

"Nice try."

For the rest of the day, Darcy evaluates her home's security and searches for black box devices meant to disrupt the power. Then she returns to the cardboard box in the bedroom and thumbs through the Full Moon Killer case files. Knowing Bronson paged through her notes sets the hair on the back of her neck on edge. What did he hope to find?

Shadows grow long by dinner time. After Hunter and

Jennifer finish putting away the dishes, she wants to throw them in the car again and drive, Hensel's advice be damned. And never stop driving. The minute she puts down roots, the killer will track them down again, so she'll just keep going.

Hensel calls ahead to warn Darcy. Detective Ames and Julian are en route to her house. She welcomes them inside, but neither Jennifer nor Hunter want anything to do with them. Looking like he finally grabbed a few hours sleep in recent days, Ames confers with Julian in the living room over a list of names. These are the recent home renters Officer Faust located. Darcy wants to trust Ames and Julian, but the wounds from their accusations run deep. She senses suspicion when they watch her from the corners of their eyes, and Darcy worries Julian and the detective are only here to gather evidence on Hunter.

Ames spies Darcy staring and breaks away from Julian to speak with her.

"I'm putting undercover surveillance on the house tonight. See the blue sedan at the end of the block?"

Darcy rests her hands on the sill and follows Ames' arm.

"The Camry?"

"That's the one. Officer Faust is in the car, and another officer will relieve her after midnight. If anyone approaches your house tonight, we'll see them coming."

Darcy doubts they will, though she keeps the thought to herself. The killer evaded the cameras before he disabled them, and none of her neighbors noticed. Not that Gibbons or any of the others would want to help Darcy, but she's certain they're always watching.

Dusk is deep at the window, the color of ocean waters a hundred fathoms beneath the surface. The nearly full moon is a red giant over the village, its light harsh as it washes out the trees.

Intending to head to the station, Ames is halfway out the

door when Darcy's phone rings. Another unknown number. She answers in the hallway and freezes. It's Bronson.

The detective steps inside and edges the door shut. The police haven't set up a trace, but when Ames reads Darcy's eyes, he calls headquarters and gives them her phone number.

Bronson sounds drunk, his speech slurred and lethargic.

"You used me, Darcy. I protected you, and you threw me out of your life. You're a little cunt, you know that?"

Darcy swallows.

"You invaded my privacy and went through my belongings."

Bronson laughs, a sound like brittle claws dragging across weathered board.

"Paranoid as always. What use do I have with the Full Moon Killer case files? You're losing your mind."

Ames winds his arm in a circle, a signal to keep Bronson talking.

"You lied about the newspaper article. That guy's arm you broke. You hurt him on purpose, and that's why the department forced you to retire."

"Someone is listening to Detective Ames. Is he there, Darcy? Tell him I'll break both of his goddamn arms along with his pencil neck."

Ames turns away and cloaks his conversation with the GCPD. Julian nods at Darcy, a subtle prod of encouragement.

"Tell me what you were doing at the cove the day I saw you fishing."

"What do you think? Relaxing under the sun and catching fish."

"Seems strange you showed up on a private beach bordering my neighborhood after you figured out where I live. You could have gone to the public beach or the river."

"And miss a chance encounter with the pretty woman from class?"

"You admit you were there to find me?"

"I wanted to get to know you outside of class. Shoot me for pursuing a good looking woman. You act like I committed a heinous crime. Next you'll say I murdered those girls."

"Did you?"

Silence. Darcy glances at Ames, who mouths *keep talking*.

"You're a sick bitch, Darcy Gellar. No wonder you failed as an FBI agent. Now you see killers in every shadow."

"You didn't answer the question, Bronson. Explain how the killer knocked out my power, unhooked the generator, and jammed the camera signals under your nose. Or did you do it?"

"The only mistake I made was not snapping your neck. Stop blaming me for all your problems."

The line dies. Darcy's hand trembles as she lowers the phone. From the frustration on Ames' face, she knows they didn't trace the call. She wants to reach through the phone and slap the taste out of Bronson's mouth for playing on her fears.

"He ditched his listed phone and switched to a pre-paid," Ames says, scanning the list of suspects. "You don't do that unless you have something to hide. We're sending an officer to his address, but I'd bet anything Bronson is in the wind."

Darcy cocks her head into the hallway. The kids' doors are closed.

"You think Bronson is the killer?"

"He had opportunity. But what's his motive?"

Darcy almost drops her phone when it rings again. Julian points at Ames to begin the trace, but Darcy waves him off. It's Gilmore Systems.

Clamping the phone between her cheek and shoulder, Darcy takes the call in the kitchen.

"Ms. Gellar, this is Scott with Gilmore Security Systems. Sorry it took so long to get back to you. We had a rush of orders this week, and it was all I could do to keep up with installations."

"It's not a problem."

"I want you to know I talked with Marylin about the camera issues. Given the amount of problems you've experienced, I'm prepared to offer a full refund, if it pleases you."

Darcy sits on the edge of the table.

"That's a kind offer, but I believe someone tampered with the cameras. I can't blame Gilmore."

"Marilyn mentioned a device attached to the breaker box. Did you ever get a resolution on the item's origin?"

"The police says the device disrupted the power and caused the generator to switch on. As far as the cameras go, the working theory is an intruder jammed the signal."

Scott lowers the phone and says goodnight to one of his employees.

"My apologies, Ms. Gellar. I'm concerned because our signal is proprietary. Jamming a Gilmore system is no small task. You're not dealing with an ordinary criminal."

"I appreciate the concern, Scott. For what it's worth, your team was professional and thorough from the day you installed the system. I was especially impressed by the gentleman who stopped by a few days later to ensure I was happy with the work."

"That's good to hear, Ms. Gellar. If you need anything else..." Scott goes quiet. "Did you say one of my tech crew checked on your installation?"

"Yes."

"We don't do follow-up visits. The Gilmore systems are plug and play and work right out of the box. Let me check our records."

A hollow sickness burns inside Darcy's stomach as Scott types at his keyboard. Voices rise in the living room, prompting Darcy to check on the commotion. Julian runs out the door as Ames talks on the phone and writes something on his notepad.

"As I figured," Scott continues. "We installed five systems that week. I don't see a repair order or anything to indicate one of our technicians visited your house. We worked from dawn until dusk. I don't know where we'd find the time. Do you remember the technician's name?"

"No. He was a younger man. Red hair. I remember he had a small scar above his eye."

"Nobody matching that description works here. Are you certain?"

"He wore one of your uniforms."

"Ms. Gellar, somebody stole one of our uniforms from the back of the van during—"

Darcy ends the call and rushes to catch Ames before he leaves. She gave the killer a tour of the house and invited him to look inside the kids' bedrooms.

"I need to go," the detective says. "Remember, Officer Faust is right outside."

"I met the killer, Detective."

He's torn between what she tells him and his need to rush to the cruiser.

"Give me a name."

"I don't know his name. He came to my house disguised as a Gilmore technician."

"You're certain of this?" Ames runs his hand through his hair. "This is Officer Faust's phone number. Tell her everything you remember about the man."

"There's another body, isn't there?"

"I need to go."

Darcy watches the whirling lights of the cruiser as it speeds toward the coast road. She's too focused to notice Aaron's sedan take its place. This time the boy doesn't come alone.

As she turns away from the window, the glass implodes.

24

T he brick blasts past Darcy's ear and gouges a fist-sized hole in the wall. Yet she does not escape unscathed. Glass shards lacerate her skin and leave her bleeding on her hands and knees. Tires shriek as the sedan disappears down the block.

Her ears ring from the sudden blast, and it surprises Darcy when Jennifer crouches beside her and touches her bleeding arm. But Darcy's daughter hasn't come to her aid. Jennifer yells incomprehensible words, something about Darcy needing to stop him. It's too late when she makes sense of Jennifer's screams. Hunter blurs past and sprints out of the house before she can struggle to the entryway to stop him.

"Call the police, he's going after Aaron and his friends! Please, they'll kill him!"

But another murder investigation ties up the police. Somewhere, a young girl's body bleeds out on the sand.

She's forgotten about Faust before the female officer pushes the door open, her gun drawn. Faust scans the room and pockets the weapon.

"Are you injured, Ms. Gellar? I'll radio for an ambulance."

"My son went after the car. You know what those boys will do if Hunter catches up."

"I already called in the plate number."

Faust tries to ease her onto the couch, but Darcy pulls her arm away.

"We both know you don't have the numbers to pursue a vandal. The FBI and the rest of your officers are at another murder scene."

Darcy shrugs into a leather jacket and zips it over her sweatshirt. Faust doesn't spot the concealed gun, but the officer's eyes follow Darcy from the closet to the kitchen, where she gathers her keys.

"Let's go," Darcy tells Jennifer.

"Don't leave," Faust says. "Let us handle Aaron Torres."

Faust's admonitions follow them through the door and into the driveway. Darcy backs the Prius past Faust's vehicle and follows the path her son took.

The road between Darcy's neighborhood and the village center is shadowed and twisting, the curves serpentine. Darcy thinks she is skilled enough to maintain highway speeds. She isn't.

The back end of the Prius veers around a bend, centrifugal force ripping the car toward the guard rail. She tugs the steering wheel and rights the vehicle when the tires spin along the gravel shoulder, her heart in her throat.

The Torres family lives a mile from downtown. Darcy memorized the address after Aaron began harassing Hunter. She doubts Aaron will go home as he'll need to explain to his parents where he's been tonight and why Hunter chased him across the village. No, Aaron and his friends will celebrate their juvenile victory at a private, secluded location. Leaving no witnesses when they gang up on Hunter.

"Is there somewhere Aaron and Sam Tatum go to drink and party?"

Jennifer jumps at Darcy's voice.

"Come on, Jennifer. Think. Where do they like to go?"

A blind curve takes Darcy by surprise. She stomps the brakes as the car crosses the dividing line.

"Sam's parents own a cabin on route 41. I know Aaron and the others go there to drink."

"Tell me how to get there."

Jennifer gives a quick nod and grabs the door handle as Darcy speeds through a stop sign. While Jennifer gives directions, Darcy pictures the road network in her head. If she takes the county road, they'll miss the village traffic.

The phone rings. She hopes it is Ames or Julian.

"It's a beautiful moon tonight, Darcy."

The voice makes Darcy's head swim. Michael Rivers. Her limbs go cold, and she tilts her gaze at the moon. The glowing face seems to follow her along the dark road.

"Darcy? Don't give up on me now. The horror show is just beginning."

Jennifer knows something is wrong. She glares at Darcy from across the seat. Her mouth moves, but Darcy can't hear what she says.

Darcy wants to toss the phone out the window. Holding the phone with Rivers on the other end is like clutching carrion.

"I saw the killer's face. I know who he is now."

Rivers cackles.

"If you knew who served the moon, the police would have caught him already. But he isn't alone."

Another killer? Or is someone helping him?

Bronson. It makes sense. He must be the one who gave Rivers her phone number. Hell, he knew her address from the moment she walked into the martial arts center.

But who keeps giving Rivers phones at the prison? Warden Ellsworth or a guard?

"What color is the moon tonight, Darcy? Is it the color of fresh blood on a sandy beach? I always preferred to hunt under a harvest moon."

"You'll never hunt again. I hope you rot in that cell."

"What a terrible thing to say. I have only compliments for you. You're striking in the moonlight. Almost as pretty as Laurie."

The memory of her phone call with Laurie pierces her heart. Laurie said she had a stalker in Georgia. No, it can't be the Darkwater Cove killer. He can't be in two places at once.

Except Rivers told her the killer wasn't alone tonight.

"Stay the hell away from Laurie. She's done nothing to hurt you."

"I told you I'd take your entire family, Darcy. I keep my promises."

Rivers ends the call. Jennifer's mouth hangs open. Did Jennifer hear Rivers' voice over the phone, or has the perceptive girl figured it out by listening to Darcy's end of the conversation?

Before Jennifer crumbles, Darcy presses her foot on the accelerator and hurtles toward route 41. Busy work keeps her daughter sane, and Darcy encourages her to continue messaging Hunter in the hope he'll come to his senses and tell them where he is.

"How much farther?" Darcy asks, sweeping her gaze across the desolate countryside.

"Two or three miles."

The cabin rests on a hillock and overlooks an inlet river five miles from the coast. A long gravel driveway bisects a small grove of apple trees, the fallen fruit clumped around the trunks and rotting. No lights shine from the windows, and the driveway is devoid of tire tracks. A dead end.

Where else to look? The Torres residence, the high school...

She sits in the car with the motor running and considers her next move. As she interrogates the dashboard GPS, her phone vibrates with a new message arrival.

Jennifer looks over Darcy's shoulder as the messages arrive in rapid succession.

Alder Park at 10 PM. Take the rim trail.

I have Hunter.

No police or he dies.

Jennifer covers her mouth and cries. Darcy can barely hold the phone in her trembling hand. She types back.

Let him go, Aaron.

A minute passes without a reply, then—

I'm not Aaron.

The clock reads nine. Alder Park sits on the northern point of the cove. She ran its trails when they first moved to the village. After climbing the rim trail to its peak, she looked down upon the blackest waters of the cove where two cliffs block the sun and starlight. She can make it there in twenty minutes and buy herself enough time to scout the park. Darcy accepts she's walking into a trap.

"What are you going to do?" Jennifer asks.

"I'm calling the police, then I'm going after Hunter."

"You saw the message. He'll kill Hunter if we bring the police."

He'll kill him regardless, she thinks. At least she has a fighting chance to save Hunter if she hurries. As Michael Rivers promised, the horror show is just beginning. But she refuses to play his game.

Darcy is a caged animal. She needs to break free. Run. Protect her kin. What will she do with Jennifer? She can't leave her alone in the car and run off to face a murderer.

She takes a composing breath and touches Jennifer's shoulder. The teenage girl turns her head, Jennifer's eyes desperate. Darcy scrolls through her contacts and finds Julian. Her finger hovers over the number. She's putting a lot of trust in a man she doesn't know. Darcy trusted Bronson, and it came back to bite her.

After a brief hesitation, she changes her mind and calls Hensel.

"Where are you?"

She gives him their location and reads the messages.

"This whole night was a set up," Hensel says, starting his engine. "The body turned out to be a false alarm. Somebody threw a dummy along the coast outside Smith Town and covered it with blood. Damn convincing until we turned on the flashlights. The ruse was a diversion, something to keep us busy."

Darcy backs out of the driveway and turns the car toward Alder Park. As she drives, she tells him about the phone call from Michael Rivers and the messages.

"Wait for me," he says, raising his voice so she can hear him over the background conversation. Darcy recognizes Ames in the background. "I'm following Ames and his team to Alder Park. Keep your cool, Darcy."

"If it was your son, could you?"

"No, but do it anyway. You're not helping Hunter by walking into a trap. And don't hang up the phone. Keep the lines of communication open until we're at the park."

Hensel is right. Darcy has no argument. But she's not waiting for him. She'll beat Hensel to Alder Park by thirty minutes by the time he fights traffic and crosses the coastal bridge.

The dashed white dividing line arrows at the windshield. The moon loses its red tinge and hides behind a forest, but she knows it's there like the pallid face of a vampire concealed in the fog. She blinks to break the spell the dividing line casts upon her. Genoa Cove's village lights sparkle on the horizon. Hensel is five miles behind her and closing fast. Now and then Hensel radios Ames, and she eavesdrops on their banter. Anything to distract her from the terror she feels whenever she imagines Hunter alone with a serial killer. The killer caused the distraction at the cove, so he must have watched her house until Aaron Torres provoked Hunter.

Which leaves another mystery. Hunter wouldn't climb into a stranger's vehicle. Who picked him up?

"You there, Darcy?"

"Never left, Eric."

"Just checking. Think positive thoughts and remember how good we were as a team."

She knows what Hensel is doing. Keep her talking, remind her of their partnership with the FBI. Eventually, he thinks, she'll come to her senses and leave it up to the FBI and police to rescue her son. By then Hunter will be dead.

"A match made in hell."

"Unbeatable, and you're still an expert profiler. Your description was dead on. We know who the guy is."

He wouldn't have shared this information under normal circumstances. He's desperate, trying any ploy to bring Darcy into the inner circle and turn her into a team player. It's too late. Spotting the turn ahead, Darcy engages her signal.

"You found him?"

"Guy's name is Richard Chaney. Born in Nebraska, but he rents a house a half-mile south of the public beach."

He lived within walking distance of Darcy's house. How many times did she pass him on the beach?

"Explains how he got from the cove to your house so quickly," Hensel says, continuing. "Chaney flamed out as a network systems engineer and wandered from job to job the last two years. But get this. He purchased three round trip tickets to Buffalo, New York over the last eight months."

"I think we know who he visited."

"The next question is why he isn't on the visitor logs. More evidence Rivers has someone on the inside working for him."

The terrain glides higher before it drops into the valley bowl. Alder Park is only a mile away now. Darcy douses the headlights and shifts the motor over to electric. She's a silent shadow, at one with the night.

"I can't see the road," Jennifer says, leaning forward.

"Don't worry," Darcy assures her daughter. "I can see it. Keep your seatbelt on."

"Good God, Darcy," Hensel says. "You have your daughter in the car with you?"

"Where did you expect her to be, Eric? She's safe with me."

He exhales and radios Ames about Jennifer.

"You damn well better wait for me, Darcy. It's one thing to put yourself in harm's way. Don't put your daughter at risk."

"I'm killing my lights, Eric. I suggest you do the same when you get here, unless you want Chaney to see you coming."

For a terrifying moment, the dark swallows the car. Cuts them off from the world. She wishes Hensel would speak and settle her nerves. And hurry. Darcy will need Hensel to survive the night.

"The trail begins on the north end of the entrance," Hensel says, interrogating a park map on his phone. "I'll go in first. Detective Ames will take the high ground east of the rim trail. We stationed a police boat outside the cove in case this bastard has water transportation waiting, and Officer Haines will stay with your daughter and make sure nobody gets past the entrance. We've got all the bases covered, so hang in there a little longer."

"Eric, there's a turnoff on the left about a hundred yards

ahead of the park entrance. I'm parking there and going on foot the rest of the way."

"Shit. You're really going to do this, aren't you? Darcy, think this through."

She stops the car on a gravel turnoff down the road from the park. Ahead, the forest thickens and deflects the moonlight. Too dark to see inside.

Darcy slips out of the car and stands with Jennifer. The few remaining crickets keep beat with the night.

"Okay, Darcy. We'll be there in twenty minutes. Stay where you are, and we'll go in together."

"A serial killer has my son, Eric. If you want to help, you better drive faster."

He's mid-protest when she cuts the call and silences the phone. She glances at her daughter, and reality crashes down on her. This is too dangerous. She can't rescue Hunter and protect her daughter at the same time. Darcy's eyes adjust and pull the moonlit road into sharp clarity. Nothing about this meeting feels right. Hunter is here—she can sense him in the park—but Chaney brought her to Alder Park for one reason. To murder her and avenge the lunatic he serves. Darcy won't see the light of day.

"Don't leave my side," she tells Jennifer, gripping the girl's shoulders for emphasis. "And whatever happens tonight, I want you and Hunter to get to safety. The police are coming soon."

The parking lot is vacant when she steps from the car. Too dark. Too much of it. The night slithers around her body and paralyzes her, takes her breath away.

"It's okay, Mom."

Darcy glances at Jennifer. She doesn't think she can move, but her daughter holds Darcy by the hand and pulls her forward. Into the night. Into the unknown.

A red trail marker on the far side of the lot leads Darcy to the rim trail. Sticking to the shadows of old trees, she wonders who watches. Before fear freezes her again, she steps into the moonlight and starts up the trail.

The dirt path radiates silver and gray. Ahead, the trail climbs and disappears over the ridge. The overlook rests on the far side of the ridge, the trail lined by dense forest. A good place to spring a trap.

"Hunter?"

No answer comes. A stream gurgles beyond the trees to her right. Darcy's gaze moves over the eastern hill. If the killer watches her approach, she doesn't see him. Instinct urges her to remain cautious, but she won't slow until Hunter is safe. With Jennifer by her side, Darcy breaks into a jog, knowing one misstep in the dark will snap an ankle. A necessary risk.

She quickens her pace. The cold burns her lungs and numbs her legs, yet Jennifer keeps up and encourages Darcy to run faster. The park entrance is far behind as she outraces the dead whispers of doubt in the back of her mind: Hunter isn't here, the killer fooled us again.

Grasping the back of Jennifer's shirt, Darcy slows to a stop halfway up the ridge. Her endurance is strong, but her sixth sense warns her to look before she advances.

Jennifer's eyes widen and struggle against the night. She holds the strained, brittle look of a girl on the verge of crumbling if their rescue attempt fails.

"I heard something," Darcy says, pulling Jennifer off the trail and into the forest.

A canopy of old pines loom overhead and stretch skyward, the scent cloying. For a long time, Darcy listens. Silence. She's ready to creep back to the trail when a sound comes from the top of the ridge. A voice. They're not alone.

A bed of pine needles cushions the forest floor. It silences her steps and allows her to move through the forest without drawing attention. Placing a finger over her lips, Darcy looks at Jennifer and tilts her head up the hill. The girl understands and follows as Darcy weaves between the trees, careful not to bump into low hanging branches and give them away. Traversing the forest takes longer than following the trail, but it gives Darcy her best chance to free Hunter and get Jennifer back to the car unscathed.

The Glock feels solid against her hip. She draws the gun when something rustles the needled path, probably an animal.

The sound comes again. Two voices, not far now.

No Hunting signs on the trees glow like dozens of eyes. She draws the dark hood of her sweatshirt over her head and motions at Jennifer to do the same. An extra measure of camouflage.

The voices become louder. And there are more of them. Darcy moves faster, keeping to a crouch as she moves behind the tree line. She pulls up when she recognizes a voice.

Aaron Torres.

She assumed the message came from the killer. Though she's terrified Aaron and his friends already hurt Hunter, confidence thaws her frozen bones. She can handle a group of teenagers.

The wet smack of fist against flesh gets her moving. A blow to the head is a game of Russian Roulette for Hunter. Another trauma could cause a brain bleed or seizure. Or worse.

She stops short of the clearing and clamps her hand over her mouth. Don't scream, she repeats to herself. Stay calm and line up the shot.

Hunter kneels on the trail, body limp and supported by the three teenagers grasping him around the arms and chest. Aaron stands over him with his fist cocked back for another punch. A string of bloody drool connects Hunter's lips to the earth. His face is a lunar landscape of bruises and cuts.

"What the hell are you waiting for, you piece of shit? Finish him."

That voice. She recognizes it. Darcy swings the gun toward the darkness and spies the large figure silhouetted against the tree line. He was so close she almost led Jennifer into his path.

Bronson.

"Back behind the pine," Darcy whispers. Jennifer shakes her head. "Do it. If anything happens to me, run as fast as you can and wait for Agent Hensel at the park entrance."

When her daughter backs away and crouches behind a stand of pines, Darcy edges toward the clearing. She keeps one eye fixed on Bronson. He hasn't noticed her yet.

Aaron leers at Bronson and spits on the ground. Then he turns his fury on Hunter. He won't hurt her son again.

Darcy pulls the trigger. The bullet decimates the bark of a tree on the other side of the clearing. The warning shot scatters the teenagers and drops Aaron and Sam Tatum to their bellies. Hunter sways and coughs blood.

"Looks like we have a visitor," Bronson says, walking into the clearing. "You can come out now, Darcy."

Stepping into the silver light, Darcy swings the gun between Bronson and the teenagers. The two thugs aiding Aaron and Sam are the football players who spray-painted her car. Not wanting any part of Darcy and her gun, they back away to the railing overlooking Darkwater Cove. Sam glances uncertainly between Bronson and Darcy, but he doesn't flee. Emboldened, Aaron crawls to his feet and smirks. When he walks toward Hunter, Darcy aims the gun at his chest.

Aaron halts and raises his hands, but the grin remains.

"Oh, for Christ's sake," Bronson says, shaking his head at the boy. "It's not like she'll shoot."

"Like hell I won't." Darcy motions at the railing with the gun. "Aaron and Sam, go stand with your friends. Now."

Darcy kneels beside Hunter. His body slumps against hers. The glaze of his eyes hints he doesn't know she's there. She wants to put a bullet in each of the boys' heads. Make them pay the ultimate price for what they did to her son. Then a shot between Bronson's eyes. The son-of-a-bitch must have fooled Hunter into thinking he wanted to help. Once Bronson lured Hunter into the truck, he fed him to Aaron and his wolves.

But Bronson didn't come unarmed. He raises his gun before Darcy can react.

"You didn't think I'd come unprepared, did you? Drop the gun."

"Not a chance."

"How good of a shot are you, little lady? I bet I take you down first. Fast and hard."

His comments sound vulgar, a double entendre meant to demean her in front of the laughing teenagers.

"I understand that you hate me for throwing you out of my life, but there's no reason to take it out on Hunter. Let him go."

"He's in no condition to walk. The amount of times these boys clubbed his head, he's got to be a goddamn vegetable."

Bronson's eyes are wild...unhinged. She can't reason with him. Only one of them is leaving the clearing alive. Darcy can beat him to the draw. She's never seen him shoot, but she has faith in her quickness and accuracy. But she can't be certain Bronson will fire at her. He'll turn the gun on Hunter and shoot her son instead. That's the most direct route to shattering her.

"I don't get it," Darcy says. "The police will charge you with kidnapping. Why help these kids settle their petty dispute? It has nothing to do with you."

Bronson snickers. The laugh grows until it echoes off the trees. Yes, he's lost his mind.

"I don't give a shit about these kids. But I figured, what the hell...let them have a go at your boy. Right place, right time. You know why we're here. Right, Darcy?"

Aaron and Sam share a look. Sensing something is wrong, the other boys eye the path. They're close to abandoning this sinking ship.

"The police are on the way. None of you are getting out of here, so lower the gun and let me take my son home."

"Not a chance. Even if I wanted to let you go, and I don't, *he* would spill your insides before you got off the ridge."

Is Chaney here?

Aaron leads his friends past Darcy. Bronson swings the gun at them.

"Where the hell do you think you're going?"

"We don't want to be part of this anymore," Aaron says, raising his hands to mollify the suddenly hostile man who delivered Hunter. "We're getting out of here, and if what she said about the police is true, you'll follow us."

"Don't take another step."

The other boys look pleadingly at Aaron. He straightens his back and calls Bronson's bluff.

"You plan to shoot all of us if we leave?"

The gunshot explodes and spins Aaron around. He drops to his knee, clutching his shoulder.

Darcy's finger closes on the trigger, but Bronson fixes his gun on her head. Her chance came and went, and Bronson won't feel a bit of remorse for murdering all of them. Hopefully Jennifer is halfway down the ridge and running for help.

Aaron opens his hands and stares at the blood, disbelief etched on his face. Bronson grins, arrogant in his power.

"Yes, that's exactly what I plan to do—"

Bronson squeals and grabs at his eyes when Hunter slings a handful of dirt and stone into his face. Darcy squeezes off two shots. One clips Bronson's shoulder in a spurt of red. The second barrels through the man's chest and knocks him flat. The scream that rips out of Darcy causes the three boys helping Aaron to scurry backward. She wants to unload every bullet into Bronson. His eyes lock on hers. Even entering death throes, he can't accept she beat him.

Bronson's gun lies a step away from his grasping hand. Choking sounds echo off the trees as he looks up at Darcy. She nudges his gun away with her toe and stands beside Hunter.

Another cry tears a hole in the night. Jennifer.

Panic surges through Darcy. She abandons Hunter in the clearing and sprints into the forest, leaping over a log as bramble claws her skin. She spots the stand of trees where she left Jennifer. But she's gone. Vanished.

Darcy spins around and calls out to her daughter.

The moon screams down at her.

25

T ired eyes project phantom images of Jennifer at the periphery of Darcy's vision with a cruel trick of the mind. But her daughter isn't here. When she swings around, she sees only forest and suffocating darkness.

Stumbling amid the trees, she loses her direction as the cold saws through her bones. This can't be happening. The Darkwater Cove killer has Jennifer, and Hunter hangs by a thread beside Bronson's dead body. Fate pulls her down opposite paths, but she can't save both of her children.

She's familiar with Alder Park, but she'd never ventured off the trail. The forest runs three miles through the valley. She could wander all night. Jagged branches and bramble take pieces of her. Death by a thousand cuts.

A rumble in the sky spins her around. It's not thunder. The noise grows louder, and she recognizes the *chuff-chuff-chuff* whirs of helicopter blades.

As she searches for a break in the canopy, a hand reaches out of the night and clamps over her mouth. Darcy swings her elbow and kicks out as the figure drags her into the shadows.

"Shh. It's me."

She twists her head and sees Hensel staring back at her in his dark blue FBI windbreaker and cap.

"He took Jennifer," Darcy says, shrugging free of his grip. "And Bronson shot Aaron—"

"We know. Haines is with Hunter and the boys back in the clearing, and an ambulance is en route. The roadblocks are up, and we've got police guarding every exit in the park. Chaney isn't getting past us."

A branch snaps inside the forest. Hensel presses a finger to his lips, then points up the ridge where the noise came from. Keeping his voice low, he radios Ames.

"East end of the forest, a hundred yards south of the rim trail."

He motions Darcy forward, and she follows Hensel into the forest. He draws his gun and puts his back against the trunk of a rogue elm tree sprouting out of the sea of pine. When he spies Darcy with the Glock, he scowls and shakes his head.

"He's got my daughter," she mouths, just as a bough rustles in the dark.

Not waiting for Hensel, Darcy races ahead and crouches behind a stand of witch hazel. He assails her with a tight lipped grimace and hurries to catch up, but she's off and running toward the next shrub before he can grab hold of her.

She hears the cove lapping at the shore now. Smells the briny air rising off the water. They must be close. The cliffs loom ahead, no escape unless Chaney takes a hundred-foot plunge into shallow waters.

As Hensel closes the gap, Darcy motions him to sweep around to the left. He sets his jaw and glares at her. Darcy refuses to waver. Seeing no alternative, he complies.

Adrenaline carries her up the ridge as Hensel circles toward the cliffs from the opposite direction. She should see breaks in the trees by now, but the forest appears endless.

Darcy worries she's lost her direction again when the wooden shack materializes out of the gloom. A blank window stares back at her like the eye of a sleeping cyclops. There must be a door on the other side. A thump inside the cabin brings her to a stop. Darcy throws her back against a tree as she sneaks glances around the trunk. If only she had a radio to contact Hensel.

But she has a phone.

After sliding behind the next tree, she drops to one knee and sends Hensel a text message.

Supply shack in the woods near cliffs. Chaney inside.

She gives Hensel a chance to reply, but he doesn't. Searching the forest, she expects to see his silhouette converging on the shack. Darcy can't wait any longer.

She darts from the tree to the rear wall, avoiding the sight lines from the window. Ear pressed to the wooden exterior, she listens. It's quiet inside until she hears the noise again. Softer this time. It's impossible to stop her teeth from chattering. The November night wicks the heat from her body and drains her strength. She can't feel her fingers and worries she won't be able to shoot. Hypothermia is a growing concern, but she'll worry about that after she has Jennifer and Hunter at her side and this nightmare ends. Standing in the dark, her mind contrives an image of Michael Rivers behind her. If she spins around, she'll find him towering over her, the chains around his wrists and ankles snapped and dragging, his toothy grin bloodstained.

When the sound inside the shack comes again, Darcy slides along the wall, careful her sneakers don't crunch the fallen leaves scattered outside the frame. Around the corner, she locates the door—paper thin and brittle. Even if it's locked, she can kick through. Though every second lost brings her daughter closer to death, Darcy isn't fit to fire her weapon. Shoving her hands under her shirt, she crams her fingers against her skin and wills them to thaw until the numbness abates. Still no sign of Hensel.

Finally able to control her gun, Darcy takes a step toward the door. Chaney underestimates her. He terrorized Darcy for weeks and stole Amy's life, but she's the woman who shot the lunatic he worships. She'll take Chaney down the same as she did Bronson.

Darcy touches the doorknob and gives it a gentle twist. Locked. No, not locked. The knob is jammed from disrepair.

She rears back and kicks the door. It blasts open in a shower of splinters and smashes against the wall.

Darcy passes through the gates of hell.

26

P itch black and rotting wood smells roll out of the interior. A bulk juts out of the far corner—a closet. Pulling open the door, she aims the gun inside and finds the closet empty. There's a long, rectangular crate on the floor, disturbingly coffin-like. Chaney etched a crude smiley face on the lid. Darcy passes it off until the thumping sound comes from inside, followed by a muffled moan.

Jennifer?

Darcy pries her fingers under the lid and yanks the top off. Jennifer lies inside, wrists bound and positioned over her chest in the position of final rest. She's breathing. Alive, thank God. The girl's eyelids pop open as she screams into the gag.

Ropes snake around Jennifer's wrists and shins. Darcy drops to her knees and unravels the knot around her daughter's ankles.

The panic on Jennifer's face warns Darcy too late. Chaney's shadow fills the doorway a moment before he thunders across the room. She fires the gun at the same time he kicks her arm. The bullet blows a hole in the roof as she stumbles backward. Her head slams against the wall. She sees the mud-crusted underside of his hiking boot a second before he stomps down on her hand. Her fingers swing open in white agony as the gun bangs off the floor. Reaching for the weapon, she searches with growing desperation. A switch blade flicks open.

"Don't you see? You can't kill all of us. He'll never stop until you're dead."

Jennifer thrashes to free herself inside the crate. A wicked smile curls the corners of the serial killer's mouth. Then footsteps clamber through the brush outside and divert Chaney's attention.

The pause is all Darcy needs. Her fingertips brush over the Glock, and she snatches the weapon, aims, and pulls the trigger in one motion.

The bullet rips through Chaney's collarbone and spins him around. Yet he stays on his feet and slices the blade across her forearm. Hot lifeblood soaks her shirtsleeve. She sees her daughter's frightened eyes as Chaney grabs the bubbling wound and grits his teeth. They're both injured and teetering. He's close enough to kill her if he finds the strength to swipe the blade across her throat. And she can't control her hand below the laceration.

Anger surges through Darcy. Jennifer isn't dying in Alder Park tonight, and neither is Hunter. When Chaney lunges, she switches the gun to her uninjured hand. Without a second hand to aid her with the shot, the bullet veers wide and blows a hole in the wall. Chaney drives her against the closet. Her head cracks against the hardwood, and she slams to the floor with his full weight atop her.

His head snaps backward as Jennifer tugs him from behind with her bound wrists around his neck. Scrambling to her knees, Darcy swings the Glock and knocks Chaney's head sideways.

"Run!"

Jennifer meets Darcy's eyes. She won't run, won't obey her mother's command to save herself. Because she's a fighter. In her daughter's eyes, Darcy recognizes the pain Chaney and Bronson brought upon them, and with the pain comes hatred and a molten fury that knows no boundaries.

Chaney swats Jennifer aside with his free hand, the other gripping the switch blade. Jennifer falls back, brings her knees to her chest, and kicks out, driving the air from Chaney's lungs.

His blood drips through the floor and stains the slats. He's still conscious, but he's mortal. They can beat him.

Darcy's spasming right arm is useless. It hangs limp at her side as she shakes the murk out of her head. When he clambers to his feet, Darcy raises the gun with her left hand, her arm braced over her knee to steady the weapon.

She squeezes the trigger.

Two gunshots ring out. Darcy's shot cuts through Chaney's gut. The second blast deafens Darcy. A geyser of blood splashes from Chaney's face as the bullet explodes into one cheek and exits through the other. She doesn't remember pulling the trigger twice. Studying her hands in confusion, she draws in her legs before the killer crashes face-first against the floor. The moonlight frames Hensel from behind in the doorway, the gun fixed on the murderer.

Hensel speaks into his radio. Help is on the way. The killer twitches and gags on the blood gushing down his throat as Hensel stands over the fallen killer. The bloody switchblade glows in the moonlight beaming through the doorway. His fingers reach for the weapon, but the knife lies beyond his grasp, and his body no longer serves him.

Darcy pulls Jennifer into her arms. She wants to yank her daughter out of this house of horrors, find Hunter, and forget she ever brought her family to Darkwater Cove. The fight drained from her body, Jennifer quivers in Darcy's arms. She's broken. Something inside her daughter shattered that Darcy can never repair. Chaney did this. He deserves this gruesome death. Darcy wishes she could make him feel more pain.

She squeezes Jennifer's hand and eases her against the open door. Hensel glares at Darcy as she crawls over Chaney and sticks the gun barrel into his ear.

Darcy leans close to the serial killer.

"What you said before—*you can't kill all of us*. I want the name of the guard helping Michael Rivers."

"Darcy, let it go."

Ignoring Hensel, she presses down with the gun. A cracking noise like broken egg shells forces Hensel to grab her arm.

"Who is involved besides Bronson Severson?"

A low cackle comes out of Chaney. Then he coughs, spraying Darcy's pant leg with blood. While he writhes and twitches, Darcy reaches under his chest and fishes her hand into his coat pocket.

"What the hell?"

"I need to know," she says, shooting a death stare at Hensel.

She pulls out Chaney's phone.

"That's evidence, Darcy. Drop the phone."

"Evidence for what? He'll be dead in a few minutes. There won't be a trial."

Chaney's face turns to look at her. The floor flattens his torn cheek and bulges his lips. His eyes blink as death approaches. Watching Darcy. Still assessing.

His phone is locked. Even if the bastard could speak, he wouldn't give her the passcode. She grabs Chaney's left arm and wrenches it backward. Grabbing his thumb, she presses it against the home button. She needs to wiggle the thumb until the phone reads the print and unlocks.

His arm slaps off the floor when she lets go. Scrolling through his contacts, she locates Bronson's phone number.

There's no name attached to the listing, just a single-digit number. *Three.* How many others are involved?

Chaney's eyes freeze on her now. Unblinking. Gone. She won't be able to question him further.

His phone battery runs low, but when Darcy interrogates his contacts, she stops on another vague contact. *Four.* Before Hensel realizes what she's about to do, Darcy calls the number. A man with a deep, gravely voice picks up on the first ring.

"Speak."

Her voice catches in her throat. It's not Rivers. Is this the prison employee who helps him?

"Who is this?" she asks.

A pause. Then the line goes dead. It's another burner. Nevertheless, she hands Chaney's phone to Hensel, who groans and grasps the device with his hand inside his shirtsleeve. Without an evidence bag handy, he slides the phone into his pocket.

"Did you expect him to tell you his name? Think, Darcy. You don't even know if the guy aided Rivers."

Darcy hears sirens. More emergency vehicles continue to swarm into Alder Park.

A moment later, Ames arrives with Julian at his side. The detective takes in the carnage—bullet holes blasted through the shack walls, the floor slick with blood, Chaney's ruined form crumpled at his feet—and hisses through his teeth. His face softens toward Darcy and Jennifer, the girl's arms wrapped around her mother. He couldn't pry them off with a winch and chain.

"I'll need your weapon, Ms. Gellar."

"Take it," she says, handing Ames the Glock.

Ames drops the weapon into a plastic evidence bag.

"Let's get that arm wrapped. You'll need stitches to stop the bleeding."

"I don't care about that. Where's Hunter?"

"Your son is at the hospital. He's groggy, but he'll be okay."

Darcy tilts her head up at the ceiling and closes her eyes.

"What about the other boys?"

"County General removed the bullet from Aaron Torres' shoulder. He'll live, but I don't think anybody will give a shit what happens to him next. The other three are at the station. They won't bother your family again."

The walk from the shack to the trail only takes five minutes, but it seems to last hours. The moon drops below the tree line, and the chill that crawls down from the black sky and stars feels winter-like and unforgiving. Darcy can't feel her fingers and toes by the time she reaches the clearing, where a GCPD cruiser waits with flashing lights. An ambulance already took Bronson's corpse, but a dark imprint in the grass serves as a reminder of where she ended his life.

Darcy and Jennifer struggle into the back of the cruiser with Julian at the wheel. Her car remains at the bottom of the hill, but it's the last thing on her mind as Julian executes a tricky turn to direct the cruiser down the trail.

"You were right about Bronson," Darcy says, and Julian's eyes find hers in the mirror. "But I never would have thought he'd aid a serial killer."

"Some people will do anything for money—"

He stops. His eyes burn with alarm, but he's looking away from Darcy.

She doesn't know what's wrong until Jennifer sags lifelessly against her shoulder.

27

"Jennifer, please stay with me."

In the ambulance, Darcy hovers over her daughter, who lies incognizant on the gurney. The girl's face is ashen, lips the color of dusk on a winter's night. A female paramedic fixes an oxygen mask over Jennifer's face and tells her partner to start an IV.

"She's in shock," the paramedic says, drawing a blanket over Jennifer.

Darcy's college roommate went into shock during their junior years. The girl binge-drank on a ninety degree day and came a whisker away from heatstroke. Darcy knows the next half-hour is crucial. The paramedics need to stabilize Jennifer, keep her warm and hydrated. But they cannot cure the root cause of Jennifer's shock.

Darcy holds the female paramedic's eyes.

"How long until we get to the hospital?"

"Ten minutes."

With the emergency lights of Julian's cruiser and the ambulance swirling, they reach County General in less time than the paramedic's optimistic prediction. As they wheel the gurney into the emergency entrance, Jennifer's eyes swivel toward Darcy, who hasn't let go of her daughter's hand since entering the ambulance. And those eyes are lucid, though terrified. A good sign.

"You're doing great, hon. You're safe, and I'm here for you. I'll always be here for you."

The paramedics hand her off to the hospital staff once she's inside. Darcy waits with Jennifer in a small room with white walls and a curtain instead of a door. The young male doctor assigned to Jennifer is calm and knowledgeable, but it's the confidence he instills that convinces Darcy her daughter is out of the woods.

"BP is up a little since the ambulance ride," he says, scribbling on her chart. "It fell too low, but it should continue to rise now. Pulse is stronger. And you'd better get that looked at." The doctor points his pen at Darcy's arm.

"Do you need to raise her blood pressure?" Darcy asks.

"Not as long as it continues to trend higher. She looks stronger already." The doctor sits beside Jennifer on the edge of the cot. "You're breathing too fast, Jennifer."

"I can't get enough breath," the girl says, clutching her chest.

"Actually, you're getting too much. Does your chest hurt? Do you feel light-headed?"

Jennifer nods and swings her eyes toward Darcy.

"Look at me," the doctor says. "Okay. I'm going to take a deep breath, nice and easy, and I want you to follow along with me."

Jennifer hitches and makes a whistling noise while inhaling.

"Let's try again. Watch me," he says, inhaling through his nose and making a winding motion with his hand. "That's better. Again."

The doctor has Jennifer repeat the process until she's breathing normally. Her color is back, and her eyes are no longer glassy.

Maybe it's the bright lights and warmth inside the hospital, or the steady stream of nurses and doctors checking on Jennifer that speed her recovery. An hour later, Jennifer feels strong enough to sit up on the cot and talk. She asks if Hunter is okay, and like all teenagers, she wants to know where her phone is. Darcy can't help but laugh as she cups a hand over her mouth to stifle a sob. Jennifer will be okay. They're all going to be okay.

Darcy gets a month's worth of exercise traveling between her kids' hospital rooms. Between trips, she consents to a doctor treating the slash wound. She needs seven stitches.

Bandages wrap around Hunter's head, and purple mounds rise off his face where Aaron and his friends beat him. But he's strong, resilient. Like his sister.

"I chased Aaron's car to the coast road," Hunter says once the attending nurse exits the room. "Two miles from home, Bronson's truck came up behind me. I never liked the guy, and I figured he'd done something bad for you to throw him out of the house."

"But you accepted the ride when he offered," says Darcy, straightening the blanket draped over his stomach.

Hunter shrugs.

"He told me he recorded Aaron throwing the brick on his phone, and he'd take me to the police station. I figured, why not? I didn't have to like the guy to accept a ride, and I didn't want Aaron to get away with smashing our window. You're not in trouble for shooting Bronson, are you?"

Darcy grabs Hunter's hand.

"The police will question me, but I'll be fine. I think we have a few people on our side now."

Hunter glares into the corner of the room, remembering what happened.

"I knew something was wrong when he headed north. I kept telling him he was going the wrong way. When I saw Torres' car following us, I figured it was a setup. The scumbag had a gun. Nothing I could do."

Darcy touches her lips against the back of his hand. The puzzle pieces fit now. Rivers was an electric contractor and taught Chaney to design the power disruptor. In turn, Chaney possessed the skills to mess with the cameras and alarm, and posing as a Gilmore installer allowed him to study the layout of the home and sabotage the power. How Bronson met Rivers, she hasn't decided, but Ames and Hensel will figure it out soon. Bronson worked for criminals running the Smith Town underbelly, and Rivers had the financial resources to keep Bronson solvent despite his legal issues.

As for Aaron Torres and his friends, they had nothing to do with Chaney and the Full Moon Killer. Bronson used them to hurt Hunter, nothing more, and Bronson tossed the boys aside when he finished with them.

Darcy stands at the vending machine when Ames arrives. He has Julian and Faust with him. A few days ago, Darcy would have taken one look at the trio and decided they were here to arrest Hunter and spin Bronson's death to implicate Darcy and her family. It's good to have people on her side for a change.

"Officer Haines told me about your daughter," Ames says. "How's she doing?"

"The doctor called it psychological shock. She's better now, but the doctor wants to keep her overnight."

"And your boy?"

"Hurting, but he's a survivor. I worry about the long-term effects of multiple concussions, but he'll be able to go home with Jennifer."

Ames no longer recognizes his sleepy village. He brushes the hair across his head and exhales.

"Once you get the kids settled, I need you to stop by the station tomorrow."

"You have questions."

He gives a non-committal reply, something between a nod and a shrug.

"I think we've reconstructed the events from the park, but I'll need your statement. You should get your gun back by then." He turns to leave and stops. "Oh. Agent Hensel turned over Chaney's phone for evidence. I understand you called one of Chaney's contacts using his phone."

"I did."

"Any idea who answered?"

"None." He stares at Darcy as if he thinks she's holding something back. For once, she isn't. "But I'm positive he's involved like Bronson was."

"After you left, someone sent a message to Chaney's phone. Anonymous, of course. The sender wanted to know, and you'll excuse my vulgarity, if the bitch and her kids were dead yet. We're trying to determine who wrote the message."

"I'll give you a hint. He lives in federal housing outside Buffalo. Small room. Low rent."

Darcy expects a chuckle, or even a smirk. Instead, Ames pulls his jacket tight and buries his hands inside his coat pockets.

"Tomorrow then."

"I'll be there."

It's after midnight, but the trauma-induced energy charging through Darcy seems limitless. Eventually, the adrenaline will flee her body and she'll collapse, but for now she roams between the rooms of her sleeping children and takes comfort in the bright lights of the busy medical center.

The hospital cafeteria finished serving food hours ago. It's empty of patrons and a good place to sit for a while and reflect on the night's events. She takes a window seat and thumbs through news stories on her phone. A slender man in a dark blue janitorial uniform mops the floor while the moon, an old villain she'll never escape, leers at her through the glass.

When her phone rings, she expects another anonymous caller. A flood of relief follows when Laurie's name appears on the screen. She's checking on Hunter and Jennifer, Darcy assumes. But when Darcy's cousin speaks, the room turns a shade darker.

The police are at Laurie's house in Georgia. Her stalker escalated.

"Did he hurt you?" Darcy asks, leaning forward and touching her heart.

"He came while I was at work, Darcy."

"Are you sure it was him? Did he break in or take anything?"

But in the roiling pit of her stomach, Darcy already knows the truth before her cousin continues. There's a painting on the back of Laurie's house. A bloody, dripping smiley face.

The hand holding the phone drops to her side. Her reflection stares back at her in the window. Pallid, exhausted.

And determined.

Michael Rivers rules over a kingdom of cutthroats and lunatics bent on destroying Darcy and everyone she loves. He's left her no choice.

She will burn his kingdom to the ground.

Thank you for being a loyal reader!
Ready to find out what happens to Darcy?

Read Bury Her Bones today

GET A FREE BOOK!

I'm a pretty nice guy once you look past the grisly images in my head. Most of all, I love connecting with awesome readers like you.

Join my VIP Reader Group and get a FREE serial killer thriller for your Kindle.

Get My Free Book

www.danpadavona.com/thriller-readers-vip-group/

SHOW YOUR SUPPORT FOR INDIE AUTHORS

Did you enjoy this book? If so, please let other thriller fans know by leaving a short review. Positive reviews help spread the word about independent authors and their novels. Thank you.

ABOUT THE AUTHOR

Dan Padavona is the author of the The Darkwater Cove series, The Scarlett Bell thriller series, *Her Shallow Grave*, The Dark Vanishings series, *Camp Slasher, Quilt, Crawlspace, The Face of Midnight, Storberry, Shadow Witch*, and the horror anthology, *The Island*. He lives in upstate New York with his beautiful wife, Terri, and their children, Joe, and Julia. Dan is a meteorologist with NOAA's National Weather Service. Besides writing, he enjoys visiting amusement parks, beach vacations, Renaissance fairs, gardening, playing with the family dogs, and eating too much ice cream.

Visit Dan at: www.danpadavona.com

Made in the USA
Monee, IL
27 October 2024